Reaper & The Lioness

Lone Star Mavericks MC Series
Book 1

Rachel Esterline

Venturesome Publishing

First Edition

Ebook ISBN: 978-1-968862-00-8

Papercover ISBN: 978-1-968862-02-2

Hardcover ISBN: 978-1-968862-03-9

Cover design by Mel Purdy of PawsitivelyPurdy (etsy.com/shop/PawsitivelyPurdy)

Content editing by Pinpoint Editing (pinpointediting.com)

Venturesome Publishing

PO Box 144

Haslett, Michigan 48840

VenturesomePublishing.com | VenturesomePublishing@gmail.com

Glen Esterline

1966–2021

To my dad, who told me to embrace being called a bitch because it meant I didn't take shit from anyone, taught me how to shoot because a restraining order is just a piece of paper, and showed me it's not the big, bad bikers you need to be scared of.

Trigger Warnings & Content Reassurance

Scan to view trigger warnings or visit
rachelesterlineauthor.com

The dog featured in this story is <u>never</u> in danger and lives happily ever after.

Key Terms

Church: Official club meeting attended by officers of the motorcycle club where business, rules, and votes happen.

Cut: The sleeveless leather vest worn by members with their club patch.

Old Lady: A wife or steady girlfriend of a club member.

Patch Over: When one club merges into or is absorbed by another. May be voluntary or forced.

Prospect: A potential member undergoing a probationary period before becoming a fully patched member. Often required to do grunt work for fully patched members to prove their loyalty to the club.

Rockers: The curved patches above (top rocker) and below (bottom rocker) the club emblem.

Sweetbutt: A woman who is sexually available to club members but doesn't hold the status of an Old Lady.

Playlist

Listen on Spotify:

Straight Up • Kelsey Hickman
Play with Fire (feat. Yacht Money) • Sam Tinnesz
killer queen • Mad Tsai
The Devil in Me • Anthony Mossburg
Only The Strong Survive • Sam Drysdale
Lock Me Up • The Cab
Baby Outlaw • Elle King
Sweet 'n' Savage • Kxlly
Little Girl Gone • CHINCHILLA
R.I.F.P. • MOTHICA
Horns • Bryce Fox
We Are Warriors • Avril Lavigne
You Are Enough • Citizen Soldier
Addicted • Saving Abel
Blue Jeans • Silvertide
Made Me This Way • Loren Rosko
That Girl Right There • Creed Fisher
never til now • Ashley Cooke, Brett Young

Chapter One

Frustration charged through me so strongly that I could shoot someone. I slammed my phone to the counter, pain searing through my wrist as I aggravated the not-quite-healed fracture.

It was as I'd suspected. The prosecutor had dropped all charges against Hale Abell, and now I owed thousands in legal fees alongside my lost hope for justice.

I glanced at my watch as I dabbed a tissue at the streaks of mascara on my cheeks. The call had lasted longer than I'd expected, mostly because I'd tried to argue with my lawyer before tearfully begging for other options.

Now, I'd risk a speeding ticket. Arriving late to this meeting would make a terrible first impression, and I couldn't afford to jeopardize the chance of landing a new client. Especially now.

I jogged to my firecracker-red Jeep and peeled out of the driveway. The warm Texas breeze whipped through my open windows as I sped along the backroads. The mid-January temperature had hit the sixties today, a welcome change from the icy Northeast winters I'd endured the past decade.

I breathed in the sweet scent of winter honeysuckle, driving ten over the speed limit until the steel sign with pitted edges came into view. It stood surrounded by open land, swaying grass, and gnarled trees.

The Lone Star Mavericks Motorcycle Club.

Gravel crunched beneath my tires as I turned into the long driveway. My hands shook as I released a long exhale. I rolled my shoulders back, trying to release the crushing sense of anxiety in my chest.

What the fuck was I thinking?

I'd signed questionable clients before. I'd handled crisis communications for a senator after his drunk driving arrest. I'd managed a corporate PR disaster for a Fortune 500 company that was so bad my NDA didn't even allow me to acknowledge I'd been a part of it. I'd defended countless CEOs who certainly didn't deserve a positive spin on their actions. Could a group of men who liked motorcycles really be that much worse?

I swallowed hard before shifting the Jeep into park beside the massive pole barn. I killed the engine and stared at the line of parked Harleys.

Two leather-clad giants stood to the side of the building. Smoke curled from their lips as the unmistakable scent of weed seeped through my cracked window. Another biker swaggered over, swigging straight from a fifth of Jack Daniel's like it was sweet tea.

Jesus Christ. It was barely one in the afternoon. If this was their Wednesday matinee, I couldn't imagine the midnight show. The Lone Star Mavericks Motorcycle Club was a far cry from the polished corporate world I'd left behind.

When Rhetta Blackwell had asked if I could support the club's businesses, I'd said yes without a second thought. Now, I wondered what exactly it might entail.

Nervously, I swept invisible lint off my navy pinstripe blazer and turned to stride toward the clubhouse. My spiky heels wobbled on the stones, and I cursed myself for not choosing more sensible shoes.

Rhetta stepped out of the door, soft blonde curls shaping around her face. She radiated confidence with a weathered edge that hadn't existed in high school.

"You made it! Welcome to Texas, sugar."

Rhetta hugged me, her black leather vest cool against my skin. In the photos she'd posted to Facebook, she'd referred to the vest as her cut—a piece of biker lingo I'd somehow retained.

I pulled back to look into blue eyes that sparkled with a familiar warmth. "I'm so happy to see you. It feels like it's been a lifetime. I'm sorry I couldn't make it to your wedding last year."

We'd stayed in touch since high school, but I hadn't visited Rhetta since she'd moved to Conroe, a growing city an hour outside the heart of Houston. It was her photos—sunlight dappling through the pines onto the still surface of the lake, open fields dotted with wildflowers—that convinced me to move here shortly after the hospital discharged my bruised, broken body.

The impulsive decision had shocked everyone, including myself.

"You missed one hell of a party. But I know you were busy with that fancy job. You were the PR director at that private equity firm, right? There was a major crisis that weekend. It's why I told Thane we needed to hire you."

I forced a smile to my face, but my gut turned to a block of ice at the reminder of my time with Abell Enterprises. "I appreciate the referral. Building a solid client base is taking longer than I expected," I said tightly. The small retainers from a local nonprofit and a few family-owned businesses weren't enough to pay the bills.

Rhetta's brow furrowed, but she didn't press. "Life has really changed for both of us, hasn't it? I can't wait to catch up. Maybe we can grab dinner this weekend?"

"I'd love that." A genuine smile replaced my strained one.

Knowing Rhetta lived nearby, a friend and ally as I rebuilt my life, brought more comfort than I cared to admit. Making new friends in your thirties was a bitch. Making new friends in your thirties in a new city while building a consultancy, fostering a puppy, and getting your shit together? A fucking nightmare.

I hesitated as I walked into the clubhouse behind Rhetta. I'd expected a grimy, smoke-filled den. Instead, a wide-open lounge sprawled before me. Eclectic fixtures hung at varying heights, casting pools of warm light across the space. The high ceiling featured flat-black industrial ductwork crisscrossing overhead, and the polished concrete floors were shiny and clean. The smoky air mingled with the sharp tang of motor oil and the richness of soft leather.

I followed Rhetta's confident stride as she approached the bar, a massive slab of polished obsidian that devoured the light. A vintage motorcycle, mounted above the bar like a chrome-plated deity, commanded attention. The sprawling liquor selection beneath the mechanical altar rivaled even the ritziest bars I'd visited on the East Coast.

"Can I get a tequila on the rocks and a whiskey for Thane?" Rhetta asked the bartender. "Anything for you, sugar?"

I hesitated. Liquor before lunch sounded reckless. But when in Rome, right?

"Whiskey for me as well."

As the bartender poured our drinks, I absorbed the gentle hum of conversation drifting from the corner, punctuated occasionally by the muffled thud of a pool cue striking a billiard ball. The group of bikers glanced our way, gazing up and down my body with a hunger that left me both flattered and wary. My eyes scanned the large space, taking in the TVs and clusters of worn leather sofas. A group of dartboards hung in one corner. In the other, a pair of classic pinball machines gleamed beneath a neon Mavericks sign.

The bartender slid my drink across the bar, and I gripped it as I thanked her. My heels echoed through the clubhouse as I followed Rhetta down a long hall. With a subtle nod, she ushered me into a well-lit office. Rich, knotty pine paneling lined the walls, adorned with framed posters of bikini-clad women posing on gleaming motor-cycles. I breathed in the faint whisper of cigar smoke as I took in the man sitting behind the large desk.

He appeared in his late forties, his face weathered by sun and wind. A salt-and-pepper goatee framed his jaw, and tan lines traced around his eyes where sunglasses must have usually sat. His black leather cut hung loosely on his shoulders beneath his dark flannel shirt. The worn president's patch on his broad chest gave away my suspicion that this was Rhetta's husband—the leader of the Lone Star Mavericks Motorcycle Club.

He reached a hand across the desk. Surprise flickered across his face as I matched his firm grip, quickly replaced by a hint of respect.

"Thane Blackwell. Please, sit."

His gruff voice matched his imposing presence, but the politeness surprised me.

"Rhetta tells me you do PR. She thinks you can help us with a bit of a challenge." His eyes, a deep brown, bore into mine as if trying to gauge my fortitude.

I offered a smile. "Absolutely. What kind of challenge?"

Thane pulled a newspaper clip from a folder.

This was how it always started with clients. They rarely thought about their reputation until a reporter wrote a headline that pissed them off. Then, suddenly, they wanted to order every service on the PR menu to change people's minds. If only it worked like that.

He slid the clip across the desk so I could read it.

"Grassroots Coalition Calls for a Boycott of Lone Star Mavericks MC businesses."

I recognized many of the storefronts listed, having even visited a few of them without realizing they were associated with the club.

Maisie's Bakery. Onyx Taproom. Jack's Car Repair. Sterling Jewelers. Elysia Salon. Grimm Construction.

"Any idea what prompted the boycott?" I asked.

Thane slid a stained manila folder across the table and scattered a few photos and a background check before me.

"Danielle Beone. She's always hated the club. Her ex was a member. He died three months ago—motorcycle accident during a fundraiser. Their kid was on the back of the bike and got pretty messed up, too. Ever since, she's been claws out."

Thane spread printed screenshots from the local Facebook group, each dripping with hostility and contempt. "Initially, she just posted her rants on social media, but this month she got traction with the local newspaper. The boycott is hurting the businesses owned by my club's members. They're losing customers. Losing money."

"Are you interested in having me represent the club? Or the businesses?"

"I'm not worried about the club's reputation," Thane said, sitting back and crossing his arms. His biceps strained against the sleeves of his shirt.

He seemed doubtful I could help, evident from the set of his brows. I bit back a smirk as I considered how similar the leader of a motorcycle club was to every CEO who had been a client. They were always overly confident, certain the small bumps would never dethrone them.

Sometimes, they were right. But small issues often snowballed into full-blown PR crises. Too often clients waited until it was too late to salvage their public perception.

This project was more than a simple reputation issue. It would take months of work and a serious retainer if he expected to shift the tides.

I tilted my head. "Putting the club in a more positive light could help the businesses as a whole. I can outline a formal proposal, but I can tell that you're a skeptic, so let me break it down for you."

I spread the papers across his desk, pointing at headlines and screenshots.

"Misperceptions about your club and its members are the root cause of your issues. People see the patches and bikes and think trouble. We need the community to see the big picture. These family-owned businesses create jobs and bring in tax dollars that support Conroe—paying for roads, schools, and county services. It makes the Mavericks an integral part of the community. That's the story you need me to tell."

The slight uptick of his brows and the grin on Rhetta's face confirmed I'd piqued his interest.

"And this isn't a one-and-done strategy," I continued now that I had his attention. "We need a steady drumbeat of positive stories. I don't want you to read a newspaper, turn on the TV, listen to the radio, or open up Facebook without seeing the face of a Maverick doing something that makes Conroe a better place to live."

I sat back, pressing the tips of my fingers together, displaying a confident power gesture common in my old world. "The answer isn't to separate the club from the businesses. It's to show the interconnection between the club and the community. People need to see how your members create a positive impact."

Interest flickered in his eyes.

"We'll show Maisie's giving fresh-baked bread to the soup kitchen, Jack's shop giving a car away to a single mom, and the construction company building a ramp for a disabled veteran. News crews will eat it up. It will help the community view your club in a new light."

Rhetta laughed and crossed her arms. "I told you she's a PR wizard."

I leveled a cool gaze at the club president. "It's not magic. It's strategy."

"Darlin', this ain't Wall Street or Capitol Hill, or a slick corporation run by suits in a boardroom," Thane said, narrowing his eyes. "We're just a bunch of grease-stained locals running shops all over town. It's more of a goat rodeo than you can imagine. You really think you can wrangle that?"

Irritation flooded my chest at his challenge. I inhaled a centering breath and offered a smile, hoping to shield my annoyance. "I've handled PR and crisis management for Fortune 500 companies, global nonprofits, and politicians. I can manage a few small businesses. The real question is, will you allow me to tell the stories that will make an impact? Because if not, I wouldn't want to waste your time or money."

Thane stared at me for a beat as he processed my words. It was true. While I needed the money, I wouldn't beg anyone to see the value I brought to the table. Skeptical clients sucked, and Thane needed to agree with my recommendations if we worked together.

A slow grin spread across his face. "I like you," he said with a gravelly laugh. "You've got balls. What's the price tag?"

His approval sent an unexpected thrill through me.

"I don't like to nickel and dime my clients, so I recommend you sign a contract for a $10,000 monthly retainer. In addition to the consulting and ongoing work to improve the reputation of the businesses, I'll be on call for you twenty-four seven."

Thane stood, hand outstretched. "Deal. Bring the contract over tomorrow. We're having a cookout. We can introduce you to everyone then."

As I shook his hand, excitement and trepidation filled my chest.

I'd come to Conroe for a change, and I was about to get a hell of a ride.

Chapter Two

"You fucking hired someone to do PR?" I growled, my voice cutting through the murmur of conversation. "You didn't think to run that by us first?"

The cigarette smoke and testosterone-fueled tension in the room stirred memories of my time in the Marine Corps. I leaned against the clubhouse wall, my arms crossed over my leather cut—a constant reminder of the weight of responsibility I carried. As always, Thane nonchalantly shared this decision during Church, our weekly club meeting, with the expectation we'd fall in line.

Thane's face hardened, his tone laced with irritation. "The businesses are suffering. The members who work for them are fucked if they fail. Not many people want to hire a Maverick right now. And I know you've lost at least two contracts this month alone."

The room fell silent except for the soft clink of ice in Thane's whiskey glass as he took a sip. His eyes bore into mine in challenge. The other club officers shifted uneasily, their eyes darting between us.

While they might also disagree, they wouldn't voice it like this. The club operated under a similar hierarchy as the military, with expectations for respect and authority by rank. I was the only one in the room who could challenge the president this directly. Though he was about fifteen years older than me, he was my best friend, and I'd served as his VP for the past five years.

I'd earned the right to speak my mind.

A twinge of frustration curled in my gut. I'd kept Grimm Construction separate from the club, building it from the ground up since leaving the Corps. However, Thane was right. Work had slowed with the boycott.

Pushing off the wall, I straightened to my full height. "And you don't think bringing in an outsider is risky? Especially with the Rangers sniffing around our territory?"

The Hill Country Rangers Motorcycle Club predated the Mavericks by nearly a decade, and they'd been a thorn in our side since day one. I remembered one of the club's founders, Maxwell Morris, endlessly bitching that they didn't have a shred of respect for our codes. Their lack of a moral compass made the Mavericks look like goddamn choirboys.

Linc, my younger brother who also served as the club secretary, piped up. "Reaper's got a point. We're sitting on a powder keg here. A few Rangers were in the Woodlands last night. They stole a Benz, and they're stripping it down in that old warehouse near our turf."

The Woodlands stood at the center of our most lucrative theft operation, with no shortage of luxury cars and bikes we could steal to strip down for parts faster than law enforcement could track. We could strip a Range Rover to the frame overnight, the owner none the wiser and the parts sold and scattered before the police report was finished.

"I hacked into the Houston PD system, and reports say they're also dealing downtown again," Linc added. "They're selling fentanyl to high school kids, according to what I've read."

"We need to press them out of Conroe," I spat. "They're goddamn drug pushers, and I don't want them doing business in our territory."

Our no-drugs policy—a stance I'd pushed for when I became VP —set us apart from other clubs, giving us a twisted sense of honor in this fucked-up world. But it also opened opportunities for rival clubs to grow in our backyard.

Hatchet Perry leaned forward. His bright blue eyes glinted with a hint of anticipation. "What's the play?"

"We start by torching their warehouse to remind them that Houston is our territory."

Hatchet offered a wicked grin. "I just put a new set of pipes on Detective Rodriguez's bike. All right guy, for being a cop. I'll reach out to him with some intel about the Rangers' coke distribution. The heat will keep them on edge."

Merrick Morris, our sergeant at arms, crossed his arms and leaned back in his chair. His sharp brown eyes focused on me as skepticism colored his scarred face. "What about the shipment coming in next week? We can't afford any extra attention right now."

The tension in the room ratcheted up a notch. The shipment was my orchestration—my contact bringing us a container of "lost" military-grade weapons to be sold off the books. This delicate operation demanded finesse. A single fuck-up would land us all behind bars in Beaumont. The weight of their gazes fell on me, waiting for my response.

"Thane," I said, my voice carrying a note of authority that caused everyone, including the president, to pause. "I get that we need to deal with this boycott shit. But the fucking Rangers are pushing into our territory, and we've got a club to run and deals to broker. You sure you want to complicate things with some PR stunts?"

I held Thane's gaze, unflinching. This dynamic defined our leadership—my steel to his flexibility.

"The PR support will be for businesses associated with the club," Thane explained, annoyance clear in his tone. "The club stays separate, as always."

I ground my molars like I chewed on broken glass. The news coverage of the boycott had just flushed a juicy construction contract down the shitter, but I still didn't want someone poking around in the business I'd worked so hard to build. And I hated the idea of working with someone who thought they could make us out to be something we're not. We'd rightfully earned our reputation for ruthlessness.

"I'm not working with some motherfucker who thinks he can spin a story that the big, bad bikers are really the good guys."

Thane let out a laugh. "I think you might be in for a surprise if that's who you think I've hired. Linc, tell us what you've found out about our new consultant."

My brother snickered as he spread the contents of a folder onto the table. "Eva Harland, thirty-two years old, born in Michigan. Went to Boston University on a full ride. Just bought a house off 1484."

Fuck me. The photograph hit me like a sledgehammer. Her stormy, blue-gray eyes pierced my soul. Her heart-shaped face was framed by a cascade of dark hair that begged to be wrapped around my fist. She wore an expensive navy power suit, her arms crossed over her chest as if she dared the world to fuck with her.

Linc continued, pushing through the pages of the background check. "Owner of Harland Communications & Marketing, a new LLC she just started." The stack of printed pages rustled as he dove deeper. "She started her career in Washington, D.C., working at a crisis communications agency for political figures and big-name CEOs. Named to a thirty-under-thirty list at twenty-four. Won a few awards for campaigns she managed. She worked at Abell Enterprises up until November. She quit after an attack put her in the hospital."

The following pages of the dossier, information he'd discovered using his skills as a hacker, hit like a punch to the gut. The police report presented a clinical, detached account of a brutal attack. The battered woman in the photos looked nothing like the polished, corporate ice queen in the headshot Linc had shown moments before.

They showed her swollen face and neck, distorted with a palette of sickening purples and yellows. One arm lay trussed up in a cast.

The close-up of her side revealed a canvas of black-and-blue carnage. Bootprints had been stamped into her flesh.

I'd witnessed my share of brutality. Hell, I'd dished out plenty myself. But to do this to a woman? My trigger finger itched, and my blood ran cold all at once.

"She named her attacker immediately. Hale Abell."

"Why does that sound familiar?" I asked.

"He's the son of millionaire CEO Benjamin Abell. They were in the news a lot last year. Some insider trading shit. Anyway, his mountains of cash and army of lawyers made sure junior stayed out of jail. The charges were dropped this week."

The familiar burn of rage built in my chest. "The whole goddamn attack was caught on camera. How does a rich cocksucker get away with something like that?"

The disgust in Linc's eyes mirrored my own. He pulled out his phone. "Here's the footage."

The video flickered to life, the glow of fluorescent lights casting an eerie pall over the concrete parking garage. A figure wearing a hooded jacket slunk into the frame behind the woman in black heels, a white blouse, and a pencil skirt. In a heartbeat, he attacked, yanking her back by her long hair like a rag doll.

But this fireball of a woman was no one's prey. She exploded into action, a whirlwind of elbows and nails like her life depended on it.

"Damn. Girl's got some fight in her."

Linc nodded grimly. "It ain't enough. Watch. His face is never shown. Angles are all wrong. When he takes her down—there—she cracks her head. Bad concussion. His lawyers used that to say she couldn't ID him for shit. He wore long sleeves and gloves, so no DNA under her nails, either."

"Convenient," I growled. My breath hissed through clenched teeth as I watched the savage attack continue, the kicks vicious and relentless. Once she hit the ground, her attacker wrapped his hands around her throat.

"Cowardly piece of—" I bit off the curse as a vehicle's headlights swept across the scene. The attacker bolted, leaving her crumpled on the cold concrete. Blood bloomed across the white silk top she wore as a figure hovered above her and dialed 911.

Linc slipped his phone back into his pocket after the video stopped. "She lives alone. Probably jumps at every shadow. She doesn't have many friends here yet. Mainly chats with Rhetta and some hotshot investigative journo from her college days. Matt Byron."

I shook my head at Thane. "No fucking way can we have someone who's friends with a journalist hanging around here. Might as well invite the goddamn feds for a tour."

Thane's face remained impassive, but I caught the slight tightening around his eyes. He shared my concerns, even if he wouldn't admit it.

Linc shrugged. "I dug through her emails and text messages. They keep a pretty solid boundary between their work and friendship. She shuts him down hard anytime he sniffs around her clients. He generally respects it. Doesn't push her for more information."

"What the hell are they yapping about all the time then?" I demanded, not buying this squeaky-clean bullshit for a second. Someone with deep connections to a reporter was the last thing the club needed.

Linc's expression darkened. "The Abells. Eva and her buddy are on a crusade. Ever since her attack, she's been trying to dig up dirt and get other women to expose Hale for the bastard he is. And, from what I've found so far, it's a rabbit hole of hush money and NDAs."

Thane stood, clearly done with the debate. "Eva's coming to the cookout. You can get a read on her then. It'll be fine. Rhetta will keep her focused."

"And if she sees or hears something she shouldn't?"

"Then we'll deal with it. Like we always do."

Chapter Three

I lobbed another ball across the yard. My foster puppy, Hawk, launched after it on gangly legs.

"That's it, buddy. Wear yourself out."

I'd scrolled through multiple calls for puppy fosters from the local rescues and shelters since moving to Texas. The promise of puppy breath soothed my aching need for connection. Shortly after submitting the application, the shelter had offered me a young German shepherd mix.

I laughed when I met Hawk at the shelter. The inexperienced staff were either wrong or lying. Years of watching my dad train military working dogs gave me confidence that this tornado of fur, claws, and fangs was a full-blooded Malinois.

The pitter-patter of Hawk's oversized paws on the hardwood floors, the jingle of his collar tags, and even his occasional howls eliminated the oppressive silence that had filled my home when I moved here. While the quiet was a welcome change from the urban chaos I'd survived for years in my Washington, D.C., studio apartment, Hawk's presence helped soothe my nagging doubts that abandoning my high-profile PR career had been a colossal mistake.

As he played, my mind drifted to the freshly printed contract on my kitchen counter. Apprehension curled in my chest as I recalled the deep dive of news clips and public information I'd read after meeting with Thane. The Mavericks were outlaws. Real-deal one-percenters with a history of violence.

But I would be working with the club's members and their legitimate businesses, not the club itself.

And I *really* needed the money.

I glanced at my watch and sighed. Time to go.

"Come on, little guy," I said as I attempted to wrangle the ten-week-old terror that the shelter called a puppy.

Hawk bounded back, drool dripping from his chin. His whiskey-colored eyes gleamed with mischief as I grabbed for the ball. I cursed under my breath as the tiny menace swerved out of reach to begin an impromptu game of tag. Dirt flew from his paws as he ran laps around my yard.

After a few minutes of chaos, I finally bribed Hawk close enough with a treat to scoop him up. He yipped in excitement and overstimulation, nipping at my hands and face as he squirmed in my arms.

"I promise I'll be back in a few hours," I murmured, nuzzling the spot between his ears and pressing a kiss to his tiny snout. The sweet scent of puppy fur mixed with the earthy smell of the yard filled my senses. "We can play ball again before bed."

As I carried him into the kitchen, my eyes fell to the bills stacked on the counter. My stomach clenched as I considered the latest—a new air conditioner installed last week after the original one had taken a shit. My severance and PTO payout were gone, and I'd begun to dip into my savings to pay my new mortgage. My checking account dwindled with each unexpected repair the lazy home inspector missed.

But not anymore. The contract with the Mavericks would keep me out of the red.

I pushed Hawk into his crate, my heart twisting as he let out a plaintive whine. I hated leaving him home alone, but I trusted he would fall asleep when I left.

The Mavericks' parking lot was packed this evening, with bikes and trucks lining the drive. Heavy rock blared from the speakers, and a small group of bikers stood around a fire pit, drinking beers and smoking.

I tugged at the hem of my leather jacket. I'd aimed for biker chic but had landed squarely in "corporate queen attempting to be edgy," wearing my Loft jacket with gold zippers and Lucchese cowboy boots. I looked like a teenager playing dress-up in a world of grit, grease, and gasoline.

I might have been out of my element, but it wouldn't be the first time. The Mavericks were no different than the dirty politicians and greedy CEOs I rubbed elbows with at fundraising galas in Washington, D.C. Strip away the leather and ink, and you'd probably find the same hunger for power, thirst for respect, and desire for control.

I squared my shoulders. My job hadn't changed. I was here to tell stories that built bridges between worlds. Whether those worlds were separated by political ideologies or lifestyle choices, it didn't matter. Still, as I approached the gathering, the butterflies in my stomach turned into angry hornets.

Rhetta materialized from the crowd, greeting me with a hug that reeked of cigarettes and sweet amber perfume. She wore her cut again, and I noticed the bottom rocker across her back. "Property of Thane." I internally cringed at the patriarchal statement.

"Glad you made it, sugar," she drawled, her eyes twinkling with amusement as she took in my attire. "Come on, let's get business out of the way first."

She led me through a gauntlet of curious stares before we arrived at Thane's office. He scanned the contract with unnerving speed. I held my breath, half expecting him to change his mind and rip it in half, but instead he reached for a pen and signed at the bottom of the page, the scratch anticlimactic to my spiraling anxieties. He handed it back to me and smiled.

With this client, I finally had a viable consultancy.

And I could finally pay my bills.

Thane reached into a drawer and pulled out a thick envelope. "First month's payment," he said, his voice gravel and smoke.

I fought to keep my face neutral as he handed it over. The envelope was heavy. Cash. Of course, it was cash.

"Rhetta will handle introductions tonight," Thane said, standing to kiss his wife's cheek. "Keep her out of trouble."

I wasn't sure if the grumbled warning was for Rhetta or me. Thane closed the door behind us, and I followed her back into the main room.

The envelope of cash pulsed in my hand, a tangible reminder of the line I was about to cross. This wasn't Corporate America, with its paper trails, digital transfers, and off-the-record secrets shared by staffers over coffee. The rules the Mavericks lived by were different, and Thane's decisions weren't made in boardrooms or over games of golf. I doubted the man even owned a set of clubs, and, if he did, they were probably used for beating the shit out of anyone who crossed him.

I shook the violent vision from my mind.

"Can we swing by my Jeep? I'd like to lock this up. I don't want to carry it in my back pocket all night."

"Sure thing, sugar," Rhetta said, throwing back the rest of her tequila and sliding the empty glass down the bar as we walked past.

As we stepped outside, I sighed. I was making a conscious decision to entangle myself with an outlaw motorcycle club. But, if I were honest, my former world had never been safe either, the men I'd worked for far from innocent.

I shoved the envelope into the glove compartment, slamming it shut and silencing my hesitations and doubts.

"Time to mingle," Rhetta drawled, her arm snaking through mine, dragging me toward a grizzled, bearded biker beside a woman in her sixties with short gray hair and deep laugh lines around her blue eyes.

"Don, Maisie, this is my friend, Eva. She's going to be doing PR for all the businesses."

I shook their hands. I'd had no idea Maisie's Bakery was associated with the club until yesterday's meeting. I'd stopped there several times for a muffin and a latte and salivated at the thought of the sweet bursts of flavor from her baked goods made with local fruits.

"I have a few ideas on how we can help your business," I said with a warm smile. "Maybe I can drop by for coffee this week, and we can go through them?"

Maisie's eyes lit up. "I would love that, dear. Business has slowed a bit with the boycott. That means Don is eating all the extra cinnamon rolls." She patted the beer belly on the biker with a laugh.

He grinned, looking down at her in adoration. "My old lady makes the best cinnamon rolls in Texas."

I laughed and promised to try one the next time I visited.

Rhetta guided me through the crowd as the clubhouse filled, leading me through a series of introductions like I was speed-dating the entire club. Each greeting offered a snapshot of the lives affected by the boycott.

Jack Patino, a young mechanic barely into his twenties, had grease under his nails and determination in his eyes. The faint scent of motor oil wafted from his clothes.

"Business is slower than a three-legged dog in a marathon," he confessed with an underlying southern drawl, his boyish face at odds with the weight in his voice. "A lot of people are taking their cars to the big, corporate shop—even though they don't do shit for the community. I let high school kids use my shop and tools, for fuck's sake."

This piqued my PR senses, and I dove in, asking Jack to tell me more about his partnership with the local high school shop teacher. I jotted down a few notes and his phone number on the small notepad I carried in my back pocket.

As another group swept Rhetta away, I found myself adrift in the sea of leather and chrome. The bar beckoned, promising the liquid courage I'd need to get through a night of networking.

"What can I get you?" the bartender asked. She looked barely twenty, with pink hair and bright blue eyeliner.

"Whiskey. On the rocks," I replied, surprised by the smoke in my voice. The night had taken its toll, despite my experience working a room. As an introvert, I found it exhausting to be surrounded by so many people.

A presence loomed behind me with an oppressive aura of danger. The hairs on my neck stood as I turned, finding myself face to chest with a wall of muscle radiating heat and hostility.

My eyes traveled up, taking in the snaking tattoos that covered his arms and disappeared beneath his T-shirt. His right arm featured a dark grim reaper, its scythe poised above a macabre bed of intricate skulls. His left bicep featured the unmistakable emblem of the Marine Corps—an eagle, globe, and anchor.

As the man's cold gaze bore into my eyes, my intuition told me I stood before someone who had experienced—and likely participated in—more than his fair share of violence.

"Eva Harland," he said, his tone low and threatening.

I raised my brows in surprise. We hadn't been introduced, but he knew who I was. The weathered patch on his cut indicated he served as the club's vice president. This was Thane's right-hand man.

"And you are?"

His eyes narrowed at me. "Reaper. Mavericks VP."

The air between us crackled with tension. I sensed his distrust and the frustration that his attempt to unsettle me with his predatory gaze was failing miserably. I offered Reaper a smile and a handshake. This biker, menacing as he seemed, presented just another challenge. And I loved a challenge.

My smile shifted into a smirk as my eyes met his, unflinching, and I sipped my whiskey. I savored the burn as it slid down my throat and into the pit of my stomach. "Reaper? I'm guessing that's not the name your mother gave you."

Reaper's lips twitched almost imperceptibly. "What gave it away?"

"Your warm persona," I replied, my tone light. I probably shouldn't have needled him, but my drink emboldened me.

He raised a brow as he lifted the glass to his lips, drawing my gaze to how his crisp white T-shirt stretched across the planes of his chest. I bit my lip as I tried to refocus on the conversation.

"Let me guess ... you're not thrilled about an outsider like me coming in to help clean up this boycott mess."

He leaned against the bar, his muscular frame towering over me. "I'm not. Thane shouldn't have hired you. We don't need your help. And you won't be working with my company at all. PR isn't my style."

"And what exactly is your style?" I stared up at him with a disarming smile as if I were facing a harmless librarian rather than an ex-Marine biker with a penchant for violence. "Intimidation? Maybe some light torture? Sharp knives and bullets?"

A low chuckle rumbled through Reaper's chest as he tilted his head. His dark eyes studied mine. "You're not easily rattled."

I scoffed, rolling my eyes at his observation. "You can try to intimidate me all you want, but I've dealt with much worse than bikers with an image problem. You're not nearly as scary as you think you are."

"Is that so? And what exactly have you dealt with that's worse than us?"

A shiver licked down my spine, but I schooled my face into a neutral expression. Memories I'd tried to bury clawed their way to the surface, making my heart race as the conversation drifted into a pool I had no intention of swimming in with this stranger.

"My non-disclosure agreements prevent me from discussing client details. All you need to know is that I'm here to help. My job is to improve your club's image and manage the fallout from this boycott."

"How?" Reaper asked, his tone challenging.

"By showing this town there's more to the Mavericks than they think. You're not just hardcore bikers. The businesses impact the community in a real way. My job is to reveal your softer side. To show the good you bring to Conroe."

Reaper scoffed. "What if we don't have a softer side? What if we aren't the good guys you want to pretend we are?"

I leaned in, close enough to catch the scent of leather and cedar emanating from his chest. "Then I guess I'll have to dig deep, won't I?" I raised a brow in challenge.

Reaper was silent for a moment, appraising me before he straightened to his full height. A condescending smile played on his lips. "Good luck, PR girl. You'll need it."

Annoyance coursed through me. Some people thought of Samantha Jones from *Sex and the City* when they heard I worked in PR. They didn't realize the closer comparison was Beth Dutton from *Yellowstone*. My job wasn't schmoozing over cocktails. It was ruthless strategy, calculated moves, and playing the long game.

He continued to stare at me quietly. I knew I shouldn't ask my next question, but I couldn't resist.

"Tell me, Reaper. What does a VP do?" My curiosity would kill me one day.

"None of your fucking business." He turned his body back toward the bar in dismissal.

I shrugged, unsurprised by his reaction. "Well, I'm on retainer. Call me when you need me."

His gaze burned into my back as I returned to Rhetta. Her eyes twinkled with amusement as I approached.

"You met Reaper," she said, nodding toward the bar where he stood, his massive frame a dark silhouette against the neon signs. "He owns Grimm Construction."

"He's pleasant. A real delight," I said dryly as I glanced at him.

Rhetta laughed heartily as she noticed his steely gaze focused on me. "Thane told me he's skeptical. Where Thane sees opportunity, Reaper sees risk."

While I found it annoying, it didn't faze me. I'd often been hired by leaders, much to the dismay of their teams. I didn't aim to make friends or mince words when calling out shitty practices that would make reputation repair harder for an organization. Reaper wouldn't be the first man who didn't want to work with me. He sure as fuck wouldn't be the last.

"Wait? Is his last name Grimm?" I tried to stifle a laugh, but it slipped out anyway. "And he goes by Reaper?"

Rhetta offered a small smile. "I wouldn't make jokes about it. Especially not where these men can hear. Road names are earned. From what Thane told me, Reaper's had that name since he was a Marine sniper. It stuck for a reason."

I glanced at the man in question. The weight of his name settled in my mind. He looked every bit the personification of death, and I wondered how many people one would need to kill to earn that type of road name.

As more members walked in, the air thickened. The scent of cigarette smoke mingled with sweat, leather, and stale beer. Gruff laughs and the low timbre of conversations competed with the TV in the corner. Sweat began to bead at the nape of my neck as the clubhouse started to feel crowded.

As we wove through the room, I glanced over my shoulder, catching Reaper's intense stare. Our eyes locked, making my heart thunder in my chest.

"So, how are you settling in?" Rhetta asked, drawing my attention back as Reaper turned away. "I know it's a change from the big city."

I smiled, hearing the twinge of concern in her voice. "I like it here. It's nice to finally have a chance to breathe. All I did before was work and sleep. It doesn't feel like home yet, but D.C. never felt like home either."

"How's the foster pup? Have you decided to keep him yet?"

I gave Rhetta a fake grimace. "Hawk is a heathen. He's already destroyed a throw pillow and a pair of shoes. He'll be up for adoption once he gets his last round of shots."

Rhetta laughed. "You're in love already. I can tell. Fifty bucks says you end up adopting him. You should bring him by sometime. The guys might act tough, but they're suckers for dogs."

"Maybe I will," I mused. Bringing Hawk to the clubhouse could humanize me, making me more than an outsider in expensive boots.

A sudden crash cut through the air like a gunshot as the clubhouse door flew open. Heads whipped around as two men stumbled in, half dragging a third whose face was a mess of blood and bruised flesh. The coppery scent of blood hit me, turning my stomach.

The atmosphere in the room shifted. I watched as several Mavericks, including Rhetta and Reaper, moved to assist. Rhetta cleared a spot on a table, allowing Reaper to help lift the broken man onto the oak-grain surface. There was no panic or fear—just cold, precise action that spoke of far too much experience with situations like this.

I retreated to the bar, setting down my empty glass with a soft clink. The pink-haired bartender raised an eyebrow, silently offering another, but I shook my head. I had to drive home.

The commotion overwhelmed me, a maelstrom of raised voices and male aggression. I needed air, space, and a moment to process.

I slipped away from the crowd, finding a dim hallway near the bathrooms. The sounds from the main room were muffled here, allowing me a moment of relative peace.

Photos and newspaper clips from the past few decades lined the walls, along with a framed vest, the weathered patch indicating it had been worn by one of the club's founders nearly fifty years ago. Most of the newspaper clips highlighted photos from rallies or funerals attended by hundreds.

I breathed in, enjoying the quiet moment, until boots scuffed behind me. A figure loomed in the shadows at the end of the hallway. He took a step forward, and I noticed the prospect patch on his cut. Not a Maverick, but someone aspiring to be.

"Well, well," he drawled. "What's a pretty little thing like you doing all alone back here?"

I straightened my spine, forcing steel into my voice. "Just getting some air."

He moved closer, blocking my path to the main room. "We haven't been properly introduced."

I squared my shoulders, refusing to cower despite the alarm bells clanging in my head. "Unless you're a club member who owns a business, there's no reason Rhetta would have introduced us."

As I moved to push past him, the man grabbed my arm roughly. I pulled back as another voice cut through the tension.

"What the fuck are you doing back here, Scott?"

The man released his grip on my arm. Relief flooded through me as Reaper stepped into view, his massive frame filling the hallway. Irritation rolled off him in waves as his eyes fixed on the prospect.

The man's menacing demeanor changed in an instant. "Just welcoming our new friend, VP," he mumbled.

Reaper's gaze flicked to me, a silent question in his eyes, before returning to the man.

"Why don't you go make yourself useful at the bar." It wasn't a question.

The prospect didn't need to be told twice. He scurried away, leaving Reaper and me alone in the hallway.

Chapter Four

I'd watched Eva since our introduction. She was magnetic, and each person she met warmed up to her within minutes. Periodically, she would pull a small notepad from the back pocket of her jeans, jotting down notes from a conversation or handing it to the other person for their number.

When the chaos erupted—thanks to a bar fight between Cash and a Ranger—she slipped away.

My instincts screamed "threat." I'd fucking told Thane this was risky, and now I'd have to clean up the mess. I followed, expecting to catch Eva attempting to break into one of the offices.

Instead, I found her transfixed by our club's history, studying each photo with genuine interest.

After sending Scott packing, I turned to Eva, who had already refocused on a yellowed newspaper clip from the eighties.

"What are you doing back here?" I asked, my tone sharp.

Her glance back to me appeared inquisitive, not guilty or suspicious. "There's a lot more history to the club than I thought," she mused as she looked closer at club indicia from the early years.

I stepped closer and glared at her expectantly. She hadn't

answered my question. Eva studied me for a moment before she realized I waited for an answer.

"I just needed a minute away from the crowd. The noise. The
chaos. It was a bit much." She pulled her long hair away from her
neck.

For a moment, her mask slipped, and I could see the clubhouse
environment overwhelmed her.

I stepped closer. Eva stood barely a foot away now. I could smell
her sweet, citrusy perfume, a heady mix of orange blossom and
vanilla filling my senses. Most women would be fidgeting, seeking an
escape when facing a man like me. Instead, her ice blue–gray eyes
met my gaze with a hint of challenge.

"You shouldn't go into dark hallways alone. It can be dangerous
for a girl like you." My voice rumbled through the empty hall with a
slight echo.

She turned to face me, pursing her lips in a way that made me
want to bite down on them.

"I'm not scared of the dark. Or you, for that matter."

"You should be."

She raised a brow at me and stared directly into my eyes. "There
are a few men in this room who I should be scared of"—she paused,
poking her pointy little fingers into the center of my chest—"but you
are not one of them."

Un-fucking-believable. In one swift move, I had her wrists pinned
above her head, her back against the wall.

A slight sound pushed out of her, and heat curled in my gut as I
realized it wasn't distress. The expression on her face confirmed
she didn't have a shred of hesitation or fear when it came to me.
She instinctively pressed her body toward mine instead of pulling
away.

Fuck me.

I invaded her space even more, a growl rumbling in my chest.
Rather than alarm, her eyes lit up in delight. She flashed her teeth at
me in a wicked grin.

"Careful," she taunted. "I don't give a warning growl before I bite."

"Is that so?" I leaned in.

Her breath hitched. "Or maybe that's what you need," she joked. "Someone to bite back when you try to get all dark and menacing."

"Maybe you need someone to teach you some manners."

She barked out a laugh. "Good luck with that. I'm not a dog that you can clip a leash on and handle."

I pulled back, searching her face. Her eyes revealed unmistakable desire, accompanied by something else—a challenge, a dare, a darkness.

"Trust me, darling," I said, a free hand trailing down her side while I held her wrists with my other. "I'm more than capable of handling you."

She arched an eyebrow. A surge of heat coursed through me as her body subtly pressed closer.

"Big words from a man who keeps trying to intimidate me. A man who hasn't made a move yet."

I chuckled, releasing her wrists but keeping her pinned against the wall with my body, my arms caging around her. "Oh, I'll make my move. But not here. Not now. When I do, you'll be begging for it."

"Don't threaten me with a good time," she breathed. She brushed her hands across my shoulders before moving them down my chest.

The tension between us crackled, charged with a dangerous cocktail of attraction and defiance. I should walk away, but something about this woman drew me in like a moth to a flame. Or maybe like a fly to a black widow's web.

I leaned in, lowering a hand to wrap it softly around her throat to pull her closer. Her lips parted slightly, and I could feel the warmth of her breath.

I sensed a savage edge beneath her polished, corporate persona. A dark side she kept hidden away. This woman was lethal, but there was a softness between her sharp teeth and claws. She drew me into her deadly web, but damn it all to hell. I wanted to kiss her anyway.

As our lips were about to meet, Thane shattered the moment, his thundering voice echoing down the hallway.

"Reaper! We need to handle the Ranger situation. Now."

I shifted back, but my eyes remained locked on Eva's. She deftly stepped away and moved around me, smoothing her clothes with practiced ease.

The transformation happened instantly. She glanced toward Thane, who had already walked away, not caring to see what woman had captured my attention. She ran a hand through her long hair and inhaled a steady breath. The woman who'd just been pressed against me, all heat and challenge, shifted back to the cool, collected professional I'd first seen in Linc's file.

"Goodnight, Reaper," she said as she sauntered past me, the sway of her hips a deliberate taunt.

As I watched her disappear around the corner, it became clear I was in trouble.

Eva fucking Harland was about to become my own personal hell.

Chapter Five

The cool night air hit my flushed skin as I drove home with the windows down.

The Mavericks weren't what I'd expected. Sure, they exuded that tough biker image, but beneath the leather and ink, I'd met business owners, family men, and community members. It was a welcome shift from the soulless weasels, bloodthirsty hyenas, and political vultures I'd dealt with in D.C. Throughout the evening, I'd built connections and walked away with a few solid leads on stories to develop.

I'd also crossed a line in the clubhouse. Reaper was a client, which meant he was off limits. No matter how much replaying our encounter in the hallway sent shivers down my spine.

His intensity both thrilled and unnerved me. I'd dealt with powerful men before, but Reaper was different. He didn't hide behind a sharp suit or boardroom bravado. He didn't bother with masks or manners. Reaper personified raw, untamed power. He embodied the fears whispered about outlaw bikers—making him intoxicating and achingly tempting. God, what was it about bad boys and beasts that caused women to lose all common sense?

Pulling into my driveway, I gripped the steering wheel tighter, forcing myself to focus, and drew a deep breath. I couldn't afford to blur the lines between professional and personal. I had to remind myself why I was here: to rebuild my life and escape the shadows that had chased me from D.C.

As I braced myself for the whirlwind of puppy energy waiting on the other side of the door, I made a silent vow. I would give this project my all, pouring every ounce of my skill and determination into it. And I would maintain my professional boundaries, especially with Reaper—no matter how my skin tingled at his touch or how my heart raced when I looked into his dark eyes. I couldn't risk compromising the contract.

The Lone Star Mavericks Motorcycle Club was now my client, and I had a job to do.

* * *

The sun beat mercilessly as I pulled into Jack's Car Repair, the gravel crunching under my Jeep's tires. Thane's quick green light on my ideas represented another small victory for my growing PR business.

Even better, the reporter responded to my pitch within a day, practically salivating at the chance to cover a story associated with the boycott. The news outlets were starved for the kind of gritty, humanized narratives I planned to package for them—even if they featured stories showing only a carefully orchestrated side.

Hawk's excited bark pierced the air as we stepped out, his tail wagging at the sight of the lanky high schoolers milling about outside the repair shop. I couldn't help but smile at his infectious enthusiasm.

Jack rolled out from under a red 1950s Ford truck, his face a mix of grease and apprehension.

"Hey, Jack."

His hands twisted together, and he cleared his throat twice. He smiled at me, clearly nervous about today's interview. I'd expected as much; he'd only agreed because his president insisted.

"It's good to see you. You brought a friend." He wiped the grease from his hands on a stained red rag and smiled at the wiggling pup in my arms.

"This is Hawk. He's my foster puppy. I'm trying to expose him to more people and teach him some manners."

Jack relaxed as he ruffled Hawk's ears, earning an excited nip. The tension in his shoulders eased, and I made a mental note: Hawk proved an excellent icebreaker. I lowered the puppy to the ground and hooked the leash around a belt loop to keep him anchored nearby.

"The reporter will be here in about an hour. I wanted to run through a few things with you first."

Jack regularly opened his shop to a few local high schoolers, giving them the space, tools, and mentorship to help them restore an old Ford Bronco. The story I'd pitched to the local news highlighted how a Maverick gave back, significantly impacting his community.

As we practiced for the interview, the story took shape. Jack's journey from local high school grad to young yet respected business owner made for a compelling narrative, but his mentorship was what really shone. His eyes lit up when he talked about teaching the boys the basics of restoration and helping them breathe new life into the old Ford.

"If they veer off-topic, especially about the Mavericks, use the response we practiced," I advised, adjusting his collar. "Keep it simple and redirect to the restoration project."

Jack nodded. "Got it. Stick to the talking points."

I patted his arm. "I know you usually don't wear it while working, but we should have the reporter capture some b-roll of you talking to the kids while you wear your cut. It will help us show your affiliation to the club without calling it out."

A flicker of pride crossed his face, briefly overshadowing his nervousness.

I squeezed his shoulder in reassurance. "You've got this. Just be yourself."

Jack's warm and genuine demeanor would be great on camera. I hoped his would be the first of many stories to show the community the softer side of the Mavericks—the side Reaper insisted didn't exist.

I stepped away with Hawk and started my Jeep to let the air crank on high. I settled the pup in the back, safely locked in his crate with a peanut butter–filled toy. Following the attention and excitement, I expected him to drift off to sleep in minutes.

The news van pulled up, and I greeted the reporter and her crew as they unloaded their gear from the back.

The thunderous roar of a Harley shattered the relative calm, drawing all eyes to the sleek matte white bike with black pipes pulling up beside the news van. The scythe emblazoned on the gas tank left me with no doubt about the rider's identity.

My heart performed a series of traitorous flips as Reaper dismounted, his presence dominating the space. His black cut and inked arms offset the crisp white T-shirt he wore beneath. Instead of a helmet, he wore a backward baseball cap.

The reporter tensed, fear flashing in her eyes. She strode away behind her cameraman, eager to put as much distance between her and Reaper as possible. While Jack offered a warm, welcoming vibe, Reaper's presence was chilling in the Texas heat.

I ground my teeth. "What are you doing here?"

"Thane asked me to come."

Irritation swept through me. "Why?"

He offered a saccharine smile that didn't reach his eyes. "Because it's my job to be here, according to the prez. So here I am."

I sighed. I couldn't argue with Thane. At least, not yet. "Fine. Just keep your distance. You're making the reporter nervous."

I spun on my heel and walked away without giving him a second glance. I didn't find it surprising Thane wanted a club representative present, but sending his VP seemed excessive.

Despite Reaper's looming presence, the story came together

nicely. The high school boys raved about the hands-on, real-world skills they'd learned throughout the project. Jack's personal account of how the shop teacher had been a lifeline for him just a few years ago, inspiring him to pay it forward, added a touching depth to the narrative.

Reaper stepped beside me as the crew captured b-roll of the boys and Jack talking and laughing in front of the shop. The reporter glanced up at his imposing form and voiced an excuse, saying she needed to check in with her producer.

"I think she's scared of you," I said dryly.

Reaper smirked. "Of course she's scared of me. What I want to know is why you aren't."

I met his gaze, unflinching. "Because the true monsters are usually the ones you least expect. They hide behind smiles, handshakes, and bibles, not leather and patches."

* * *

The setting sun cast a warm light across the wood floors in my home office as I hunched over my laptop, sifting through a digital labyrinth of police reports, employee announcements, and email leads.

My eyes burned from hours of screen time. I'd already spent a day on video calls, meeting with clients and talking to editors. But I couldn't stop my investigation at night. Each piece of information added another fragment to the mosaic of Hale Abell's mistreatment of women, and I believed we had nearly enough information to break the story.

A soft whine drew my attention to Hawk. He stared at me with his soft brown eyes. I reached out to scratch behind his ears, guilt twinging in my chest. Sometimes I became so deeply entrenched in my work that I'd forget I had a puppy—at least while he napped. If I didn't take him out to play soon, he'd either piss on my floor or find his own entertainment by chewing on something he shouldn't.

"Sorry, buddy," I murmured. His tail thumped against the floor, a plea for attention. "I promise we'll go for a long walk in a few minutes. I just need to talk to Matt, and then I'll be done for the day. I promise."

He let out a low whine. As if on cue, my phone screen lit up as the cheery tone rang through the air. I took a deep breath before throwing in my earbuds.

"Hey, Matt."

"Eva!" His voice boomed, full of its usual enthusiasm. "How's life in the Lone Star State? Are you line dancing in a cowboy hat yet? Maybe joining a rodeo?"

I laughed, picturing myself stumbling through a crowded dance floor with my two left feet. "Definitely not. There isn't enough tequila in this state for me to try line dancing. But I'll keep rodeo clown as a career option if my consulting business fails."

Matt chuckled. "Have you found yourself a cowboy yet?"

His tone was less teasing, and I rolled my eyes. While only a friend, Matt often seemed all too concerned about my romantic interests.

"No, Matt. No cowboy."

Just a sinfully hot, tattooed biker with a bad attitude, I added mentally.

I shifted the conversation, not wanting to get into my new association with the Mavericks with my friend. He'd ask far too many questions.

"Listen, I have to fly to Houston soon for a few interviews. I'm digging into some tips about corruption at one of the big oil companies. I'll be in town for a few days. We could meet for lunch." His excitement was palpable.

I double-clicked on my desktop calendar. "Sure, I'm flexible almost every day next week. I think we have enough that we can map out the story."

"I like the way you think. We're getting close. I can feel it."

My adrenaline surged at the thought of finally bringing Hale's crimes to light. Matt's story in the Washington Post would expose the pattern of violence and abuse I knew all too well.

"I wanted to let you know I've turned up a new source. We have a call scheduled soon, but ..." I hesitated, knowing Matt would be irritated at this next revelation. "She only wants to talk to me. And only on background. We won't be able to use her in the story, but I think she could shed light into the patterns we've uncovered."

Matt paused on the other end of the line. When he spoke again, his voice had lost some of its zeal. "Who is she?"

"I can't tell you. She insisted on complete anonymity. She's terrified of what might happen if word gets out that she's talking."

"Come on," Matt said, frustration creeping into his tone. "You know my editor won't let us use her if we can't identify her."

I rubbed my temples, a headache brewing. "I know, I know. But let's see what details she shares first. She worked for Abell Enterprises for a long time. Longer than most. She's probably seen a lot of women come and go. Maybe we can find a way to corroborate her information without revealing her identity."

Matt's sigh crackled through the phone. "Fine. Just don't make any promises."

"If she has good information, I'll see if I can convince her to go on the record," I promised. "Maybe we could use a pseudonym in the story."

Matt groaned. "We'll need to validate the facts before we publish. Hale's lawyers are going to be on our asses when this gets out. Everything has to be by the book. I can't let your little side project end my career."

I ground my teeth at his comment. "I'll update you later, okay?" My response came out tighter than I intended as I ended the call.

Heat prickled at the back of my neck. When he'd offered to partner with me on the story, Matt thought it could elevate his career. Now, he acted like it was a favor.

I hooked the leash onto Hawk's collar. I needed a walk as much as he did. My phone rang as we stepped out the door, and I tensed—

until I read the name on the caller ID. I fumbled to answer the Face-Time call while juggling my keys.

"Do you miss me yet?" Kenna asked immediately as I answered.

I laughed, feeling the tension releasing from my shoulders as the familiar face of my best friend filled the screen. "I do. I'm sorry I haven't called. Between my new client and the story with Matt, I've barely had time to sleep."

"You need to make time for a personal life," Kenna chided, tossing her auburn hair over her shoulders.

I laughed, squinting at my screen in the bright Texas sun. "You're one to talk."

"Valid point. It's not the same here without you," she said, her voice softening. "Are you moving back?"

"Nope. Maybe you should move here," I joked. "The weather is better, and so are the tacos. Plus, you need to come meet my foster pup before he gets adopted." I pivoted my phone down to show Hawk trotting alongside me with his nose to the ground.

"Cute!" she squealed. "But you had me at tacos. Tell me about this new client."

I hesitated. "They aren't exactly mainstream corporate."

Kenna perked up. "Wait, is this another weird software start-up? I can't work with another techbro CEO."

I laughed, remembering the horror stories of one of her former clients who considered himself a cooler version of Mark Zuckerberg. "I'm working with the Lone Star Mavericks. Reputation repair and crisis management, mostly."

Kenna set down her phone, and I watched the ceiling for a moment as I listened to her tap a keyboard. She gasped before picking it back up to look at me.

"Eva. You can't be working with a biker gang. These guys are dangerous."

"Not all the headlines are true," I said defensively. "I have a story running today about a Maverick that mentors high school boys."

A few more clicks and Kenna hummed. "I see that. Jack Patino. He's cute. Is he single? You should go out with him."

I laughed. "I can't date a client."

"Sure you can," Kenna said nonchalantly. "You own the company. That means you make the HR rules and you can do whatever you want. It's been a while since you've let your hair down. And these guys certainly look like they know how to have some fun."

I rolled my eyes. "Jesus, you sound just like Rhetta."

Kenna cackled. "Has she handpicked a biker for you?"

I groaned as Kenna continued to prod.

"Please tell me he has tattoos. And that he's packing more than a gun." Kenna waggled her brows suggestively.

I hesitated a second too long.

"Oh my God. Are you blushing? Who is it? Tell me everything."

I tried to sound casual. "It's not like that."

"Uh-huh," Kenna drawled, not buying it for a second. "I'm looking at a group photo of the club I found on a news site. So, which one is he? Is it the brooding one with the murdery eyes? Or the one with the scar on his cheek? The blond one is too pretty for you. He's more my type. Maybe I should move to Texas ..."

I nearly tripped over Hawk as I laughed. "Kenna!"

She giggled with delight. "So, what's his name?"

I sighed. "Reaper."

Kenna stayed quiet for a beat. "You're making that up."

"I wish I was. That's his road name. I don't know his real one."

Kenna whistled. "Reaper. Jesus. That's not intimidating at all. Is he hot?"

I hesitated again, which was answer enough.

"Oh, he's hot. You have to at least send me a picture. For HR purposes."

I shook my head. "You're impossible. Nothing can happen. He's the VP of the club. My HR director says he's off limits."

"You should fire that bitch."

I chuckled as I shook my head. "This is the biggest contract I've landed so far. I can't risk it."

"Bummer. Promise me you'll call if you need me to move to Texas to be your backup. Or if you need bail money."

"Deal. But if you join my company, you can't veto my HR decisions."

"Rude. Love you."

"Love you too, Kenna."

I hung up. The pressure in my chest eased, replaced by the familiar warmth of my best friend's teasing echoing in my mind. Ever since college, we'd dreamed about starting a consultancy together during late-night study sessions fueled by cheap wine, cold pizza, and wild ambition.

Kenna had considered moving to Texas to start this consultancy with me. I understood why she'd stayed behind, though. She was still piecing herself together. She tried to hide it, but I noticed the weight in her eyes. Kenna needed space to breathe, to figure out who she was when grief wasn't the loudest part of her story.

I missed her. Not just her wit and friendship, but the way she always saw straight through me. She was the one person who would call me on my bullshit—my doubts, my fears, and my stupid crush on a biker.

It had always been the two of us against the world. But lately, we'd been living parallel lives—close enough to see each other's struggles, but too far apart to help in the ways that mattered.

Still, every time we spoke, the spark in her eyes flared brighter. Like the Japanese art of kintsugi, where broken cracks are filled with gold to create something stronger and more beautiful, maybe moving to Texas and building a business together could be the gold she needed to fill the cracks in her heart.

Hawk tugged at the leash, pulling me back to the present. I glanced down at him, his tail wagging as he sniffed a fire hydrant. I smiled, a little wistful. Selfishly, I hoped she'd consider moving so we could finally make our dream a reality—together.

Chapter Six

Each interaction with Eva left me with a gnawing sense of irritation.

My patch prompted either fear or fawning from most women—she gave me neither. She acted unafraid of who I was or what I could do, and she hadn't attempted to flirt her way onto my bike or into my bed. It unsettled me.

"Flip to twenty-six," I barked across the room to Leah, our bartender. She changed the TV channel just in time for us to watch Jack's smiling face and the story that painted him as your friendly neighborhood mechanic and high school mentor.

Linc sidled up beside me and pressed a cold beer into my hand. "So, what's your read on Eva?"

I shot him a sidelong glance. The story on screen drew my attention back as I watched the clips of Jack pretending to work on the truck wearing his cut, proudly showing his membership to the club. I had to admit it was brilliant of Eva to ask him to wear it.

"I'm still figuring her out. How deep was her background check?"

"Standard-level shit."

"Go deeper."

Linc raised his eyebrows at my request. "Why?"

I took a long pull from my beer. "Something she said in passing. My gut is telling me there's more. Go back further. Check into her family. Her friends. Her fuck buddies. Hell, look into where she went to high school. We're missing something."

Linc looked skeptical, trying to work out what exactly I sought and why I cared.

"Good fucking story, right?" Thane's meaty hand landed on my shoulder, gripping tight before releasing. He nodded to the TV. "I want you to be there for the next one."

I bristled. "What do you mean, the next one?"

Thane pulled a pack of smokes from the front pocket of his flannel, taking a Marlboro between his lips and lighting up. "Maisie is delivering muffins and coffee to the women's shelter Thursday morning. Reading to the kids, too. You're going."

My stomach dropped and I groaned. "Fuck me. Why?"

"First, I want one of us there to make sure the publicity doesn't stir up any unwanted attention—from the Rangers in particular, but also if Danielle shows up spouting about the boycott. Second, I'm not entirely sure we can trust Eva yet. She's good at what she does, but she's an outsider. I need you to make sure she's not digging too deep or asking the wrong questions."

"Don't you have someone else you can send?"

Thane shook his head. "Nope. I need Linc to put together plans for our next run, and Merrick is heading to Illinois for Merci's graduation. It was canceled in December because of that ice storm and they rescheduled it for this weekend."

"No shit. The kid is graduating from med school already?"

Thane nodded. "Top of her class at Northwestern."

"Yeah, Merrick can't miss that. He's worked too hard to get his baby sister to the finish line."

Thane continued his line of thought. "I know you have your reasons for not wanting to, but I need you there. You're the VP. I trust you to know when to step in."

Memories flashed through my mind. Off-brand grape juice boxes, threadbare sheets on a cot, and stuffed animals that'd seen better days.

I ran a hand across the back of my neck in frustration. My jaw clenched at the thought of shadowing our consultant while she paraded around town, stirring up fuck all. I had better things to do with my time—a company to run, weapons deals to broker, rivals to keep in check.

It was just like Thane to delegate something like this to me. Hiring the consultant was his shitty idea, not mine, but I understood the necessity of having a club officer on site. If Eva started to head in the wrong direction, someone needed to run interference. And since Thane planned to retire within the next few years and wanted me to become president when he stepped down, he'd begun to give me more responsibility.

"Fine," I growled, not bothering to hide my displeasure. "I'll babysit the consultant."

Thane chuckled at my outburst. "At least the view is good. She's got a nice rack and wears those tight jeans. I apologize for making you suffer, brother."

I ignored his comment. The last thing I needed was to think about how Eva filled out her blue jeans. I drained the last of my beer and slammed the glass bottle to the bartop harder than necessary. "If this goes sideways, I'm pulling the plug. Not just on whatever story she has reporters out to cover, but this entire goddamn PR circus. I'm not fucking kidding."

Thane nodded, his expression serious. "That's why I'm sending you." He crushed his cigarette on the clay ashtray. It was godawful, but he loved it because his nephew made it. "You've got the judgment to know when to step in. And you'll know if we need to stop working with Eva entirely."

As I left Thane's office, the familiar burden of club leadership settled on my shoulders. He respected me like a brother, trusting me with the club's present and future.

I knew he thought Eva's efforts would ultimately help the club, but the truth didn't make this assignment any less of a pain in the ass. I couldn't shake the nagging thought that this woman would cause more trouble than she was worth. But the club came first, always. If keeping an eye on Eva was what we needed right now, then that's what I'd do.

* * *

The rumble of my Harley announced my arrival, and I couldn't help but grin at the flash of irritation that crossed Eva's face as she realized it was me.

Before I could even kill the engine, she tore into me, eyes blazing.

"Absolutely not. You're not coming in to intimidate another reporter."

I swung off the bike. "I'm not here to intimidate. Just to make sure the right story gets told."

I liked how the fury built in her eyes. She squared off, hands on her hips.

"That's my job. Storytelling is my lane. Yours is ... whatever you do as a VP." She waved her hand at my bike dismissively.

I opened my mouth to retort, but Maisie's van pulled up, defusing some of the tension. She stepped out, wearing her cut for the news crew, and opened the back door to reveal boxes of fresh pastries and two large disposable jugs of hot coffee from the grounds she roasted at her bakery. I wrapped an arm around her in a hug.

"I promise not to intimidate anyone. I'll carry these in and stay at the back of the room." I smirked as her eyes narrowed at me. Maybe she did have more bite than bark.

"Fine," Eva growled. "But if at any fucking point I notice someone is uncomfortable with your presence, you leave. This isn't about you or your little club. These women have been through hell, and I will not let an eight-foot-tall ogre intimidate them."

Maisie laughed as she patted my arm. "Come on, dear," she said, handing Eva a coffee jug. "Let the ogre do the heavy lifting. We might as well take advantage of him."

I raised a brow. "Yes. Please, take advantage of me."

Eva blushed and then huffed, mumbling under her breath and walking away without a second glance.

The familiar scent of industrial cleaner, thrifted clothing, and desperation cut through me like a set of throwing knives as I carried the boxes into the shelter. I sucked in a shallow breath. This place stirred up memories I'd fought for years to bury. I sighed as I set the boxes on the table, trying to steady the emotion that threatened to rise.

I scanned the room, taking in the worn furniture and scattered toys. I shifted my weight from foot to foot and clenched my fists. Maisie gave me a knowing glance as if she sensed the turmoil rolling in my gut. She probably remembered what she'd seen the day Don had called the club to come to my mother's rescue.

A few women cast wary glances at me, but most ignored my presence. I could sense the suffocating weight of their stories mixing with my own dark history.

"Text me if you need anything else. I'll wait with my bike." My voice came out rough and too loud in the quiet room. I didn't wait for a reply. I stepped outside and let the door thud shut behind me.

Leaning against my bike, I tried to shake off the ghosts of my past. Mom, Linc, and I spent time in a shelter just like this. It might have even been this one. I couldn't recall.

Linc, young and resilient, adapted quickly. But I was old enough to recognize the haunted look in Mom's eyes. I could still hear the tremor in her voice as she spoke to the crisis counselor when she thought we slept. The snapshot of her bruised and battered face flashed before me, and I clenched my jaw, willing the images away.

That was a lifetime ago. She was safe now.

Desperate for a distraction, I pulled out my phone to skim through emails. The potential contract for Conroe's new charter school loomed in my mind. It would be a game-changer for my construction company—new hires, including a project manager, and a chance to make Grimm Construction a bigger fish in the Greater Houston market.

If the boycott didn't threaten my chance at winning the bid.

I shook the thought from my mind. My company would recover. Even if we didn't get the charter school contract, others would come along. The boycott would fade from memory, and the social media warriors would find something else to be angry about.

I didn't need to complicate my life by allowing Eva to help.

Finally, nearly an hour later, Eva emerged with the reporter. She offered smiles and handshakes to the news crew before walking toward the southern magnolia I stood beneath.

I slipped my phone back into the pocket of my cut as I watched her approach, a strange feeling stirring in my chest.

Eva's eyes shone bright with enthusiasm. Her work fueled her, filling her with a radiating energy. "Maisie wants to stay a bit longer. The kids adore her. She read a book about motorcycles and even made her own sound effects. It was so damn cute."

I glanced back at the building, my expression stoic. I moved to my bike, swinging a leg over and turning my baseball hat backward.

"One of the little boys even asked to try on her cut," she added. "Then he said he wanted to be a motorcycle when he grows up." She let out a small laugh, gazing at me as she waited for a response. I remained silent.

"She wants to offer at least one of the women a job at the bakery. She said Don would swing by in a few minutes, so you can leave."

I nodded, pressing the ignition on my bike. The sooner I left this haunted place, with its echoes of a past I'd rather forget, the better.

"I guess I'll talk to you at the next one?" Her tone seemed almost taunting. It was as if she wanted to push my buttons, to remind me I had no interest in being her chaperone. "Thanks for coming."

I huffed. "My pleasure." My voice dripped with sarcasm and dark malice that usually sent most women skittering. But instead of flinching, Eva smiled, throwing me off balance as she climbed into her Jeep.

This woman was dangerous—not because she feared me, but because she didn't. And a part of me was starting to like it.

* * *

The dim light of the back office cast long shadows across the room as I closed the door. Dixon's boot tapped on the floor impatiently. Thane was away, but I'd asked Dixon to meet to discuss a potential contract before Merrick hit the road.

I spread my palms across the top of Thane's desk as I stretched my neck from side to side, my muscles still tense from the morning. "All right. You've been itching for a job. One just came in this morning."

Dixon leaned forward, his eyes gleaming with excitement and desperation. He'd probably lost all his money at the casino in Livingston last weekend. "About fucking time."

Merrick laid out a dossier, spreading a handful of pages across the clean desk. "The target is a high-profile exec in Houston. Oil company bigwig," I explained. "Seven figures. The kill needs to be clean. This can't be like the San Antonio fiasco last month."

Contract killing jobs were rare but lucrative, and we had a reputation for handling contracts with discretion and efficiency. Only the club's officers and Dixon knew about this particular "service" we offered.

Dixon broke the silence. "So, am I taking this one or what?"

Merrick and I exchanged glances. His expression was unreadable, as always. "It's yours," I confirmed. "The club gets twenty percent, as always. And this time, you follow the plan. No cowboy shit."

Dixon grinned. "You got it, boss."

"If I have to send Merrick in to unfuck this job after you make a mess, I'll kill you myself."

Dixon leaned back in his chair, unbothered by my threat. "Speaking of unfucking things, what's this I hear about some PR chick sniffing around the club? Hatchet said Thane hired her as a consultant?"

Merrick's face darkened, contrasting with the scar slashed across his cheek. "It's a fucking mistake, if you ask me. Having some outsider poking around? It's asking for trouble."

I ground my teeth. "You're not wrong. But ..."

"But what?" Dixon pressed.

"She's good at what she does," I admitted. "I've been watching her work. So far, she's sticking to what Thane wants—helping the businesses."

Merrick's gaze narrowed, his eyes piercing in the dim light. "And if she gets out of line? Finds out something she's not supposed to know?"

His voice was calm, but there was an underlying tension, a sense of readiness. It was why we'd selected him to serve as our sergeant at arms.

I shrugged. "Then you know my orders. Protect the club at whatever cost necessary."

Chapter Seven

Watching the stories I curated for my clients air on TV always sent a rush through my chest—even after all these years of working in PR. The two-minute story on ABC 13 was a far cry from the media placements I'd earned on *Good Morning America* over the years, but it was no less fulfilling.

Immediately after the story aired, my phone pinged with a text.

Rhetta: Nice work! Thane is thrilled.

Me: Happy to hear!

Rhetta: You should swing by the clubhouse next Thursday. We're having a birthday party for Thane. Live music, open bar, BBQ.

Me: Thanks for the invite … I'll think about it.

Rhetta: Get your introverted ass out of the house, or I will drag you out myself.

I laughed. Rhetta had hauled me to more parties than I could count in high school. Even though I always wanted to stay home with a good book, I had fun when she got me out of the house.

> Me: Fine. I'll be there.

I settled at my desk, readying myself for a virtual meeting with another of Hale's victims.

Amy Sullivan had spent several years working at Abell Enterprises and left shortly before I was hired. She had an impressive background, having worked for some of the top executives on the East Coast. Former colleagues on LinkedIn raved about her ability to solve problems, manage difficult schedules, and multitask. She seemed like the kind of person you'd want at your side if you led a multimillion-dollar company. It was probably why they'd recruited her.

As I waited for Amy to join the call, a familiar knot of anxiety tightened in my stomach. I'd agreed to this one without a second thought, but I hesitated in these moments before the discussions. I straightened my ink pens and notepads on my desk to steady my nerves. Each interview dredged up memories of my time working at Abell Enterprises, a torturous form of exposure therapy.

I hated how listening to others recount their experiences under Hale's tyrannical management made my heart thunder. While my rational side knew I was thousands of miles away, the memories filled me with dread.

I sipped my coffee as I skimmed through the list of questions on my main screen and launched the transcription app on the other. The video screen flickered as a curvy blonde wearing thick black glasses joined the call. "Hi, Amy."

"Hi." Her tired eyes and nervous energy tore at me, reminding me of the importance of this story.

"Thank you for agreeing to speak with me. I understand how difficult this must be."

She bit her lip before responding. "I'm just hoping I can help.

Becca told me about you. Said you're trying to expose Hale for who he really is."

"I am. How long did you work for him?"

"Three years. I covered the front desk, mostly. I managed his calendar and screened his calls."

I leaned in. Her tenure was longer than most. "Can you tell me about your time there? What was it like?"

Amy's expression tightened. "I thought I was lucky at first. Avoided the worst of it. Most of the time, Hale left me alone. I did my job well, and it helped me stay off his radar."

I nodded to encourage her to continue. This wasn't new. Every woman I spoke to thought they could somehow avoid Hale's advances and abuse. But eventually, he would take notice. And, once he did, he didn't stop.

Amy took a shaky breath. "He seemed to single out one woman at a time. Once he had a target, he looked for every opportunity to manipulate them. It was like it gave him some sick sense of power. He'd change meeting times without telling them, then berate them for being late. He would 'lose' their reports and then call them incompetent. He'd tell them how great they were one day and then fly off the handle the next. It was a real Jekyll and Hyde situation."

Her words reminded me of the painful, toxic environment I'd experienced. Hale's sudden mood swings. Walking on eggshells every single day. The constant gaslighting. Rage-fueled one-on-ones followed by team meetings in which Hale showered you with praise after handing you a latte. The manipulative experience left the team tired, confused, and on edge.

I couldn't help but consider how Hale had twisted my own reality. How often had I doubted my abilities and sanity while working at Abell Enterprises? A familiar tension clawed through my chest as she spoke. I breathed deeply to center myself and focused on my list of questions.

"Did you witness any physical abuse?" I'd heard rumors that other women had been on the receiving end of Hale's unchecked rage, though I hoped none had endured an attack as brutal as my own.

Amy clenched her jaw. "Yes. His marketing director, Sarah, once left with a bloody nose. I don't know what exactly happened. But it was clear he hit her. Hard."

My stomach dropped. "What happened after that?"

"That's the thing. It was like it never happened. Benjamin Abell strolled in, pulled me aside, and handed me an envelope filled with cash. He said it was mine if I told the cop some random man ran out of the office with bloody knuckles."

My fingers froze over the keyboard. "And did you?"

Amy nodded, shame coloring her expression. "I was too scared not to. But that's not even the worst part. The cop didn't even blink. That's when it hit me. They've got the police in their pocket. That's how Hale has gotten away with this for so long."

I'd suspected as much based on how the police reports I'd read noted high crime in the buildings where Hale worked. Still, Amy's testimony provided the confirmation I'd sought for months.

I nodded, taking a deep breath before asking my final question. "You lasted a lot longer than anyone else I've spoken to. What made you leave?"

Amy's eyes dropped to her hands. She remained silent for a long moment, as if wrestling with whether to share this part of her story.

"I thought I was different. I thought I was safe because I wasn't his type. I kept my head down and did my job. Then, one night, I stayed late. I was finishing some paperwork, and Hale came out of his office. He'd been drinking. He cornered me. Started talking about how loyal I was, how much he appreciated me."

Amy took a deep breath to center herself. I stayed silent, hoping my expression showed empathy that would encourage her to open up.

"He put his hand on my shoulder, and I just froze. That's when he leaned in and whispered, 'It's time you show me just how loyal you can be.'"

I fought to keep my expression neutral.

"I panicked. I shoved him away and ran. I didn't stop running until I was in my car." Amy's eyes met mine through the screen, filled with shame. "I never went back. Left everything at my desk. Blocked his number and his email. I was terrified he'd come after me, but I guess I wasn't worth the trouble."

"I'm sorry that happened to you." I paused, collecting my thoughts. This information could help us hit national headlines. "Would you be willing to go on the record with any of this?"

Panic flashed across her face. "No! Absolutely not. I signed an NDA, and Hale has eyes everywhere. If he found out I talked ..." She glanced off-screen. "I have kids. I can't risk it."

"I completely understand and will keep this all on background. I promise." I paused before I continued. I didn't usually share my story with sources, but I wanted Amy to know. She needed the reassurance that I understood the seriousness of the situation.

I broke out into a cold sweat as memories flashed through my mind. "I worked at Abell Enterprises after you left and ended up in the hospital. Hale attacked me after a meeting. I'm glad you left when you did."

Understanding and shared pain flashed in Amy's eyes. "So this isn't just a story to you? This is personal. Promise me you'll nail this bastard. Make sure he can't hurt anyone else."

"I promise. One way or another, Hale Abell will face justice."

As our call ended, I sat back to process Amy's story. Every interview was one more piece of the puzzle I needed to hold Hale accountable for his actions and the extreme lengths he and his father would go to bury their secrets.

I closed my eyes. Dark memories flashed through my mind and fear pressed into my chest. The phantom pressure of Hale's hands grasping around my throat caused my breath to catch.

I pushed the feelings away, focusing my thoughts on the brave women I'd spoken to and those too scared to come forward. Their stories of abuse and manipulation at the hands of the Abells fueled my desire for justice.

For retribution.

* * *

My arrival at the clubhouse felt different from my first few visits. Familiar faces nodded in my direction as I parked in my Jeep, and Jack offered a friendly wave. My successful placement of his story on the news lent me credibility, helping others see the value in my involvement with the club.

Rhetta had somehow transformed the yard into a raucous birthday carnival to celebrate Thane's fiftieth. Leather-clad men and women strolled through the yard while children played under the trees. Rhetta mentioned it would be a family affair, but I hadn't quite believed her until now.

A band played a lively mix of honky-tonk and classic rock. Sweat-slicked prospects hustled around massive grills, and tendrils of hickory smoke curled through the air, carrying the mouthwatering aroma of sizzling steaks.

A tent on the other side of the building drew appreciative cheers as scantily clad women twirled around gleaming poles. I couldn't help but chuckle, picturing Rhetta's mischievous grin as she arranged this particular surprise for her husband. When she'd first mentioned hiring strippers as a birthday gift, I'd assumed she was joking—or at least exaggerating.

Weaving through the sea of leather and denim, I found Thane holding court near the outdoor bar beside an enormous Jack Daniel's–themed cake.

"Happy birthday." I handed him a bottle of expensive bourbon with a bow. While Rhetta had insisted I didn't need to bring a gift, I wanted to provide a token of appreciation to the client who had finally taken my bank account from red to black.

Thane's eyes crinkled as he grinned. "Thanks, darlin'. Glad you could make it." He gestured to a group of picnic tables under a cusp of oak trees. "Rhetta and the old ladies are over there if you want to join them."

I nodded in thanks as I strode across the yard and sat beside my friend. I traced the initials and crude drawings carved into the worn table with my fingers.

"How does it feel to be robbed from the cradle?" I began, a teasing lilt in my voice. "What are you, like fifteen years younger than the birthday boy?"

The other women laughed, and Rhetta swatted my arm. "Age is just a number, sugar. Besides, I keep that old man young."

Rhetta introduced the group of old ladies I hadn't yet met.

"This is Cora," she said, gesturing to a twenty-something blonde with a pixie cut sitting beside Maisie. "She's with Ace."

I shook her hand and noticed an intricate tattoo wrapped around her pale, scarred wrist.

"And this is Jess. She's with Reno."

Jess nodded at me from across the table, brushing her hair from her face as her green eyes assessed me.

"And I don't know if you remember her, but this is Taryn. The two of you met at my bridal shower. She's with Tomcat."

"Of course I remember," I exclaimed. "You had adorable twin girls, from what I recall."

Taryn nodded proudly. "Tilly and Talia. They're the ones using Reaper as a jungle gym right now with Cora's boy, Leo."

I glanced across the yard, letting out an unexpected laugh as I saw two five-year-old girls hanging off Reaper's large frame with a boy of about ten sitting on his shoulders. The sight of the man who commanded respect overrun by a pack of children caught me off guard.

I noticed Merrick's intense gaze from across the bar as we chatted. The sergeant at arms watched my every move with suspicion as he spoke to a blond-haired, blue-eyed biker. I tensed under his scrutiny as I brought a round of drinks to the table.

"Don't mind Merrick," Rhetta said, following my line of sight. "He's just doing his job. Even though Thane says you're good, he's still waiting for you to pull a badge out of your bra."

I laughed. "I didn't realize I gave cop vibes."

I became distracted when I caught sight of Reaper moving through the crowd. Our eyes met, and a jolt ran through me.

"So, when's the last time you had a little fun?" Rhetta asked, a sly grin spreading across her face.

I pretended to misunderstand. "I have fun every day. I have a job I love and a rambunctious puppy."

Cora chuckled. "I think she means fun with a man."

"A naked man," Jess clarified.

My cheeks warmed. "Oh, it's … it's been a while," I admitted, suddenly very interested in the label on my beer bottle. "Dating in D.C. was a nightmare."

"You're in luck," Taryn said as she pulled her black hair into a high ponytail. She gestured around the clubhouse yard. "Plenty of single guys here."

"Reaper among them," Rhetta added, the corners of her eyes crinkling as she grinned.

I choked on my drink. "Absolutely not."

Rhetta beamed as I continued to sputter.

"Reaper is frustrating and annoying and—"

"Hot as fuck?" Cora finished, raising an eyebrow.

My face flushed even deeper. I couldn't deny my attraction but pushed the thought aside. "He's a client. He owns one of the club-associated businesses that I'm here to represent. That's it."

Rhetta shrugged. "If you say so, sugar. But if you ask me, you need to loosen up and let go. Shed that uptight, professional persona and live a little. What better way to break free from those corporate shackles than getting tangled up in sheets with a man like *that?*"

A hot flush spread across my cheeks. "Stop," I insisted. "It's not happening."

"Sugar, I'm speaking from experience. A night with a biker is just what you need to forget your troubles."

As the night wore on, I found my eyes drawn to Reaper. Each time our gazes met, the same inexplicable pull teased at my chest. But I steeled myself against it, reminding myself of professional boundaries and the complications that would arise from any involvement with a client—especially one as complex as him.

The group of old ladies broke apart when the prospects yelled it was time to eat, some moving to make a plate for their children and others sitting beside their bikers.

Having already eaten at home, I leaned against the bar and nursed my third drink of the night. I watched the members interact in fascination—like a zoologist watching a pride of lions interact across a savanna.

A clean-shaven man wearing black glasses and a prospect cut approached the bar. His handsome, polished appearance felt out of place amongst the gruff crowd.

He flashed a charming smile. "Can I buy you a drink?"

His bright blue eyes raked down my body quickly before he offered a boyish grin. He couldn't have been older than his mid-twenties.

"From the open bar?" I laughed. "Sure, why not? I'll take another Woodford Reserve on the rocks."

As he ordered our drinks from the bartender who'd been introduced to me as Leah, I studied him.

"I'm Tyler Grove. I don't think we've met."

"Eva," I replied, shaking his hand. "I'm a consultant. Thane hired me. And I'm old friends with Rhetta."

"Ah, the PR girl. I've heard about you."

I offered a fake grimace. "Good things, I hope?"

Tyler laughed and stepped closer. He leaned casually against the bar. "Mostly. Some of the guys aren't sure about you yet, though. You're not what I expected."

That piqued my interest. I tilted my head. "What did you expect?"

He took a drink as he considered the question. "Reaper has complained endlessly about having to shadow you. And Hatchet said you were all business, no fun."

I rolled my eyes. "I'm plenty of fun. What about you? You don't exactly fit the Maverick mold."

Tyler chuckled. "I hear that a lot. I moved back to Texas after law school. Never thought I'd join, but here I am. My dad was one of the founding members."

My eyebrows jumped in surprise. "You went to law school?"

Tyler shot me a self-deprecating grin. "Don't be too impressed. I failed the bar exam. Twice. Now I'm working construction to pay the bills while I figure out my next move."

As we continued chatting, I enjoyed Tyler's harmless flirtation. The alcohol had loosened me up, and his attention was a welcome shift from my tense exchanges with Reaper.

Tyler wasn't my type, but perhaps the old ladies were right. A no-strings-attached night with a biker could be fun—as long as they weren't one of the business owners.

Tyler moved closer, his hand brushing a rogue hair out of my face. "Maybe I can take you for a ride. Texas looks better from the back of a bike."

A flush crept up my neck. "I would love that. I've never ridden on a motorcycle before." The whiskey made me bold, and I swept a hand across his forearm, tracing his nautical tattoo.

Before Tyler could form a response, a shadow fell over us. Reaper scowled as he glanced between me and Tyler. I dropped my hand and stepped backward, my heart thudding in my chest.

"Everything all right here?" Reaper growled, his eyes fixed on Tyler.

Tyler stepped back, and his throat bobbed as he swallowed. His easy confidence faltered under Reaper's menacing glare. "Yeah, boss. We were just talking."

Reaper's jaw clenched. "Go talk somewhere else. Now."

I watched in confusion as Tyler nodded and retreated with no contest. I turned to Reaper. "What the hell was that about?" My earlier good mood turned to dust. The nerve of this man.

His eyes met mine. "Just looking out for you. Tyler has a bit of a reputation."

I crossed my arms. "I can take care of myself. I don't need you to look out for me."

His eyes roamed over my face, lingering on my lips. For a moment, I thought he might kiss me. Part of me desperately wanted him to. Another part of me wanted to throat-punch him.

Reaper leaned in. "You have no idea what you're getting into here." His voice sounded low and rough amongst the happy chatters of the partying crowd.

"Then why don't you tell me?" I challenged. "Why did you chase Tyler away? I was having a good time talking to him. He was going to take me for a ride."

Reaper's scowl deepened. "You know what? Do whatever you want." He turned and stalked away.

What the fuck? Part of me wanted to chase after him to demand an explanation for his bewildering behavior. However, another part—my more rational side—understood that confronting him in the middle of the party would only lead to more tension.

Instead, I scanned the crowd for Tyler, hoping to pick up where we left off. But every time I tried to approach him, he vanished into the throng of partiers.

My mood soured. It was time to leave, but I was too buzzed to drive myself. I fumbled with my phone, squinting at the screen as I pulled up the rideshare app. As I waited for a driver to accept my request, Rhetta appeared at my side.

"Heading out already, sugar?"

I nodded in exhaustion. "Yeah, I think I've had enough excitement for one night. My Uber will be here in a minute. I'll get a ride back in the morning to pick up my Jeep."

"Nah, we can take care of that." She held out her palm. "Give me your keys. A prospect will drop your Jeep off in the morning."

"Thanks," I said, fishing the keys from my purse and dropping them into her outstretched hand.

Rhetta wrapped an arm around me in a side hug.

"Thanks for coming tonight. I hope you had fun."

I nodded, not wanting to let on that I was leaving because I couldn't stand the club's VP and his dominating presence.

As I walked to the end of the driveway, I could sense eyes on my back. I didn't need to turn around to know they belonged to Reaper. The weight of his gaze followed me down the driveway.

Chapter Eight

The open highway stretched before us, asphalt cutting through the barren landscape outside Houston. Thane confidently led the pack on his Heritage Softail. Merrick and I flanked him in a tight, practiced formation on our own Harleys.

My mind wandered, replaying the scene from last night. Tyler's gentle touch as he pushed Eva's hair out of her face. The way her eyes lit up as she beamed at him.

The memory gnawed at me, causing a persistent ache in my chest.

Maybe that's why I didn't notice them at first.

Merrick's sharp whistle cut through my thoughts. I glanced into the mirror before speeding up to ride beside Thane, signaling we had company. My surprise at the group of Rangers hot on our tail was why a distraction like Eva posed a danger to me and the club.

The group of three bikers rode erratically, weaving as they approached us. It wouldn't have surprised me if they were high. Rangers often were, and that made them more unpredictable.

Before we could formulate a plan, the crack of gunfire split the air. Bullets whizzed past, uncomfortably close. One pinged off my bike's frame.

I'd just paid off the custom paint job on this damn bike.

"Fuck!" Merrick's curse was barely audible over the roar of the engines as he swerved his black shovelhead. He avoided a second shot by an even more narrow margin.

In one fluid motion, I reached for my Glock. The familiar weight of the weapon grounded me. Twisting in my seat, I returned fire, the recoil traveling up my arm. Thane and Merrick followed suit, our bikes weaving as we squeezed our triggers.

The Rangers' impaired state worked to our advantage. Their shots were wild, most going wide. But they compensated for what they lacked in accuracy with a sheer volume of fire.

White-hot pain lanced through my left arm. I'd been hit. Blood seeped through my shirt, the leather of my cut growing slick and warm as it spread. I glanced down and relief washed over me as I appraised the wound. Through the blood I could see it was only a graze. I clenched my jaw. It was less about the pain and more the annoyance when I noticed the scar would cut across one of my oldest tattoos.

As we approached an overpass, Thane's voice cut through the chaos. Using hand signals and shouts, we formulated a plan on the fly. We sped up, and our engines roared as we pulled our bikes over to the right side of the highway. The concrete barrier provided cover as Merrick lay down suppressing fire.

The Rangers slowed, confusion evident in their hesitation as they noticed our disappearance. Their moment of uncertainty gave us the opportunity we needed.

My first shot caught the lead Ranger square in the chest. He slumped forward as his bike veered before crashing into the guardrail.

The second Ranger, distracted by his fallen comrade, was thrown back by Thane's next bullet. It caught him in the head, and he went down hard, his body rag-dolling across the asphalt.

The third tried to speed away, but I caught him in the side before he could escape. His bike careened into a road sign, and the metal shrieked as it twisted around him.

The silence after the firefight was broken only by our heavy breathing and the ticking of our cooling engines.

Thane's hard expression surveyed the scene. "We need to move. Now. This stretch is empty, but we can't count on it staying that way."

I flexed my injured arm, wincing at the sharp pain. "What about the bodies?"

I reached into my saddlebag and pulled out a spare T-shirt. The fabric tore easily as I fashioned a makeshift bandage.

Thane shook his head. "No time. Right now, we need to get clear. The highway patrol won't lose sleep investigating this." He paused, his gaze sweeping over Merrick and me. "We need to call everyone in for Church. Figure out our next move. I'll text Rodriguez to ask him to give us a heads up if PD points to us for this."

* * *

The ride to the clubhouse was tense. Every passing car and distant siren sent a fresh wave of unease through us. The adrenaline from the firefight wore off, replaced by gnawing anxiety and the burning pain in my arm.

The familiar sight of our brothers lounging outside the clubhouse did little to ease the knot in my stomach. Thane dismounted and barked orders to gather everyone for Church in thirty minutes.

I followed him into the clubhouse. I gritted my teeth against the searing pain. It wasn't my first gunshot wound, and it certainly wouldn't be my last.

Leah spotted me as she wiped down the counter. Without missing a beat, she grabbed the first aid kit from under the bar.

"Jesus, Reaper. Again?"

I grunted a response as she grabbed my arm to examine the cratered hole through my bicep. Club bartender and unofficial medic.

She'd patched us up more times than I could count, and while her bedside manner left a lot to be desired, she was steady as hell.

Leah grabbed a bottle of Everclear and poured it straight onto the wound. The liquid burned like fire, and I hissed through clenched teeth.

"Stop your bitching," Leah barked as she tore open sterile gauze. "I've seen worse. You got lucky. Again."

She wrapped my arm tight with gauze and elastic bandages, tying it off with an aggressive knot.

"Bleed on my floor and I'll put another bullet through you," she said, eyes locked hard on mine. No coddling, no sugarcoating. It's why she fit in with the Mavericks.

The news spread, and soon the clubhouse hummed. Cigarette smoke and tension filled the air as Thane recounted the highway ambush.

He calmly lit a smoke as he gazed around the room. "This changes everything. The Rangers have made their move. Now it's our turn."

Hatchet leaned forward with a roguish grin. "I have an idea. We've got that shipment coming in on Sunday. What if we use it as bait? Let those cocksuckers think they're gonna hit the motherlode. But we'll be waiting for them."

"It's risky," Thane mused. "But if we pull it off ..."

"We'll mow them the fuck down," I finished. "Even if their president isn't there, it'll send a message."

Merrick glanced between Thane and me. His fingers drummed restlessly on the oak table. "We've got one shot at this and not a lot of time to make it happen."

Thane's voice cut through the chatter. "You've got that right. Failure's not an option. Let's work it out now."

Chapter Nine

I slung my camera bag over my shoulder as I walked to the Main Street Market in downtown Conroe. Shoppers strolled through the farmers' and artisan market, perusing homemade candles, jewelry, and crafty signs. Local farmers proudly spread fresh fruits and vegetables across the tables. I picked up a few blood oranges from a bearded man in a straw hat as I admired the colorful display of carrots, sweet potatoes, and collard greens.

Thane texted me the night before, suggesting I capture some feel-good moments for social media at Maisie's booth. I'd talked him into launching a Lone Star Mavericks Instagram, and now we needed content.

Surprisingly, Thane had a knack for spotting good stories and even started texting me photos. I'd yet to get a selfie from him, though—I was fairly certain the gruff, chain-smoking biker didn't even know how to flip his camera phone. Still, I appreciated the way he grasped my vision for showcasing the warm hearts beneath the cool chrome. It made my job easier.

The aroma of Maisie's fresh-roasted coffee and cinnamon rolls wafted through the air. My stomach growled. It was an angry reminder that I'd forgotten to eat breakfast, and I knew I'd have to try one of the famous cinnamon rolls Don had bragged about.

The rumble of a familiar motorcycle sounded through the air. I watched in annoyance as Reaper parked and strolled casually to meet me.

I glared at him, still fuming from our interaction at Thane's birthday party. "This doesn't quite seem like your vibe."

Reaper shrugged. "It's not. Prez's orders. Again." His imposing figure, broad, leather-clad shoulders, and deep voice drew curious glances from nearby shoppers. He seemed out of place among the families and college students who frequented the market.

My irritation rose. "Is this really necessary? I'm perfectly capable of handling a farmers' market on my own. We don't even have a media interview today. I'm just shooting content for Instagram."

"Don't take it personally. We're just making sure our investment pays off," he said as his eyes scanned the market as if he were looking for insurgents.

"I don't need a watchdog."

I turned to storm away, but his calloused hand wrapped around my arm. He roughly pulled me back to face him, and I squinted in the bright sun as his eyes met mine.

"There's more going on here than you know. I'm not just here to observe. I'm here to protect. Thane wants me to shadow you whenever you're working with the Mavericks. Get used to it."

"Protect? Care to elaborate on that cryptic bullshit?"

"No. Just do your job, and I'll do mine."

I yanked my arm away and began to press past him until I noticed the gauze wrapping his left bicep. A spot of blood stained the bandage wrapped around an intricate tattoo.

"What happened to your arm?"

Reaper smirked. "Gunshot."

I reeled back in surprise. "How?"

He let out a dark chuckle. "Presumably from a gun."

I rolled my eyes, but my heart began to race. "Is that why you're here? Are we in danger?"

"You're always in danger when I'm around."

I doubted a community market would be ideal for a shootout, so I adjusted my camera bag and pressed past him.

"Fine. Stay out of my way."

As I stormed by, I could sense his eyes on me, and I couldn't shake that there was indeed more to this situation than met the eye.

Despite my outward irritation, an unfamiliar flicker of comfort eased into my mind at the idea of being protected. The thought unsettled me. I'd learned the hard way that self-reliance was the only true safeguard. Entrusting my safety to others had always been a dangerous gamble—and I'd too often been dealt a losing hand.

Yet, as Reaper's watchful gaze followed me through the market, I wondered if having someone at my back might not be such a bad thing. My past taught me I couldn't anticipate every threat, and maybe having an annoying, overbearing biker at my back wasn't a completely terrible idea.

I quickly pushed the thought aside to focus on the job at hand.

The only person I could only truly rely on was myself.

The booth for Maisie's Bakery displayed bags of fresh-roasted coffee beans, sourdough bread, muffins, and cinnamon rolls. Four child-sized tables were set beside it, overflowing with craft supplies. Maisie grinned and waved at me before returning her attention to the children before her.

I understood why Thane thought this would be perfect for social media. Maisie's black cut contrasted with the rainbow explosion of craft supplies. She warmly greeted many shoppers by name as they stopped by to say hello.

I adjusted my tripod and positioned my phone to capture the scene. Kids surrounded one of the tables with Maisie kneeling beside them. Their faces lit with joy as they adorned miniature cardboard motorcycles with glitter, stickers, and paint.

I hunted for golden moments—the ones that could punch

through the noise and actually make people feel something. They say a picture can paint a thousand words, but I think social media has changed that. People skim, they swipe, they doom scroll. My job was to make them stop just long enough to feel something. Curiosity. Amusement. Hope. Maybe even a flicker of empathy. If I could get them to see the Mavericks as something other than the villains, I'd call it a win.

Maisie guided a little girl's hands with infinite patience as they attached pipe cleaner handlebars to a pint-sized chopper. The girl held up the pink glitter-covered bike to show her parents before hugging Maisie.

This scene would form the heart of our narrative.

I began to record a new video clip that I would use to create a reel when a shrill voice cut through the cheerful chatter.

"This is unacceptable! The market should not allow a motorcycle gang here. All you do is bring violence and crime to Conroe!"

Danielle, the woman spearheading the boycott, stormed toward the booth. Her ruddy face contorted with rage as she pointed an accusing finger at Maisie.

"You might think you're fooling everyone with this little act, but I know what you and your club are really about. These parents don't understand how much your club destroys our community."

Maisie's smile faltered, and the children's excited chatter died into confused whispers.

Danielle looked around, catching eyes with the gathering audience. "Did you know that the Lone Star Mavericks sell drugs? My son's friend overdosed. The drugs he bought from them were laced with fentanyl."

Nearby shoppers exchanged uneasy glances.

Danielle continued her rant, raising her voice to attract more attention. "Is that the type of vendor you want at our market? Is that the kind of person you want around your children?"

I stepped between the slightly disheveled middle-aged woman and the craft table. "Ma'am, you're disrupting a sanctioned event and harassing a vendor. We'll be forced to take legal action for slander and harassment if you don't leave right now."

Danielle sputtered as her face turned even more red. "You can't threaten me! I know my rights!"

"And I know the law," I countered as I gestured to my phone. "You're on camera, Danielle." I made sure to enunciate her name. "When I involve Thane's lawyers, there will be no mistaking your threats and harassment against Maisie and her business. Please leave. Now."

Danielle tensed at the mention of Thane and, for a moment, she acted like she might back down. Then, her face twisted with renewed anger, and she lunged forward, hands outstretched as if to shove me.

Before she could make contact, a large figure slid between us, and she stumbled backward.

"Hello, Danielle," Reaper said. His voice sounded deceptively calm, but there was no mistaking the brutality below the surface. The tone of his voice sent a shiver through my spine, and I wasn't even the focus of his malevolence.

Danielle's face paled as recognition dawned. "I ... I was just ..."

"You were just leaving," he finished.

Reaper took an intimidating step closer and narrowed his eyes. Without another word, Danielle turned and pushed through the crowd watching the confrontation.

As the tension dissipated, I found myself standing close to Reaper. Heat radiated off his body.

"I had that under control," I muttered, stepping away to stop the camera.

Reaper's lips quirked in what might have been a smile. "While you might threaten Danielle with lawyers, she knows my mere existence threatens her."

He held out his hand. "Your phone. I need that video for Thane."

"I can send it later."

"Now."

I rolled my eyes and shoved my phone in his outstretched hand.

Reaper's fingers moved across the screen, and his device pinged. As he returned my phone, his calloused hand lingered a beat longer than necessary.

"There. Now you have my number," he said with a hint of satisfaction in his voice. "You can text me the plan for our next PR story ... or anything else, of course."

"Of course," I echoed. I tried to ignore how my pulse quickened at the thought of Reaper's number now residing in my contacts.

As he turned to leave, he paused, glancing back over his shoulder. "You did good today. But next time, let me handle Danielle. Some people only understand one language, and it ain't legalese."

I watched him walk away, the crowd parting around him. My eyes couldn't help but trace the broad expanse of his shoulders, the way his dark jeans hugged his—

No. I would not go there.

Chapter Ten

Tension hung heavy in the night air as I crouched behind a stack of wooden pallets. The weight of my Kevlar vest provided a comforting pressure against my chest.

"Snipers, check in," I murmured into my radio.

"In position," Jay said.

"Ready," Archer followed.

The distant rumble of an engine broke the silence. Right on time.

I watched as the semi-truck rolled into view. Its headlights cut through the darkness. Behind the wheel, Hatchet played his part—an unsuspecting driver with a load of our "lost" military-grade weapons.

As the truck came to a stop, I held my breath. We'd set the trap. Now, we waited for our prey.

Like rats drawn to cheese, ten Rangers pulled up on their bikes with weapons drawn. I could see the greed glinting in their eyes as they approached the truck.

Poor bastards thought they'd stumbled onto the score of a lifetime. They had no idea they'd walked right into our trap.

I pressed the radio button as they approached. "Collect their souls."

The night exploded into chaos. The staccato rhythm of gunfire filled the air as my men opened up from all sides. On the roof, muzzle flashes erupted as Jay and Archer picked off the men with cold efficiency.

The Rangers never stood a chance.

Caught in the crossfire, they fell one by one, their screams of confusion and pain silenced.

When the last echoes of gunfire faded away, I stepped out. Gunpowder and death hung heavy in the air as I surveyed the carnage. Bodies lay strewn across the ground. Their blood seeped into the cracked asphalt.

"Unload the weapons and clean this up," I ordered. "Put the bodies in the container, and we'll use it to transport them all to the incinerator. Bones left the junkyard unlocked for us."

Thane stepped beside me as we watched our men move with practiced efficiency. He took a long draw of his cigarette before speaking. "Not a single leader here tonight. They sent foot soldiers only. Fuckin' pussies."

I nodded, watching my men unload and move the weapons into the warehouse.

"You know this means the war isn't over. Things are going to get worse before they get better."

Thane took another long drag of his cigarette and nodded.

Within the hour, my men piled the Rangers' bodies into the empty container, and we wheeled their bullet-riddled bikes into the warehouse. They'd fetch a reasonable price at the chop shop. I'd even let my brothers pick pieces from the remains for their own bikes first.

The Rangers had brought the battle to us again, but we'd reaped every one and had walked away unscathed. They'd think twice before underestimating us again.

And, if they wanted a fight, we'd give them a goddamn war.

* * *

My phone dinged. The Mavericks group chat lit up with a screenshot that immediately set my nerves on edge.

The image detailed the action agenda of an upcoming City Council Special Meeting. Linc had circled one agenda item: "Discuss and consider the allowance of businesses associated with criminal enterprises."

Another screenshot followed. It was a post from Danielle, who was crowing on Facebook about meeting with the city administrator. She bragged about her "victory" in getting her boycott on the city council agenda. The comments section was a dumpster fire of middle-aged women clutching their pearls and waving their pitchforks.

God-fucking-damn-it. A flurry of curses escaped me as I informed the group I'd call our PR consultant and lawyer. We'd want them there.

> Me: Have you seen this?

> Eva: Shit. Call me.

I stared at the phone for a beat. The audacity of this woman, barking orders at me like I worked for her. The phone barely rang once before she answered.

"Hello?"

Eva didn't bother with a greeting. She dove in without a preamble, using her bossy consultant tone that amused, irritated, and aroused me all at the same time.

"I need you to get every Maverick who owns a business to show up to this meeting. If they have a family, I want them there. Kids, wives. Hell, they should bring their sweet old grandmothers if they're still around. And I want them dressed like they're going to church. No cuts this time."

I ground my teeth. "Why? What's your plan?"

"Sorry, I'm leaping ahead. My mind's moving faster than my mouth. These meetings are performative. We need a show of support.

If the council sees a crowd of families—normal people, not bikers—they'll realize it's more trouble than it's worth to create a policy against your businesses. I have some other angles I'll work on while you call your members."

"Care to share?"

"Not yet. I have less than twenty-four hours to pull this off, so I need you to just do as I ask."

Eva hung up. My fists clenched as I slammed my phone down. *Are you fucking kidding me?* The nerve of this woman.

I fired off orders in the group chat. I told the members to leave the cuts at home and dig out their Sunday best. Then, I called our lawyer, ensuring he'd be front and center, ready to shut down any slander.

This wasn't the kind of fight I enjoyed. No fists. No bullets. But it was a fight just the same.

And for once, I didn't think I'd be the most dangerous person in the room.

That honor belonged to Eva.

Chapter Eleven

City Hall filled to capacity just before the meeting began, the fire chief closing the doors and instructing a line of latecomers to wait outside. The standing crowd buzzed with energy beneath the harsh fluorescent lights.

I shot Reaper and Thane a satisfied grin as I scanned the crowd. Mavericks and their families packed the front rows. Jack's high school shop boys clustered in their letterman jackets at the back. Women I recognized from the shelter visit filled an entire row with toddlers perched on their knees, and a group of elementary school moms crowded around Cora. Maisie moved about the crowd, hugging customers she'd asked to attend on her behalf when they ordered their morning lattes and cinnamon rolls.

Reaper leaned in. "How did you get all these people here?"

I shrugged nonchalantly. "What can I say? I'm charming as fuck."

Thane's laugh rumbled as he squeezed my shoulder. "Hiring you might have been the best decision I've made all year."

Reaper scoffed and walked away. He'd never admit it, but the hint of a smile tugging at his mouth told me he was impressed.

"Call to order," shouted the mayor.

Following the roll call and the meeting agenda presentation, the city administrator opened the meeting to discuss the "facts" as they'd been presented to him by Danielle. But the smug look was quickly wiped from her face as public commenters began to form a line. Each person shared a unique story or perspective on how a Maverick-owned business had impacted their community or family.

I watched with curiosity as Sarah Knapp, the woman I recognized as the city's director of parks and recreation, moved to the mic.

"Last year, the Mavericks raised $10,000 for the new playground in Crockett Park after the tornado destroyed the old equipment. Grimm Construction, which is owned by the Mavericks VP, installed it for free. Thousands of children visit the park each year. We shouldn't let a few bad actors chase away companies that support our community."

I glanced at Reaper, and he met my gaze from across the room. I raised a brow in surprise. I watched as he picked up his phone to type a message. My phone buzzed seconds later.

Reaper: You're not the only one who can be charming as fuck.

I stifled a laugh as others stood in line to share their stories. Danielle's face grew more red by the second, resembling a boiled crawfish. She'd underestimated the support we'd bring. What she thought was a sure victory was shot to hell by our countermove.

As more supporters spoke, I watched the executive director of economic development lean over to whisper in the city administrator's ear. He blanched before standing to address the room. "Thank you to everyone who attended and shared your perspectives. You've given us much to consider. I'd like to table this discussion until further notice."

The room erupted in relieved chatter. I lingered near the door as the crowd spilled into the hall. I watched Danielle slink out, her army of Facebook followers nowhere in sight.

Reaper brushed my arm to catch my attention. "Nice work tonight, PR girl."

I grinned. "A compliment? Are you okay? Do you have a fever?" I reached out to touch his forehead in mock concern.

He snorted and swatted my hand away. "I'm just relieved no one started a riot. Then I'd have to bail you out of jail."

"Or maybe not. I look good in handcuffs." The flicker of shock on his face was worth every ounce of bravado. "But it's good to know you're here to save me from my bad decisions."

Reaper stepped a little closer. "You don't seem like the type of woman who needs to be saved."

I shrugged. "I'm not. But I like knowing I have a knight in shining leather on speed dial." I pretended to study my chipped nail polish before meeting his gaze again.

His dark eyes skimmed over my face and lingered a half-second too long on my mouth. "Have you ever even made a bad decision?"

I tilted my head, and the tension hung between us for a beat. "Sometimes I think I'd like to."

Before he could respond, Rhetta burst through the crowd and hugged me tightly. "You did it, sugar. Thane is thrilled at how you packed this place."

"I'm just glad it worked. We still have a lot of reputation repair ahead of us, though."

"Come on. Let's go to the bar around the corner to celebrate."

She tugged me away as I watched Reaper disappear into the crowd.

* * *

I gripped my steering wheel as I searched for a parking spot. Rhetta had talked me into a late dinner at Ríonach, a sleek new fusion spot downtown, and she'd nabbed a reservation during a peak hour because a member owned the place.

I hated driving downtown. I could barely parallel park even in the most ideal spots. In addition, street parking was scarce this late as the bars and restaurants filled with the promise of a fun Saturday night.

The setting sun cast shadows across the road from the tall buildings as I drove past Ríonach and the dark parking garage beside it, turning down the side street to find a spot. I'd take the peace of mind and longer walk over the anxiety and memories that would flood me if I stepped foot inside a concrete prison.

Finally, I found an open space I could maneuver into without risking my paint job or my pride. The chirp of my Jeep's lock cut through the humid evening air.

That's when I noticed two men emerging from a dented pickup truck parked a few spots down the street.

The hairs on the back of my neck raised as I watched them stalk behind me through my peripheral vision. My heart rate spiked, and adrenaline flooded my system.

Feigning nonchalance, I thumbed a location pin to Rhetta. My pulse thrummed in time with the clicking heels of my platform stilettos—a fashion decision I cursed, knowing I couldn't run in them.

> Me: Think I'm being followed. If I'm MIA in 15, start here.

> Rhetta: Hold tight. Thane is in a meeting, but I know some of the guys are nearby.

I reached into my purse to thumb the switchblade I almost always carried, though I knew it wouldn't be adequate for a woman in heels against two attackers. I kicked myself for ignoring my dad's suggestion that I carry a concealed weapon.

I quickened, watching the men close the distance between us through the reflection in car windows. Their shadows stretched long on the sidewalk. I crossed the street. Their boots scuffed the concrete as they matched my pace. Baseball caps pulled low obscured their faces in the storefront reflections.

I jumped as my phone rang.

"Hey, Rhetta! I'm just a few minutes away," I said loudly, hoping to signal to my pursuers that someone was expecting me.

"How far are you from Main Street?" she asked, her voice tight with worry.

"Just about there."

"Okay, listen for the bike. Thane is sending someone."

I let out a shaky breath as I approached the intersection. Traffic had stopped, so I jogged across. "I'm on the other side of the street now. I hear bikes."

"Good. Let whoever it is drive you the rest of the way here."

Two Harleys pulled beside me as I hung up. Relief washed over me as Reaper dismounted, a welcome sight for once. He hit the kickstand and approached me, his eyes intense as they scanned my body for any signs of harm.

"Where are the guys who were following you?" he demanded, scanning the area.

I glanced over, pointing to the two men retreating to their truck at the sight of the Mavericks coming to my aid. He nodded to the other man, the pretty-boy blond with bright blue eyes I'd seen at the clubhouse. "Follow them, Hatchet," he ordered. "Get their plate and send it to Linc."

He straddled his bike. "Get on. Where am I taking you?"

"Ríonach." I moved toward the bike, my legs shaky from the adrenaline. "I can walk the rest of the way now."

He shook his head. "Prez's orders were to give you a ride. So get on. Why the fuck did you park all the way out here? There's a garage across the street."

His bike roared to life as I settled behind him.

"Because I ... uhh ... I don't particularly like parking garages."

His jaw tensed, the muscle popping a few times before he moved his gaze to the road ahead. "Hold tighter. Unless you wanna become roadkill."

The bike lurched, and I gripped his waist. I'd never ridden on the back of a motorcycle before, and my heart jumped in my throat at the fear of falling off the back.

Within minutes, he stopped in front of the restaurant's black awnings and hanging lights, with Rhetta stepping out to greet us. I used Reaper's shoulder to balance as I dismounted from the bike, wobbling in my heels.

"Thanks for looking out for her," she said over my shoulder at Reaper, pulling me into a hug.

He nodded curtly. "Text Thane when you pay the bill so we can wait for you outside." He revved the bike, whipping it around in the middle of the street.

Rhetta peered over me, concerned. "Are you okay?"

I shook my head. "I need a drink. I don't know what those men wanted from me, but they immediately turned around when Reaper and the other guy pulled up. Please thank Thane for me."

"You can tell him yourself when he picks me up after dinner. Thane's really happy with your work so far. I know he didn't mind sending a few guys after your stalkers."

I cringed at the idea of being stalked again. "Part of me wonders if I overreacted. But I can't shake the feeling that they were coming for me, especially since they ran as soon as the bikes pulled up."

I did my best to hide my shaking hands as I read the menu. A shot of tequila and two smoky palomas later, a soothing warmth spread through me, easing the anxious dread. By the time the waitress served dinner, I had a good buzz.

Rhetta cocked an eyebrow as she stabbed another bite of enchilada. "So, when will I get you to go on a date with a real man?"

I rolled my eyes. "Just because my boyfriends haven't been bikers, doesn't mean they aren't real men."

"Please. Let's look at your history. The tech bro organized his socks by color and theme. The senator's son insisted you quit working after your hypothetical first child. The think tank analyst cheated on you at a gala. And the lawyer was married. Married!"

"To be fair, I didn't know. Did I tell you what I did right before I confronted him?"

Rhetta's eyes sparkled with anticipation. "Please tell me it was epic."

I laughed. "More devious. I poured a half gallon of milk into his golf bag because I knew he had an important golf meeting that weekend with some clients. And then I slipped my panties just barely under the pillow on her side of the bed. She must have found them because I heard they split right after that."

"Good for her. Have you gone on a date since moving here?"

I shook my head. "I gave a guy my number a few weeks ago. The first thing he sent me was a dick pic. I told him I'd just check my bank account if I wanted to see something that disappointing."

Rhetta cackled and caught me up on her dating misadventures before meeting Thane. Since I'd need to call an Uber anyway, I ordered a fourth drink with dessert. When the check arrived, my cheeks burned, and the world before me blurred slightly.

Rhetta insisted on paying, a thank you for a job well done, and we stepped out into the quiet downtown street as the waitstaff wrapped up for the night. Most restaurants had closed, and the only people milling about moved from bar to bar.

Thane and Reaper leaned against their bikes outside the restaurant. Rhetta's lips brushed Thane's cheek, leaving behind a faint berry-colored lipstick smudge. I tried thanking the men for their help earlier, but my words slurred together. The haze of the tequila coursing through my system made it challenging for me to form sentences.

"You're drunk."

Reaper's voice sounded flat and annoyed.

"S'fine. I'll Uber."

He shook his head. "I'll drive you home. Get on."

My eyes narrowed. "You're kind of bossy, y'know? You better be nicer, or I'll give this Uber-cycle a two-star review."

"Get the fuck on the bike."

My heart raced as Reaper guided me onto the back of his Harley. The world blurred as Rhetta's laughter and Thane's knowing smirk faded into the background.

"Okay, okay. I promise to give the Reaper-Uber at least a four-star review," I said with a giggle as he settled in front of me.

Drunk me thought I was funny. Reaper did not appear to agree. He moved my hands, wrapping my arms around him tighter before glaring at Thane.

"You fucking owe me," he growled at his president.

The Harley's engine roared to life. A deep thrumming vibrated through me, and I gripped Reaper's body with a desperate hold as he pulled away.

The cool night air whipped against my face, clearing some of the alcohol-induced fog.

In my drunken haze, it dawned on me that I liked riding on the back of a bike. And, if I was honest, I enjoyed being pressed against Reaper. His body radiated heat against mine, and I felt his muscles shifting beneath my hands as we navigated turns and accelerated.

Warmth pooled low in my belly—dangerous, addictive warmth. In my buzzed boldness, one of my hands slipped lower, exploring the hard muscles of his thigh. The bike swerved, and his body tensed.

"Eva," Reaper's deep voice rumbled in warning. "You're drunk. Don't start something you can't finish."

His words sent a shiver down my spine. "Who says I can't finish?" I teased, emboldened by the alcohol coursing through my veins.

Reaper's hand came down to cover mine, firmly moving it back to his waist. "Not tonight. Just enjoy the ride."

I pouted. "I thought bikers were supposed to be all about living dangerously."

He chuckled, the sound vibrating through his back and into my chest. "I do live dangerously. But taking advantage of drunk women isn't my style."

"Who says you'd be taking advantage?" I mumbled, pressing my cheek against his leather jacket.

"Ask me again when you're sober."

As he revved the bike, the sudden surge of power beneath us caught me off guard, and I let out a startled squeak as my seat began to slip. I clutched tighter around his middle, my hands pressing firmly into his leather cut. The action seemed to amuse him as a low, rumbling laugh escaped his lips.

I realized I'd never given Reaper my address when we pulled into the driveway.

"How do you know where my house is?" The realization sobered me slightly.

"Because I know everything about you, Lioness."

"Lioness?"

Reaper gave me a grin. "You remind me of a lioness. Fierce. Fearless. And fucking relentless." His gaze softened, a hint of admiration creeping into his tone. "And I don't for one second trust you to not rip out my goddamn throat."

I tried not to smile. Rarely did men see through my professional persona. I'd learned to hide my ruthless side behind a carefully constructed mask, and it sent a thrill through my body as it dawned on me he had glimpsed beyond the facade.

The tequila tore through my inhibitions, and I leaned in to meet Reaper's lips in a reckless kiss. My heart pounded in my chest, and my senses became overwhelmed by his taste and the feel of his lips against mine. Reaper pulled me closer, and the heat of his body seared against my own, chasing away the chill on my arms from the windy ride.

Internally, I cursed. He was a client. Off limits. But at that moment, it didn't matter. I pulled back and sucked in a ragged breath.

Reaper smirked at me in amusement. "Well, that's one way to

thank me for the ride home. Be sure to leave me a five-star review on … what did you call it? Uber-cycle?"

I rolled my eyes. "Thanks for the ride." I turned toward my house, and my brows furrowed.

"What?" he asked as he noticed the tightening shift in my posture.

"I left a few lights on for my puppy, but the house is dark."

Reaper pushed his cut aside to reveal a holstered gun. "Stay behind me," he growled as he scanned the shadows.

Chapter Twelve

A cold sense of dread washed over me as Eva's words registered. Though drunk, I trusted she remembered leaving a few lights on. Every instinct in me—honed from years of danger as a Marine and a Maverick—screamed something seemed off. I didn't know Eva well, yet my blood boiled at the thought of her in danger.

The familiar weight of my weapon did little to quell the unease churning in my gut. Her new association with the club made it possible that she'd become a target.

Eva keyed in the code to her lock, and I ordered her to stay outside. I nudged the door open with my foot. With my weapon trained before me, I searched the room and cataloged every shadow, every potential threat.

Ignoring my command, Eva stepped in behind me. She flicked on a light that illuminated a scarcely furnished living room with a dog crate in the corner. The occupant let out an excited bark.

"Damn it. I told you to stay outside."

Eva glanced at me, rolling her eyes dramatically as she unlocked the crate.

"Hello, handsome," she cooed.

Movement in the kitchen caught my eye. Time slowed. A figure materialized from the shadows. A balaclava obscured his face, and I caught the unmistakable flash of a chrome-plated gun.

I reacted on pure instinct. The Glock bucked in my hand as I pulled the trigger. The intruder's chest exploded in a spray of red, and his gun clattered to the floor as he crumpled.

Eva's scream pierced the air, but I couldn't afford to comfort her. Not yet. I kicked the fallen weapon away, my own gun trained on the wheezing man as I yanked off his mask. The unfamiliar face stared up at me in pain and shock.

"Stay there," I ordered over my shoulder as I cleared the rest of the house before calling Thane. He answered on the first ring.

"I need cleaners to Eva's house," I said.

"What the fuck happened?" Thane asked. "What did you do to Eva?"

My tone turned to ice. "I saved her goddamn life. Someone broke into her house."

"Was it a Ranger?"

I nudged the wheezing man on the floor with my boot. "No, I don't think so. This is the second time tonight she's been targeted. It's not a fucking coincidence. I'm getting her out of here. Send Merrick. Maybe he can get this guy to talk before he bleeds out."

I needed to know why the fuck someone wanted to hurt this woman. Blood seeped through the man's shirt, staining the hardwood. I grabbed a white towel from the counter and pressed it against his wound. As much as I wanted him dead, I needed him somewhat alive for questioning.

I glanced at Eva, huddled on the floor with her puppy clutched to her chest. For the first time, genuine fear shone in those stormy eyes. It twisted something in my gut.

I moved to her in four quick strides. We needed to leave her house until I figured out who was targeting her and why.

"Come on," I urged, helping her up. She leashed the puppy, and we stepped outside.

"What's going on?" she asked, her voice steadier than I expected. She rubbed her bare arms and shivered.

I shrugged out of my jacket and helped her slip her arms through each sleeve. "Someone's gunning for you. We need to move."

The leather engulfed her small frame. I scooped up the puppy, zipping it inside with her. He snapped at my hands. "Fucker, stop it," I snarled, recognizing the breed. A goddamn Malinois. Of course she would have a dog as tenacious as her.

A car drove toward her house from the distance, too slow for regular traffic.

"Get on," I commanded. "Now."

She swung her leg over and pressed against me with the puppy awkwardly wedged between us. I sped away from her house, taking several turns in case anyone followed. Paranoia wasn't just a habit—it was survival. I checked my mirrors and watched the shadows. Whoever came after her tonight might not be done, and I wasn't about to lead trouble to my doorstep.

I never thought I'd have a girl and a dog on the back of my bike. The little bastard kept trying to lick the back of my neck like I was a damn ice cream cone. Eva didn't say much. She just held on tight as her pup occasionally made little yips as if he were enjoying the ride.

After about thirty minutes, I turned down a dirt road and stopped before a gate. I keyed in the code and drove through, the sound of my bike echoing against the surrounding trees.

"Why would someone be after me?"

I pushed down the kickstand and helped her off the bike. She unzipped my jacket, setting the puppy on the ground with his leash gripped in her palm.

"Pissed off anyone?"

"I mean, probably. It came with the territory of my old job, but there's no reason for it here."

My phone buzzed. I ushered Eva to my front door, punching in the lock code and pushing her in before stepping away to take the call.

"Linc? What do you have for me?" My brother had access to the cameras on my property and had likely been watching to see when I could answer.

"Dude, someone put a hit out on that PR chick."

"Who?" I glanced at Eva through the window, ensuring she couldn't listen to the conversation.

"My best guess is the Abell family. I need to do some more digging. Maybe since she wouldn't take the settlement, they want to find another way to keep her quiet."

"How's the rest of her background check coming along?"

"Still working on it. I found some juvenile records, but I need to call in a favor to get a hold of them."

"Interesting. So she has a record?" This confirmed my suspicions that there was more to Eva than she let on.

"She must. It's sealed, but I should have it by tomorrow or the next day."

"Okay, Linc. Call me if you find anything else." I slipped the phone into my pocket as I turned to my cabin.

Eva stumbled back onto the porch, her puppy zigzagging between her unsteady legs. She'd kicked her high heels off, appearing even smaller before me.

"What did you find out?" she asked, her eyes still wide and glassy. She'd sobered up a bit, but the mixture of adrenaline and alcohol would cause her to crash soon.

I settled onto the split-log porch swing I'd built a few weeks ago, the wood creaking under my weight. I patted the spot beside me. She hesitated for a moment before accepting.

"There's a bounty on your head because you've apparently pissed off some very rich, influential people. Care to explain?"

She leaned her head back. Her eyes fluttered to a close as she drew in a long breath. "That means we're getting close to the truth."

I flexed my jaw at her vague response. "The fuck is that supposed to mean?"

Her eyes snapped open, and she pulled my jacket tighter around herself like armor. "I've been working with a friend. He's an investigative journalist. We've been trying to find women who have worked with someone I used to know. We're trying to get them to speak out so he can be held accountable for what he's done."

"You mean Hale Abell? The asshole who attacked you?"

Her jaw dropped. "How do you know about that?"

I smirked. "Like I said, Lioness, I know everything about you."

She had the audacity to roll her eyes, a spark of her usual fire returning. "Well, it came as a surprise that someone wanted to kill me, so I'd say you still have a few things to learn."

Beneath her snark, I sensed the uncertainty roiling within her. For a split second, she dropped her mask. She appeared panicked. Scared. Confused.

I stood, guiding her into the house. "You'll be safe here. Only Rhetta, Thane, Linc, and my mom know where this cabin is."

"Wait? I'm staying here? Why can't I just stay at my house?"

I pressed my fingers across my forehead. "Because, in case you've already forgotten, someone has offered $1 million for you to be killed, and three men have already tried to earn that payout tonight. Give me your phone."

She handed it over without argument, watching as I powered it off. "We can't risk you being tracked. I have enough cameras that we'll know if someone shows up, but I'd prefer not to have to bury any bodies out here yet."

Eva's impassive expression suggested she understood I wasn't joking.

I handed her my phone. "Send Rhetta a text with whatever you need from your house. You can stay here until we eliminate the threat."

She took the phone and then paused to process what I'd said. "Eliminate?"

I smirked as I strode toward my bedroom. "If you're not ready for the answer to that, I suggest you not ask the question."

Within thirty minutes, I'd showered, changed the sheets on my bed, brought a stack of blankets and sheets to my pull-out couch, and served Eva and me each a heavy pour of Jack Daniel's. Hawk gnawed on my fingers as I watched Eva stare at the wall, lost in thought.

The rumble of Thane's truck broke the silence. Rhetta burst through the door, enveloping Eva in a hug.

"Sugar, I don't know whose Cheerios you pissed in, but I'm glad Reaper was there. He'll keep you safe."

I stepped outside beside Thane, who pulled a dog crate filled with bowls, food, and toys from the bed of his truck.

"Well, this escalated quickly," he joked with a Marlboro hanging from his mouth. "Are you ready to play house?"

I glared at him as I took the duffel bag Rhetta had packed for Eva. "Glad you find this amusing."

Thane chuckled. "Rhetta thinks you'd make a good couple. Some mean-ass babies, too. Eva's one of her oldest friends, so keep her alive for me. Otherwise, Rhetta will cut my balls off—and yours."

"Yeah, yeah. I know who really runs the Mavericks. Rhetta can keep her steak knife away. She'll be safe here."

Thane crushed out his cigarette. "I know she will. I wouldn't trust anyone else. By the way, I asked Linc to add me to your security system for now. If there's any activity, I'll lead the entire cavalry to your door."

I shook my head as he shoved the crate across the front porch. "No one knows about my cabin, and no one needs to know."

As they left, the silence settled around us. I turned to find Eva watching me. A complex mix of emotions I couldn't quite decipher flashed through her expression. Exhaustion was winning, though. She started to head to the couch, her movements slow and uncertain. After a moment, it dawned on me she thought I wanted her to sleep there. The idea of her within reach of anyone who could walk through the front door sent an unexpected surge of protectiveness through my chest.

"You can take the bedroom," I said, my voice rougher than

intended. I cleared my throat. "I changed the sheets. There are towels in the closet beside the shower."

She started to protest, her stubbornness pushing through her fatigue. "I can't—"

I leveled a stern look at her as I picked up her duffel bag and tossed it on the bed with a soft thump. "Get some sleep."

Eva rubbed her bleary eyes and sighed as she disappeared into my bedroom, closing the door behind her with a soft click.

Chapter Thirteen

The weight of the night's events crashed over me. The fabric of my shirt clung to my skin, still damp with cold sweat.

I moved mechanically, shedding my clothes for a shower. The hot water cascaded over me, steam rising in billowing clouds that fogged the glass. But even as it soothed my tense muscles, it couldn't wash away the reality of what happened. I could have died tonight. Hale was dangerous, but I never imagined my investigation could result in this situation.

I stepped out of the shower and slammed the glass door shut harder than necessary. As I toweled off and brushed my teeth, my mind raced. The moment Reaper shot the hitman in my kitchen replayed in my mind. He hadn't called an ambulance. Reaper had wanted Merrick to question him before letting him die. And I had no idea what they would do with the body.

The thought should have horrified me. Instead, numb acceptance filled my chest. This was the world I'd stumbled into. As much as I'd hoped to separate the businesses from the bikers in my work, the two were intertwined.

A wave of conflicting emotions washed over me. Part of me recoiled at the casual brutality and the ease with which Reaper had pulled the trigger. I'd intellectually known what an outlaw motorcycle club was capable of, but witnessing the violence that simmered beneath the surface firsthand hit differently.

A darker part of me swirling below my facade of corporate professionalism and achievement embraced the grim satisfaction. The man had come to kill me, and he'd bled out on my kitchen floor. There was a certain poetic justice to it.

If asked to choose between my life and the life of a killer, I'd choose my own. Every. Fucking. Time.

I sat on the edge of Reaper's bed, running my fingers through my damp hair. Each recent lead ran through my mind, a twisted maze of cover-ups. In addition to Amy, I'd spoken to several other women who'd worked for Abell Enterprises. Their stories echoed the same patterns: humiliation, gaslighting, and brutality.

Katelyn had been the head of sales for one of Hale's companies. Like Amy, she was terrified to go on the record. Hale had berated her in front of the staff, called her incompetent, and when she'd finally resigned after a late-night confrontation, he'd attacked her. She'd drifted in and out of consciousness as the Abells covered their tracks, fabricating alibis and using their influence to shield Hale from consequences.

Another victim, Sarah, was a promising executive in accounting who'd discovered evidence of fraud. When she brought it forward, Hale had responded with violence. She'd left his office with a scar across her forehead, her injuries blamed on a workplace accident and her silence bought with a settlement.

The pattern was clear: anyone who threatened to expose Hale's secrets was swiftly dealt with.

My hand unconsciously went to my throat, recalling Hale's grip as he'd attacked me—all because I'd refused to be his puppet, to spin lies. The flashpoint occurred when I'd professionally told him to fuck off in a meeting. The memory of his face, twisted with rage as he fought to control his wrath in front of the board, still burned in my mind.

"We're not in the business of lying to investors," I'd told him, Hale's board chair shifting in discomfort at the confrontation. "I won't spin this report just so you can sell the company. Your proposal violates so many ethics and maybe a few laws. We have to tell the truth."

I lay in the hospital a few hours later in a haze of pain and confusion, the details of the attack blurred under the pain medication. Still, I remained adamant to the police that Hale was my attacker. They took my report and said they had enough to make an arrest.

I clenched my fists so tight that my nails dug into my palms. How many more women were out there, silenced by the Abells' money and influence? How many more stories of violence and intimidation remained buried? And how could I bring all of this to light without ending up in the ground?

I curled up in Reaper's large oak bed and tightened the quilt around me. Exhaustion warred with adrenaline, leaving me wired and drained all at once. Reaper's scent clung to everything in the room. The smell of cedar, campfire smoke, and leather reminded me I wasn't alone.

My mind drifted back to the kiss we'd shared outside my home. The memory of his lips against mine still burned, and the searing heat of his body lingered on my skin. I could almost feel the rough texture of his leather jacket beneath my hands and how he'd pulled me to his chest with a possessive intensity. The kiss had left me breathless and wanting more.

But, even as I replayed the moment in my head, I couldn't shake the feeling I was playing with fire.

He'd saved my life tonight. No hesitation, just action. It should have scared me. And maybe it did, a little. But it also made me feel safe in a way I couldn't explain.

I chewed my lip, staring at the unfamiliar shadows on the ceiling. If anyone came through that door tonight, I had no doubt Reaper would end them before they took a single step toward me.

The brutality of the thought should have unsettled me.

Instead, it filled me with a sense of peace.

Chapter Fourteen

The first slivers of dawn cut through the pines as I tossed Hawk's ball. The pup launched after it like a furry missile, all chaotic joy and reckless momentum. Fucking hell. I'd watched these dogs take down insurgents in Baghdad with discipline sharper than most soldiers. This one? Pure, fearless chaos.

Just like Eva.

Hawk skidded back, mud-streaked and triumphant, dropping the slobber-coated rubber ball at my boots. "Again?" I muttered, taking a sip of my black coffee. "Fine. Last one."

I arced the ball into the tree line. Let him chase shadows for five minutes.

Leaning against the porch rail, I surveyed my domain. I'd built this cabin for solitude—tall fences, no neighbors, trails rigged with motion sensors. Now, the scents of citrus shampoo and dog filled the air. A whiskey glass soaked in the sink, smudged with red lipstick. The intrusion should have bothered me more than it did.

Hawk's bark echoed as he cornered a groundhog. My fingers twitched toward the Glock at my hip reflexively before I caught myself. Old habits. Older paranoia.

Eva's laugh played in my head. *"Who says you'd be taking advantage?"* The memory of her pressed against me on the bike, all warm curves and defiance, sent a jolt through my system.

She was a protected asset. A favor for Thane.

Bullshit.

The truth was one I wasn't ready to confront. I'd killed for Eva last night and driven her to my home without a second thought. I'd never brought a woman back here. I'd always intended to maintain this cabin as my private sanctuary—separate from club business.

And that kiss ...

I was surprised the leather on my jacket hadn't been seared off by the heat between us.

Hawk trotted back, panting. I crouched, roughing his ears. "You've got to step up, pup. If you were big enough, you would've broken through that cage and launched yourself at that fucker's throat without hesitation to protect your person. I was there this time, but you need to be ready next time."

The pup licked my knuckles and nudged the ball again, oblivious to the weight of my words.

The creak of the screen door froze us both. Eva stood silhouetted in the warm morning light, her hair sleep-mussed, eyes still heavy. My chest tightened at the sight.

She padded barefoot across the dew-soaked grass. Hawk nipped at my knees, insisting I throw the ball again.

"He's obsessed with you already," she said, her voice still husky from sleep.

"Malinois imprint fast. Train him right, and he'll die protecting you."

She reached for my cup of coffee and wrinkled her nose after taking a sip. "You sound like you're recruiting him."

"Just stating facts."

"He's a foster. Within a few weeks, I'm sure he'll get adopted, and I'll have to say goodbye."

We stood too close, and her sweet scent wrecked my focus. I stepped back and nodded toward the copse of trees and shrubs.

"My entire property is fenced and lined with motion sensors. But stay on this side of the tree line for now. It's thick, and no one can see you from the road."

Eva's lips quipped up. "Paranoid much?"

"My paranoia is what kept you alive last night."

She tilted her head in consideration and nodded in agreement. "I guess I can't argue with that. I didn't get a chance to thank you." Her eyes bore into mine, mixed emotions swirling in their blue depths.

Hawk barked, shattering the moment. I tossed the ball harder than necessary. "I have to go check on a few jobs. Linc will let me know when he makes progress in tracking down Abell. Once I know more, we can talk about the next steps."

"Next steps," she echoed, voice flat. "You mean hiding here?"

"I mean surviving."

Her chin lifted, defiance flashing in her eyes. "I don't want to hide."

"You will." I moved into her space, crowding her against the porch post and reclaiming my nearly empty coffee cup. "Or I'll cuff you to my bed until this blows over."

Her breath hitched, but not in fear. Something darker, more primal, flashed in her eyes. "You wouldn't."

"Oh, I would."

The challenge hung between us. Hawk whined and pawed at my leg. I tossed the ball again, and he yipped excitedly as he chased it.

Eva shrugged, attempting to show a calculated nonchalance that didn't quite mask her interest. She turned away, sauntering back into the cabin. "Come on, Hawk. It's time for breakfast."

The image of Eva wearing a set of leather cuffs in my bed seared into my brain. Desperate for distraction, I flipped to my security cameras on my phone, checking the perimeter. I'd have received an alert for any movement, but I needed to think of anything but Eva.

Otherwise, I'd call off work and spend the entire day figuring out what else she liked.

By the time I walked back into the cabin, Eva had stepped into the shower. I left her a note on the kitchen counter, along with a burner phone.

Do not turn on your phone. Use this one for now. The Wi-Fi password is on the back of the router. I'll be back around lunch. Also, I took your keys. I'll have a prospect pick up your Jeep from downtown and drop it off at the clubhouse.

I poured another cup of coffee, leaving half of the pot for Eva, and started my work truck. I had three construction jobs to check on, materials to order, and a meeting with an architect.

Two hours later, as I spoke to the drywallers at a custom home my company had built, my phone pinged with the chirp I'd assigned to Eva's burner phone.

> Eva: Where do you keep your food?

My brows furrowed. Did she hit her head?

> Me: Generally in the kitchen. Did you check the refrigerator and the pantry?

> Eva: I'm not an idiot. You have ingredients.
> Do you not have cereal hidden somewhere?
> Maybe a granola bar?

I'd gone grocery shopping the day before. There were a dozen eggs in the refrigerator, fruit for smoothies in the freezer, and vegetables in the crisper. Sourdough bread sat on the counter beside the toaster.

> Me: I'll be home in less than an hour, and I'll bring you lunch. Just text me what you want from the sub shop.

I went back to work, ignoring the pings that followed until the fourth one. Fuck, this woman was needy.

> Eva: Turkey sub on white. Extra mayo and avocado. Lettuce, tomato, jalapeno.

> Eva: And a bag of their pickle-flavored potato chips with a large Mountain Dew.

> Eva: And a chocolate chip cookie or two!

> Eva: And next time you're at the store, can you get some creamer? That is the strongest coffee I've ever had.

I shook my head as I went back to the blueprints.

I picked up my regular—a grilled chicken salad—and Eva's carb and sugar coma at the sub shop and headed back home.

Hawk barked at me as I opened the door, latching onto my pant leg. With my hands full, I dragged him across the wooden planks to spread our lunch across the counter, swearing as his sharp teeth scraped against my calf.

Eva spoke animatedly to the person on the other side of her video call, her hair pinned up in a professional bun and dark-rimmed glasses perched on her nose. She wore a sharp navy blazer and white top, giving lawyer vibes. But on the bottom, she wore a tight pair of leggings adorned with skulls. I smiled at the juxtaposition.

She ended the call in an upbeat, chirpy voice I'd never once heard her use and closed her laptop, letting out a deep sigh as she removed her glasses. She stood and her eyes lit up as she moved toward the feast before her on the countertop.

"Thank you! I'm starving," Eva said, unwrapping her sub and biting into it like a rabid street dog.

"Do you not know how to cook?" I scanned the kitchen as I thought of ten things she could have whipped up this morning.

"Of course I know how to cook. It's just hard to do between meetings."

Her tone sounded sharp and defensive. I raised my eyebrows at her as I took another bite of my salad. I didn't believe her for a second, because Linc's background check included her credit card statement, which mainly consisted of takeout and delivery charges.

"How do you stay in such good shape when you eat like a ten-year-old?"

"Are you saying I have a nice ass?" Eva smirked, her eyes challenging me.

I met her gaze, refusing to be baited. "I'm saying there's no way you're eating a nine-hundred-calorie sub, a hundred grams of sugar in your drink alone, and two cookies daily, and you look like that without doing CrossFit or something."

"I take Pilates classes. Speaking of, what are the chances I could go to a class this week? You could come work out with me to make sure no one, you know, offs me." She mimed drawing a blade across her neck, sticking her tongue out the side of her mouth like a cartoon.

Her cavalier attitude toward her near-death experience grated on my nerves. It was either a coping mechanism, or she truly didn't grasp the gravity of the situation.

"Zero chance. You can't go anywhere, especially to a business you go to often. Those will be the first spots they'll be watching for you."

She chewed on the straw and dragged it up and down in the cup, the sound of squeaky plastic worming its way under my skin.

My phone pinged. Linc had the rest of Eva's background check ready, and Thane wanted to talk.

"I have to go handle some club business," I said as I finished the last bite of my lunch. "I'll be back in a few hours."

The roar of my bike did nothing to drown out the chaos in my head. I prided myself on being cold, calculated, and unshakeable. Most women had a healthy dose of respect and fear for men like me, especially ones like her who spent more time in boardrooms and behind desks than in sketchy bars and back alleys. They instinctively knew I was a threat. But Eva was the first woman I'd ever met who I thought could meet my threats with her own. She stared me down with her chin held high like a dare. I couldn't decide if she was brave, stupid, or just too new to my world to know better.

I downshifted hard, gravel spitting under my tires as I tried to shake off the restless energy gnawing in my gut. I didn't like feeling off-balance. She wasn't scared of me, which made her dangerous in a way I couldn't pin down.

As I strode into the clubhouse, I hoped Linc could offer more answers about this enigma of a woman who had barreled into my life with her pint-sized furry piranha. The stale beer-and-gun oil stench of the clubhouse did nothing to ground me as I sat beside my brother. The air hung heavy with cigarette smoke, curling in the dim light.

"What do you have?" I asked Linc, cracking open the beer he'd slid across the bar, condensation spreading across the obsidian countertop.

"This woman's a walking Molotov cocktail," Linc said with a grin. "Want the long story or the short?"

"The fucking short." Linc's long stories had an irritating number of irrelevant details.

Linc laughed. He'd expected that answer. "I'll do my best, but some of these were just too good to leave out. Eva has more than a record. This pretty little vigilante has left a trail of broken bones and blood behind her since she was just a kid."

He spread the contents of Eva's folder across the clubhouse bar.

"Freshman year of high school—a classmate bragged about how he'd roofied a girl at a party. Eva followed him to the bathroom and beat the shit out of him."

A slow smile tugged at my lips as I imagined this woman facing off against a boy probably twice her size.

"She broke two of his ribs against a urinal," Linc continued. "But they couldn't prove it, and her friends claimed she had been with them. It was his word against hers, and she hadn't been in trouble before. She was a straight-A student."

I almost felt sorry for the bastard. Almost.

Linc flipped the page, showing another high school record.

"Sophomore year—she caught a senior harassing a freshman girl. She broke his nose. Got suspended this time because a teacher caught her."

"I thought you said she had a sealed record," I prodded.

Linc's grin widened. "I'm getting there. At sixteen, shit really hits the fan. This youth pastor has been groping her and some other girls. Eva reports it, but no one does jack shit."

My grip tightened on the bottle as a familiar anger stirred in my gut.

"So, one night, she waits for him in the parking lot. Takes a bat to him. He gets a few hits in, too, but she puts him in the hospital."

He slid the police report over. Even in her mugshot, I could sense her simmering fury. Her chin remained high despite her split lip and the bruise forming under her cheekbone. She'd been arrested and taken to a juvenile detention facility.

"The prosecution pushed for a more severe punishment because it had been a pre-meditated assault—not exactly self-defense. But the judge took her side, especially after other girls came forward. Gave her community service and sealed her record."

"What else?" I asked as I flipped through the pages. Linc had pulled everything he could find.

"In college, she caught the president of a frat trying to take advantage of a drunk girl. She broke a beer bottle over his head and pushed him down the stairs."

A laugh punched out of me. "Fuck. I'd have paid to see that."

"She was gone before the EMTs arrived. When the police showed up at her door, her roommates vouched for her. They said she'd been watching movies with them all night."

"Smart. Always have an alibi."

Linc's expression turned serious. "The last incident is ... well, it's an assumption. Circumstantial. Few years back, she went on a date with a guy. Turns out he's a stalker. Restraining order doesn't work. Cops are useless. Said she was being dramatic."

My jaw clenched as a protective rage rose within me. "What happened?"

"One night, he cornered her after work with a knife to her throat. He whispered all the ways he was going to hurt her. She got away and reported it to the police. They arrested him, but he was back on the streets the next day. A week later, someone broke into his house and slit his throat in the middle of the night."

I raised my brows. "You think it was her?"

Linc shrugged. "I don't *not* think it was her. Maybe it's a coincidence. Or maybe she took justice into her own hands. She had a solid alibi, but ..."

"But it fits," I finished. A new respect for Eva settled in my bones. "She's got teeth, that's for sure."

Linc's lips curled into a knowing smirk. "You've got a thing for her, haven't you?"

I shot him a warning glare but didn't dignify it with a response. "What else did you find? What about her family life?"

Linc's face went grim. "A sad story. Her parents divorced when she was three. Lived with her mom until her piece-of-shit stepfather stabbed her to death. Her mom was four months pregnant." He tapped the police report. "Eva witnessed everything. She called 911 from a closet. She was thirteen."

I stared at the crime scene photos, bloodstained floral wallpaper and a pink backpack visible under the yellow tape. "Fuck." Her childhood had been shattered in an instant.

"She and her brother moved to Maryland to live with her dad. Career military. Working dog handler. Took the ... practical approach to grief." Linc flipped to military records. "He started training Eva in Krav Maga. Her brother enlisted the next year."

"Where's the brother now?"

"MIA."

Linc tapped a deployment photo of Jace Harland.

"What about her dad?"

"Retired. They catch up every week, according to her phone records."

I shook my head as I processed the weight of Eva's past. I'd sensed her dark side the moment I met her, but I never imagined she'd been through so much. She'd been tempered by tragedy and loss at an age when most kids worried about school dances and homework.

"Shit," I muttered, running a hand over my face.

The image of young Eva calling 911 while her world shattered around her twisted something in my chest. I'd experienced my share of horrors, too. But she'd been just a kid.

"She's been fighting her whole life. I bet she doesn't even know how to relax or trust anyone at this point."

Linc raised an eyebrow. "Sounds like someone else I know."

I shot him a warning glare, but the comparison stuck. Maybe it explained my inexplicable draw to her. Life had cut us from the same cloth—survivors, fighters, people who'd seen the darkest parts of humanity and chosen to stand against it instead of succumbing.

"We need to end this Abell situation. Not just for her safety, but because it's the decent fucking thing to do."

Linc nodded, a hint of his usual grin returning. "Never thought I'd see the day when you became a white knight."

I flipped him off. "Fuck off. Track the bastards down."

Chapter Fifteen

I was a captive in a cabin, but it didn't mean I could pause everything with my growing consultancy. The constant hum of activity provided a welcome distraction from my precarious situation. As I settled into my makeshift office on the soft brown leather couch, I couldn't help but smile at the irony. Here I sat, a PR professional used to sleek city offices, now crafting strategies from a rustic hideout.

I shot Kenna a text with my new number, knowing she'd send a private investigator to find me if I went longer than a few hours without responding to her.

Kenna: Did you break your phone again? Or did you just want a Texas area code?

Me: It's a long story. Too long for text message. Shit went down and I'm somewhat in hiding until I figure things out.

Kenna: Is this a burner phone!?! Are you going into Witness Protection?

Me: More like Maverick Protection …

My computer pinged with an influx of emails. Each message reminded me of the normal world outside of the threat I faced. I had a handful of clients and projects I needed to keep on track, with several check-in calls scattered throughout the afternoon. But more than that, I remained determined to continue working with the Maverick-associated businesses. The last thing I wanted was for Thane to pull the contract or ask for a refund. Plus, I had to admit the challenge held a certain thrill.

Fortunately for my sanity and security, I could do plenty of work from the cabin. And as I edited the photos and videos captured the other day of Maisie at the market, an idea began to take shape.

I wanted to create a community report highlighting the collective economic impact of the businesses owned by Mavericks. The report would tell stories about how they helped people who lived and worked in Conroe. My strategy would change perceptions, showing the world the side of the Mavericks I'd just begun to understand.

I closed my eyes, imagining a glossy magazine-style report. The pages would be filled with striking photos. A bearded biker, his arms covered in tattoos, handing a teddy bear to a wide-eyed child in a hospital bed. A family of five—both parents wearing their cuts with pride—walking dogs at the local animal shelter. Children sitting cross-legged on a colorful rug, their faces rapt as Maisie's animated voice brought a story to life. Eye-catching infographics would tell the story, too. Jobs created, taxes paid, community programs funded.

The misperception of the Mavericks seemed unfair, and I intended to fix it. Not just because my job required it, but because I had begun to uncover the truth under the leather and chrome. These people—my clients, my protectors, my friends—deserved to have their real stories told.

I'd wrapped up my last client call when an email from Matt pinged through. He hadn't been able to reach my cell—it was still powered off. I fired off a Google Meet invite, which he joined within a minute.

"Eva, where have you been? It's like you fell off the map. Your phone just goes straight to your voicemail—which is still full, by the way." His eyes searched the room, the rough-hewn logs of the cabin behind me.

I rubbed my temples, unsure of how much to say or if Matt would even believe me. "I guess you could say I'm in hiding."

"Where?" Matt pressed, leaning closer to his camera.

I paused, realizing I didn't know. I hadn't exactly been sober when Reaper brought me here, and his driving had been erratic. I hadn't considered until now that he may have been trying to confuse anyone who was following us.

"Somewhere safe. Hale is trying to kill me."

Matt let out a tight laugh. "Come on. That isn't funny."

"Matt, I'm serious. We're getting close to exposing Hale. Benjamin put a bounty on my head. A million dollars. I'd be dead if it weren't for ... one of my clients."

His eyebrows shot up, interest piqued. "Who?"

I shook my head, a flicker of unease settling in my stomach. "Matt, you know I can't disclose client information. You shouldn't even be asking."

His expression hardened. "Don't you think at least one person should know where you are in case something happens?"

"A friend knows because of her ... association with the client. They saved my life. Twice in one night. I trust them."

Hawk let out two excited barks and a small howl as if on cue. Reaper stepped inside, scooping up the pup before he could latch onto his clothing.

Matt let out a deep sigh. "I don't like this. We need to meet up when I'm in Houston. I have more leads to share. I found two women who might be willing to talk—on the record, this time."

I hesitated but pushed on. Reaper already knew about our investigation into Hale's abuse. It wouldn't hurt for him to listen in on this part of the conversation.

"Who are they? What do you know?"

Matt rustled some papers at his desk. "Ruth Wass worked for Hale as an intern a few years ago. She filed a police report after he allegedly assaulted her but dropped the charges a day later."

He paused as he sorted through the disorganized pile of paper. Given the chaotic state of his desk, I struggled to understand how this man ever filed a story on time.

"And then Paige Villa. She'd worked as a contractor at a gala, raising money for one of their charities. She was attacked after the event. But it was dark, so Hale wasn't named. But the description of the attacker fits, and he attended the event. We need to meet with both of them."

I glanced at Reaper, who shook his head at Matt's insistent request.

"Email me the information. I can't go anywhere right now."

Matt's jaw clenched, frustration evident. "I promised my editor this story. We are so close."

I bristled at his tone and jumped as Reaper slammed a cupboard harder than necessary. I glared at him before returning to my screen.

"Who's there with you?" Matt asked, his curiosity invasive.

"My personal chef," I quipped, forcing a smirk. "And we agreed not to involve your editor until the story was locked down. So that sounds like a 'you' problem. Email me what you've found, and we'll go from there. I'll check if the information aligns with what my sources are sharing."

His eyes hardened. "Fine, I'll send the info. But these women won't leave a paper trail. They'll only meet in person. I'll find a spot to meet. And maybe you could consider giving me the names of your latest sources, too. Just to make sure we aren't duplicating work."

I rolled my eyes. It drove him crazy that I refused to reveal all of my sources. I trusted Matt, but Amy had only been willing to share her story as long as I kept her name a secret—even from the journalist who would publish the story.

"Bye," I said, ending the call and pushing the laptop away.

Reaper glanced at me as he methodically chopped a carrot into perfect bite-sized pieces. "You're not going to meet anyone right now."

I figured as much. I wouldn't press him on it ... yet.

"Who is Matt?"

"A friend from college. He's an investigative journalist. He promised to write the story if I can get enough women to speak out against Hale and how Abell Enterprises has covered up his violent tendencies."

My phone pinged, an email with attachments coming through from Matt. "We're so close. These new leads could help us break the story."

Chapter Sixteen

The scent of sizzling vegetables filled the cabin, mingling with the earthy aroma of the log walls. Eva perched on a stool at the counter. I found myself asking about her school days, hobbies, and career—genuinely curious about the woman behind the sharp wit and seeking to understand how she kept a dark side hidden beneath the professional facade.

Hawk circled our feet. His nails clicked against the hardwood floor as he hoped for a morsel to drop. I shooed him away with my foot, earning a disappointed whine.

"Can you get the minced garlic out of the fridge and add a teaspoon to the pan?" I asked Eva, my hands busy slicing chicken into even strips.

Eva brushed against me as she moved past, the brief contact sending a jolt through my system. Her eyes flicked to mine as she gauged my reaction. I kept my expression neutral, but my pulse quickened.

She rummaged through a drawer, found a spoon, then moved to the refrigerator. I watched from the corner of my eye as she dipped the spoon into the garlic container, eyeballing the measurement before flicking it into the sizzling pan. The pungent aroma intensified in seconds.

"Damn it. That's easily a tablespoon," I growled, more amused than annoyed.

She smirked. "Garlic is best measured with your heart."

This woman was as infuriating as she was adorable. I bit back a smile, not wanting to encourage her.

"You like to cook?" she asked, moving a few ingredients to the side as she hoisted herself on the counter. Hawk sat at her feet, gazing at her with hopeful eyes.

"Yeah, I enjoy it," I admitted, focusing on the pan to avoid getting lost in her gaze. "I cooked dinner every night from the time I was thirteen to when I left for boot camp. Linc is five years younger, and our mom worked long hours as a nurse. My choices were either learn to cook or eat microwave dinners every night."

Eva hesitated, reading between the lines. "What about your dad?"

I scraped the chicken into the pan. "Sentenced to life when I was twelve. Piece of shit of a human being."

After washing my hands, I turned toward her and stepped closer. "What about your parents?" I asked, curious to hear her version of the story.

"My dad was in the military, and my mom got tired of moving around, so she left him. Then, we moved in with my dad after she died. My brother, Jace, was only around for a year before he enlisted. My dad trained military working dogs. That's how I got into fostering. I like volunteering to take on working breeds. I understand them."

The vulnerability in her voice drew me in closer. "I'm sorry about your mom. That must have been hard."

A mask slid into place in an instant. It became clear Eva still didn't speak about the grief and trauma, even after two decades.

"Thank you," she said in a curt tone. "Besides cooking, what else are you good at?"

A line drawn. A topic closed. She spun the conversation back to me with practiced ease.

"Motorcycles. Guns. Construction."

Her eyes glinted with that sharp, suggestive edge I'd become all too familiar with. "So, you're saying you're good with your hands?"

Her flirtation never came across as subtle. There was always a challenge in it. A taunt and an awareness of the buttons she pushed, daring me to react. The woman was relentless. Always pushing, always testing. It both maddened and aroused me.

I'd battled a war within myself since the night I'd pinned her against that hallway wall at the clubhouse. My logical side recognized her as a distraction I didn't need.

But my primal instincts, the part of me craving a challenge and release, fought against my control. And goddamn, did I want to give in. I wanted to prove how easily I could shatter her cool composure. I teetered on the edge of a fucking cliff and knew I couldn't resist any longer.

I stepped in front of her and brushed my fingers against her knees. "I am very good with my hands."

The statement came out as a promise, threat, and challenge all rolled into one.

Eva's breath hitched. "Prove it."

I ran my fingers in slow circles on the insides of her thighs, starting right above the knees and moving upward. My lips grazed hers in a soft, teasing kiss.

I pulled back and searched her eyes for consent. Eva's gaze was a dare. An invitation to take it further. I spread my palms at the top of her thighs, pressing her legs apart as I leaned in to crush my lips against hers once again. I slid my hands under her top, savoring the softness of her skin. Breaking the kiss, I pulled the shirt over her head, then unclasped her bra. I took a moment to admire her, the curve of her breasts, the way her nipples hardened under my gaze. Eva arched her back, and a low moan escaped her lips as I took one nipple into my mouth while rolling the other between my fingers. I kissed her chest and neck as my hands moved to the waistband of her skull leggings. She lifted her hips, allowing me to pull them down—along with her lacy black thong.

"Wait," she breathed, her voice husky.

I stopped, surprised. I didn't think I'd misread the signals. Even now, her body vibrated with every touch.

"What's your actual name?"

I hesitated for a moment. I rarely used my real name anymore. I'd been known as Reaper since boot camp, and it had become my road name once I'd joined the Mavericks.

"Why do you want to know?" I asked, letting my fingers drift across her stomach. "Planning to run a background check?"

Eva's smile was trouble. "Just want to know what to scream when you stop asking questions."

I huffed a laugh. "You think you'll have enough breath left for that?"

She leaned in, her lips brushing my ear. "Fucking try me."

I liked her boldness. I liked her smart mouth even more. "Roman. That's the name you'll be begging for." Only the government and my mother called me Roman. And now Eva would, too.

She grinned, her pupils dilated and cheeks flushed. "Roman," she repeated in a low, taunting tone. "I don't beg for anyone or anything. You'll be the one begging."

I smirked as her hands started to move down my chest. I caught them, pinning her wrists between us as my lips grazed against her throat.

"You want to keep mouthing off, or do you want to find out how loud I can make you scream? And how long I'll make you beg?"

I kissed down her chest, pausing again at her pebbled nipples before running my lips down her stomach. I released her wrists and she leaned back on her elbows, flattening the surface of her body to allow better access. As my teeth scraped her hip bones, Eva arched her back with a sharp intake of breath.

I ran my hand up her thigh once more, this time brushing my

thumb against her clit. Eva moaned again, her head tilted back in the pleasure of the sensations. I dipped my head down, swiping my tongue up her center before sucking at the bundle of nerves at the apex of her thighs. She was already slick with desire.

"Oh, fuck, Roman," she said in a strained whisper as if she struggled to hold it together.

"Let go," I said before swirling my tongue against her again. "Just enjoy the ride."

Her hips bucked as I worked her with my tongue and fingers. I chuckled against her as she swore in a strained whisper. Her climax hit hard and fast, her body shuddering beneath me. As she came down from her high, I scooped her up, wrapping her legs around my waist. I carried her to the bedroom, pausing only to turn the stove to simmer.

I planted her on the bed, admiring her naked form as I reached for the back of my T-shirt and pulled it over my head.

I paused. "Please tell me you're on birth control."

She only nodded in response. Thank God, because I kept my condoms in my spare room at the clubhouse, and riding my bike to the store at this point would be uncomfortable as fuck.

Eva watched my every move, and hunger shone in her stormy eyes. I unbuttoned my jeans and kicked them to the floor. Fuck me, this woman was as beautiful as she was dangerous. My heart raced as I stood at the edge of the bed.

Crawling over her on the soft blue quilt, I began to slowly kiss her neck again. Her hands roamed all over me—running down my abs, my back, my cock. The sensations overwhelmed me, making it hard to focus, to stay in control. I sat up, leaning back on my heels to grab her wrists and pin them above her head.

Eva's eyes lit up with excitement, reminding me of our first encounter.

"Do I need to remind you of our little conversation in the hallway at the club? When I said you'd be begging me?" I teased my cock against her, and she arched her hips into me.

"Roman, please."

As much as I wanted to continue to tease her, to make her beg, I couldn't hold back any longer. I'd craved Eva since the moment I set eyes on her. I slid into her, giving her a few breaths to adjust.

"Fuck," I moaned, each letter of the word escaping my mouth slowly. I crushed my mouth to hers in a kiss as violent as our pasts.

As I thrust into her, our pace became a desperate plea to release the tension that had started building a week ago when we'd first met. I released her wrists and moved my hands to her hips, seeking leverage.

"Fuck. Oh, fuck," she said in a breathy moan. "Roman, faster. Harder." She ran her fingers over my shoulders before gripping my biceps.

She tightened, approaching another orgasm. Her pleas drove me wild. I quickened my pace, my own release barreling right behind hers. She arched her body and tilted her head back against the pillow, tightening around me like a vise just moments before I pulsed inside of her.

I moved over, leaning to my side. "Fuck me, that was ..." I trailed off, unsure how to describe how my heart raced in my chest.

"Yeah," Eva agreed, still panting. "That was really ..."

"Fucking amazing isn't enough to describe it, is it?"

She laughed and shook her head.

"You're addictive, my sweet Lioness. I haven't been able to get you out of my mind since I first laid eyes on your headshot. And now that I have you here in my bed, I don't know that I'll be able to let you go."

She grinned. "If being your captive involves sex like that every day, I'll happily stay."

Then, confusion crossed her face. Her eyes narrowed as she sat up. She tilted her head. "Wait. What do you mean by my headshot?"

Shit. In my post-fuck haze, where the blood still hadn't returned to my brain, I'd said too much. But at this point, I was a little glad. I had grown tired of talking around what I'd learned about her.

"Do you remember how I said I knew everything about you?" I sat up to face her. "Before the club works with anyone, Linc does some digging."

"Like a background check?"

I ran a calloused finger across her jaw, noting the growing tension in her shoulders.

"Yes. Just with a bit of light hacking to get the information we won't find in your standard background check."

A stoic mask slipped across her expression, and the air shifted around us. I recognized the rare panic in her eyes.

"How much do you know?"

"I know you are a fearless, fierce survivor. A woman who takes no shit. Allows no harm. And holds predators accountable for their actions—even when others don't. Especially when the authorities won't."

I leveled my gaze at her, hoping to show admiration for all she'd done. I sensed her fear and trepidation as she processed my words.

She stood and pulled my T-shirt over her naked body. "That doesn't answer my question," she said as she began pacing the room. "What exactly do you know?"

I sighed and rubbed my hand on the back of my neck. This wasn't going well. I stood and walked to her, wrapping my arms around her trembling shoulders.

"Come on. Let me make you a drink, and I'll tell you what I know. And you can fill in whatever blanks you're comfortable with. Or you can choose not to tell me anything. You don't have to confirm or deny anything you don't want to."

Eva released a shaky breath, and I kissed her forehead before slipping on a pair of gray sweatpants.

She followed me into the living room and lifted Hawk into her lap on the couch.

I moved to my small liquor bar and poured a generous amount of expensive bourbon into two crystal glasses. I sat beside her and handed her the glass. She took a long sip before leveling a gaze at me.

"What do you know? What did you find out about me?"

I brushed my fingers against her arm, needing to find some way to comfort her.

"I've read your high school records. I know about the boy you beat up as a freshman and why you were suspended your sophomore year. And Linc got hold of your sealed record."

Her jaw dropped. "How?"

I shrugged. "He's really good at what he does. We were all impressed. And it sounded like that pastor deserved it."

She only nodded as she processed the news.

"I also know a bit about the situation in college. With the frat president."

Eva gasped in disbelief. "There shouldn't even be a record of that. I wasn't arrested."

I smirked. "The cops sought you out that night. It was in their notes that you had a solid alibi. What you might not know is the type of records your college kept. Unofficial but still on their servers. The frat tried to have you expelled, but there wasn't enough evidence."

Eva raised her brows. "I didn't even know that."

"The last thing we found is ... circumstantial at best." I paused, taking another sip. "You had a stalker about three years ago. And after several calls to the police, he was killed. But you had an alibi, and your name was only referenced in the police report as a person of interest because of the restraining order."

Eva's eyes widened. Shock and vulnerability flickered across her face, and she swallowed hard. "What are you saying?"

My hand moved to cup her cheek. "My fierce Lioness, I'm saying *if* you did anything, it doesn't change my perception of you. If anything, it makes me admire you more."

She pulled away. "How can you say that? What if I was the one who slit his throat? You would be okay with that?"

I couldn't help but smile as she confirmed what I suspected to be true. The police had never released details of the murder. No public reports shared he'd been killed by a blade.

My eyes darkened as an untamed protectiveness radiated from within my chest. "Hell, Eva. I wish I could've been there to help you take that bastard down myself."

"Most people would run screaming if they knew everything I've done. My career would be over. No one would trust me." She shook her head, stroking Hawk's head as she stared at the ceiling and steeled herself with a deep breath.

"I'm not most people. I've got my own dark past. I would never judge you for what you've had to do to protect yourself. To protect others."

Eva searched my face for any sign of judgment. Finding none, she allowed herself to relax. "I never thought anyone would understand, let alone accept it."

My lips quirked into a half smile. "Justice isn't always served by the law. Sometimes, it has to come from our own hands. What you've done? That was justice."

Eva's eyes glistened with unshed tears. "I've spent so long hiding from my past, hiding who I am. And here you are, knowing it all, and still looking at me like ... like ..."

"Like you're the most incredible woman I've ever met?"

She smiled and leaned in for a kiss, the storm in her eyes beginning to clear. "So, that's it? I've beaten the shit out of a handful of men and maybe even murdered one, and it's all fine?"

I laughed. "It's more than fine. But don't ever comment on the details of the murder. The media never reported how he was killed. If you're going to commit a felony, you need to work on keeping the details to a minimum so you don't get caught."

Eva shook her head in disbelief. "I never thought anyone would put it together. No one has ever asked me about it."

"It's unlikely that anyone ever will. But you should never speak of it to anyone but me. Even Thane and Linc were unsure if it had really been you. You don't need to confirm it. If your stalker ever comes up, you can pretend to have forgotten his name. Always give people the bare minimum and then stop talking. Don't be afraid of the silence."

I stood and walked to the kitchen to stir our dinner, bits of vegetables beginning to burn to the bottom of the cast iron pan.

Eva let out a small laugh. "I give the same advice when I coach people to speak to the media during a crisis. Stick to the message, answer the reporter's question, and then shut the hell up."

A different sort of tension filled the kitchen as we ate our slightly overcooked stir-fry. Eva sat on a countertop stool, and I stood across from her on the other side.

"You're staring, Roman. See something you like?"

"Always. But it's different tonight."

"How?"

"Because now I know what sounds you make when you come." I watched her throat work as she swallowed. Her fork clattered against the plate.

She moved around the counter, pressing into my chest. Bourbon and spices exploded across my tongue as she kissed me, all teeth and desperation.

I lifted Eva and carried her down the hallway. Her legs locked around my hips as her fingernails carved half-moons into my shoulders.

This time, we were less frenzied, the sex slower but no less steamy. I savored the way she arched into me and the soft gasps and moans that escaped her lips.

Afterward, she fell fast asleep, curling against my body like she belonged there. Moonlight shone across her bare back as she lay beside me. My fingers traced the script and blade tattooed along her ribcage.

"She wasn't looking for a knight. She was looking for a sword."

The ink suited her. Fierce and unapologetic. A warrior of a woman.

Eva's eyelashes fluttered, a soft sigh escaping as she nuzzled closer. I pressed my lips to her temple, her scent of grapefruit and vanilla filling my senses. Eva's warmth seeped into my skin, and I contemplated our connection. It was more than attraction. More than lust. I'd experienced both but never felt this way about a woman.

The realization hit me like a .45 round, sudden and with devastating impact: I'd burn the whole damn world before letting anyone hurt her again. The intensity should have scared me, but instead, it seemed right. Inevitable.

My heart raced as another thought struck me. I couldn't imagine my life without her now. The idea of waking up to an empty bed, of not hearing her laughter or feeling her touch, left an ache in my chest.

This fiery woman had stormed into my life and changed everything.

Hope bloomed in my chest for the first time in years—a desire for a future that included more than just the club, my construction company, and my solitary existence.

As Eva shifted in her sleep, pressing herself closer to me, I tightened my arm around her. Whatever came next, whatever challenges we faced, one thing remained certain: I would do anything to keep her safe. To keep her by my side. Because somehow, in the span of a few weeks, Eva had become my whole world.

Chapter Seventeen

I woke to excited puppy yips and the aroma of strong coffee. I slipped on Reaper's T-shirt, abandoned on the floor last night, and stepped out of the bedroom as he measured a white substance on a small scale atop the kitchen counter.

"Is that cocaine?" I asked, rubbing my eyes.

Reaper glared at me, dumping the powder in a bowl before picking up a whisk. "I'm not a fucking drug dealer. It's monkfruit powder."

I blinked at him twice. What the hell was monkfruit powder? I stepped closer to peer over the bowl.

"Since you don't understand how ingredients work, I'm making you blueberry muffins so I don't have to be your delivery boy. Between leftovers from last night and these, you should be able to forage on your own for a full day."

I rolled my eyes. "You measure your ingredients with a scale? Are you that much of a control freak?" I examined the ingredients spread across the kitchen island. Almond flour. Coconut oil. Whole wheat flour. "Are you making me healthy muffins? Oh, God. Are you one of those 'I treat my body like a temple' guys?"

Reaper chuckled. "I promise these will be good. What do you usually eat for breakfast?"

"I treat my body like a dive bar. Usually, it's coffee with sugar and cream. If I eat anything, I'll have a bowl of Captain Crunch or maybe a slice of cold pizza."

Reaper faked a shudder and shook his head as he poured the batter into muffin cups. I dipped my finger into the mixture and brought it to my mouth. Our eyes locked as I sucked on it suggestively.

"Hmm, not bad. Could use some more sweetness, though."

Reaper grabbed me around the waist, lifting me to sit on the counter. "I can think of something sweet."

Wrapping my arms around his shoulders, I leaned in as he began to kiss my neck.

"I like seeing you in my shirt," he growled in my ear.

"Get those in the oven, and I'll let you see me out of it," I joked, hopping off the counter to pour myself a cup of the death-fuel coffee he'd brewed with a generous addition of cream and sugar.

He sighed. "I would love to, but I just got a text that there's a problem at one of my jobs. I have to head out in a minute."

Reaper slid the tin of muffins into the oven. "You'll have to take these out in twenty-five minutes. Do not let them burn."

He glared at me as if he didn't trust my cooking skills, even with the simplest of responsibilities. I laughed, making a show of setting the timer on my phone before taking off my shirt in the kitchen and sauntering to the shower.

* * *

My mind raced as I prepared to start working at my computer. The previous night's events played on repeat in my head, a whirlwind of emotions and sensations leaving me breathless.

I'd never felt so exposed, so vulnerable. Reaper had discovered everything—my fights, my sealed record, and even the darkest secret I'd kept buried for years.

It should have crushed me and sent me running for a country that offered no extradition. But instead, a weight lifted off my shoulders. For the first time in my life, someone accepted me fully—the good, the bad, the downright brutal—and didn't flinch.

My fingers hovered over the keyboard, but I couldn't focus. All I could think about was Reaper's gaze last night, his dark eyes filled with admiration instead of judgment. The way he'd called me his Lioness, like some adorable animal rather than a justice-driven vigilante who belonged in prison for pre-meditated murder.

A shiver ran through me as I thought of his touch, gentle yet demanding. The way he'd pinned my wrists above my head. The raw desire in his voice. The way I'd moaned his real name.

A connection existed between us that I couldn't explain or rationalize away.

I'd spent years keeping everyone at arm's length. It seemed safer that way. Easier. But Reaper had somehow slipped past my defenses.

It terrified me.

I stroked Hawk's fur and contemplated the feelings bubbling inside. I'd grown accustomed to being in control. I called the shots in every facet of my life. My experiences in romantic relationships were few and far between, but I sensed this could be different.

If I let it.

I needed to talk to Kenna. She had a sixth sense for my relationship woes.

Me: So, I have a confession to make.

Kenna: YOU DIDN'T

Kenna: Please tell me it was as good as I imagined.

I grinned, biting my lip.

Me: Better. Maybe the best?

Kenna: Like, ever?

Me: Yeah. I'm in so much trouble.

Kenna: DETAILS. NOW. I want adjectives. I want metaphors. I want fruit and vegetable–size comparisons. Are we talking carrot? English cucumber? Eggplant?

I snorted at her lack of boundaries.

Me: A perfectly sized banana. Thick, yet long enough to bruise my cervix.

Kenna: Hot. Also terrifying. But mostly hot. Can you walk today? Are you freaking out?

Me: Very much freaking out. He's so different from anyone I've ever been with.

Kenna: Honestly, that's a good thing. Your taste in men has been shit. You should roll with this. See where it goes. Don't run before you have a chance to find out what you have.

I stared at the screen, her words sinking in. Don't run.

I was in dangerous territory. Reaper wasn't just some guy I could have a fling with and forget. The logical part of my brain screamed at me to pull back, to protect myself, to put up the walls again. But my heart wanted more. And now that I'd had a taste, I craved every part of him.

I shook my head as I attempted to clear my thoughts. I had work to do. But as I finally managed to focus on my laptop screen, I couldn't shake the thought that my life had irrevocably changed. For better or worse, Reaper had carved out a spot in my world.

* * *

After a few hours of focus, responding to client emails, and editing copy for some ads, my burner phone pinged with a text.

Rhetta: How's life in captivity?

Me: Quiet. But less murdery than it would be at my house, I guess. You should come over. We could have a cookout or something.

Rhetta: We're free tonight! I'll have Thane coordinate with Reaper on the menu … because I know you can't cook. Is there anything you need me to bring?

Me: Snacks. Unhealthy ones. If I have to eat one more carrot stick, I'm going to stab Reaper in the eyeball with one. I'm going into candy withdrawal here.

Rhetta: We'll be there around 6. I'll bring ALL. THE. SNACKS.

Chapter Eighteen

The rain pelted my leather jacket as I jogged into the clubhouse, the familiar scent of leather, motor oil, and stale beer hitting me like a punch to the gut. My muscles ached from a morning spent fixing a leaky roof, but there was no rest for the wicked. I stepped inside and shook off the rain.

A familiar scene played before me. Thane sat at the bar with a cigarette dangling from his lips, drinking with Linc and Jack. Bones huddled in the corner with Merrick, their grease-stained hands tinkering with a bike. Archer and a few prospects hovered near the pool table.

"Well, well, look what the cat dragged in," Thane called out with a shit-eating grin across his face. He took a long draw of his cigarette. The smoke curled around him as much as his smugness did. "Thought you might've forgotten about us."

I flipped him off as I approached the bar. "Some of us have actual work to do, dickhole."

Thane slid a beer my way. "Uh-huh. And does this 'work' have long legs, pretty blue eyes, and a smart mouth?"

I cracked it open and took a long pull from the bottle, fighting to keep my face neutral. "I'm busy running a company all day. Now I'm here to talk club business."

"Oh, I know. But I also know you. I bet she's getting under your skin more than you're willing to admit. And I've seen the way you look at her. Boys, I think Reaper has a crush on our consultant."

I glared at him as I drained the bottle. He could read me like a damn book. I reached behind the bar for another beer as I ignored the jeering from the guys.

Once the rest of the club's officers trickled in, we headed to Thane's office for Church.

"Has the shit Danielle's stirred up settled yet?" I asked after calling the meeting to order.

Linc huffed. "Not according to her Facebook. But she's lost momentum. Enough people watched the city hall debacle, and some people are starting to push back. One Facebook group even kicked her out."

Thane stroked his goatee. "I've been thinking," he said, pausing as he collected his thoughts. "As much as we fucking hate her, that kid still belongs to one of our fallen brothers. Usually, we take care of old ladies and the family if a brother passes."

I gritted my teeth. "She was never a fucking old lady."

Thane leveled a look at me and held up one finger. I silenced my opposition out of respect. Barely.

"She wasn't. But I think we can make this problem go away. I think we have enough in the Maverick Widows' Trust to set up a college fund for Sebastian. Kid's only nine."

"So, we make her a deal?" Jack asked, pulling his phone from his pocket and tapping a few keys. As treasurer, he tracked our accounting and investments.

"She has a GoFundMe for the kid's outstanding medical bills," Linc added. "Says she owes $27,000. Only about $7,000 has been funded so far."

Jack turned his phone to face us, showing the cash we had on hand in the fund dedicated to helping the women and children left behind when a club member unexpectedly died. "Let's say college costs $160,000 in ten years. We could give her an even $200,000. I can write a check for $20,000 to the hospital for the bills."

Thane nodded. "I remember Russell saying Danielle blew through money like a goddamn QVC addict, so we sure as fuck aren't giving her the cash directly."

Jack slipped his phone back into his pocket. "I can set up a trust for Sebastian. He gets it when he turns eighteen. Keeps her grimy fucking fingers off it and honors Russell."

I tapped my fingers on the table. "You think she'll back off?"

Thane scoffed. "She'll have to. I'll have the lawyer draw something up. We only pay the bills if she agrees to never speak another word about the Lone Star Mavericks MC. All in favor, say aye."

Unanimous ayes rumbled through the room. It was the right move to support the kid, even though we fucking hated his mom. Had she not been a pain in our assess since the day of the accident, we'd probably have made the offer out of the goodness of our hearts—or whatever you call the thing in our chest that kept most of us from becoming complete menaces to society.

"Good," Thane grumbled. "I never want to hear her fucking name again."

"Now that we've settled that issue, let's move on," I said, changing the subject before Hatchet said her name just to piss Thane off. "What's the status on the Ranger situation?"

The mood in the room shifted. "We got a message this morning," Merrick said. "From their president."

"And?"

Thane's earlier grin shifted into a grim expression. "Hickok wants a sitdown. Wants to talk about a truce."

I shook my head. "I don't believe that for one fucking second." The Rangers were a festering wound. If we didn't deal with them soon, the infection would spread.

Thane flexed his jaw. "You're right. We'll plan it today. We take the meeting to them and give them three choices—they either stay the fuck out of Houston, patch over, or die. And no matter what they choose, they stop slinging dirty coke. Rodriguez told me two college kids OD'd on fentanyl-laced blow last weekend."

"If Hickok's calling for a truce, it's because he's scared or he's setting a trap," Merrick said. "They'll never patch over. The Rangers will never give us peace. We've been their enemy since my dad started this club."

I cracked my neck, working my jaw to release the tension. "So, we go in hot. We know we won't get peace, so we give them an ultimatum instead. I met Poe, the VP, at Sturgis. I've heard he and a few guys are tired of Hickok's shit. They might welcome the end of an era. A fresh start."

Thane tilted his head, catching my drift. "You think they'll turn on him?"

I shrugged. "Hickok's just been running the club into the ground."

Thane lit a cigarette. "Either way, we're probably sending him packing with a bullet. He's been a plague to Texas for too long."

"We'll have to decide on the spot if we give Poe the chance to write a new chapter."

As we discussed ideas and contingencies, the air grew thick with cigarette smoke and tension. We hammered out a plan to send one last message to the Rangers and end the brewing conflict between our clubs. After two hours, Thane slammed down the gavel and passed around a fifth of Jack Daniel's.

"Dinner at your place tonight," Thane informed me after taking a shot. "Apparently, the ladies made plans."

"Have they? This is the first I'm hearing of it."

Thane grinned. "Rhetta says you're in charge of the steaks. Apparently, Eva can't be trusted in the kitchen."

"Don't I fuckin' know it. I think she'd live off potato chips and chocolate if I didn't cook for her. I baked her muffins this morning." The words slipped out before I could stop myself. Fuck me.

Thane roared with laughter. "You baked muffins for her?"

"Shut the fuck up. If I don't leave her with food, she'll text me all day like I'm her snack bitch."

Thane shook his head, still grinning. "Didn't realize you were running a bed and breakfast. You're a goddamn Martha Stewart. You're losing your edge—going all domestic on me."

"I'm not losing my edge. I'm keeping her alive, just like you asked. Feeding her is part of that."

"You tired of pretending you don't want more from her than this roommate situation? A relationship would be good for you."

I shook my head. This wasn't like me. I didn't do relationships. I was Reaper, for fuck's sake. Cold. Calculating. Lethal. No attachments. No distractions.

I fought the urge to defend myself further because it would only encourage him. "I need to get back to work. I'll see you tonight."

I flipped Thane off as I walked away, and the sound of his laughter followed me out of the clubhouse.

As much as I enjoyed having Eva locked away in my cabin, my brother still hadn't updated me about where the Abells were hiding so we could end the threat on her life.

> Me: Any updates?

> Linc: Right after they put out the contract, they boarded a plane for a vacation in Switzerland. I'm guessing their plan was to return after she was confirmed dead.

> Me: When are they scheduled to fly back?

> Linc: Not sure yet.

> Me: Okay, keep an eye on them.

> Linc: Got it, boss.

> Me: By the way, Thane and Rhetta are coming to my place for dinner. If you come, bring your own beer.

> Linc: You sure it's okay if I crash your double date?

> Me: Fuck off. You're not invited anymore.

I tried to focus on the road ahead, but the wind whipped past me with my running thoughts as I left the clubhouse. This thing with Eva seemed different than my previous hookups. Not just a quick fuck to scratch an itch, but something more. My chest tightened in an unfamiliar way as I thought of her. The touch of her lips. The sound of her breathy moans and gasps. The way she fit perfectly against me. It went beyond physical, though. Eva's clever quips and the way she laughed. Her sharp intelligence. Her fearlessness.

I'd watched her warm with every interaction with the club. Maisie already treated her with the same love and respect as she did the other old ladies. She'd helped Jack feel comfortable on camera and defended us at the market. I'd even felt her eyes on me as I played with Tilly, Talia, and Leo at the cookout. She understood we were more than just outlaws with motorcycles. This woman drew me in. Every part of my dark heart wanted her. But could she want every part of me?

* * *

I kicked open the door with an armful of groceries. Eva glanced up from her laptop, and her face lit with a smile that sent my heart racing. I could overhear a man regaling her with a story about the fish he'd caught that morning. I sat the groceries down and put the cold beer in the refrigerator until Hawk started tearing at the paper bags to get to the steaks.

"Hey, asshole. Get out of there. Those aren't for you."

I moved the steaks and potato salad to the countertop before Hawk could commandeer them.

The man paused mid-sentence. "Who's there with you?"

Eva's eyes widened, and a hint of panic crossed her face. "A friend just stopped by. So, the fish?"

"Liar. That was a man's voice. You have a boyfriend, don't you?"

"Dad, stop. Finish your story."

I watched the blush creep up her neck at her dad's teasing tone. I removed my cut and hung it on the hook near the door.

"Let me meet him," her dad pressed. "If he's on vacation with you, it must be serious."

I'd forgotten she caught up with her dad each week, and apparently, she'd told him my cabin was a vacation spot. It was understandable, because the reality—that your former employer had tried to kill you and you were hiding in a cabin with the VP of an outlaw motorcycle club—wasn't exactly the kind of thing you wanted to share with a parent.

"Come on, I promise I won't scare him off," her dad cajoled, his voice a mix of amusement and curiosity.

I smirked at Eva as I stepped behind her. Her shoulders tensed, but she didn't stop me. I squatted eye-to-eye with the screen.

"Sir, it's nice to meet you. I'm Roman."

Eva gave me an exasperated expression, but her father just grinned at me, his weathered face crinkling with delight.

"I was right," he said triumphantly. "She was being so cagey. Now I understand why. Tell me about yourself."

Eva side-eyed me as if she wanted me to give him the sanitized version. I cleared my throat, choosing my words carefully.

"I own a local construction company. Before that, I spent ten years as a Marine."

Knowing his background, her dad would show more approval for my military service than my club service—which I conveniently left out.

"A Marine, huh? Glad she's finally dating someone who won't back down from a challenge," he joked. "Those boardroom types in D.C. never lasted long—always too intimidated by her."

"Dad ..." Eva said in warning, her cheeks flushing deeper.

"She certainly still tries to intimidate me, but I think she's pretty when she's pissed off. She's cute, in a honey badger sort of way," I said with a grin as I watched her shift in her seat. "Unfortunately, I need to step away. I have to prep dinner, because somebody"—I glanced at Eva before continuing—"invited a bunch of people over tonight, and they'll be here in thirty."

As I returned to the kitchen to season and prepare the steaks, Eva finished her call, her voice a low murmur punctuated by occasional laughter. I tossed some trimmings to Hawk, keeping him occupied and quiet.

After she ended the call, Eva hopped onto the stool at the counter, shaking her head. "He's going to be begging to come visit to meet you in person now."

I paused in my dinner prep, turning to face her. "And how do you feel about that?" We hadn't defined our relationship, and the thought of meeting her father in person made it more real.

Eva bit her lip as her eyes met mine. "I don't know. This situation is complicated enough without adding my dad into the mix." She trailed off. "It was kind of nice that you got along, though."

"That's good. It's important for your dad to like your boyfriend," I said nonchalantly, glancing up to gauge her reaction.

The word sounded foreign on my tongue, but not unpleasant.

"So, we're already placing a label on this?" She waved her hand between us.

My lips quirked into a smile. I enjoyed watching her squirm under my gaze. "I think so. Unless you have any objections?" I left the question hanging, giving her an out if she wanted it.

Eva bit her lip, considering. "No objections," she said after a beat with a smile. "It's just ... unexpected."

"Speaking of what people know about us, did you tell Rhetta anything?" I wondered if she'd texted her best friend about our night together.

"Not yet. I wasn't really sure what to say. Did you tell Thane?"

I shook my head, focusing on seasoning the steaks. "Nope, though he has made some insinuations. Linc is already giving me shit about you, too."

"Is Linc coming tonight? You should invite him."

I nodded as I started chopping lettuce for the salad. The rhythmic sound of the knife hitting the cutting board filled the kitchen. "Yeah, he's coming."

Eva pulled a bowl from the top cupboard for the lettuce. She moved to the sink to wash the tomatoes next. It felt so domestic, the two of us cooking together and talking about our friends.

"Can I help with anything?"

I glanced at Eva with a raised brow. "No. I don't have much confidence in your cooking abilities."

She scoffed but didn't argue as she boosted herself to sit on the counter. The memory of our first night together blasted through me. I nearly cut myself as I raked my eyes over her body.

"We should make a bet on who calls us out first."

Eva's eyes lit up at the challenge, her competitive streak showing. "What are we betting? I think Linc will be the first to say something. You two grew up together."

"Nah, it'll definitely be Rhetta."

I paused as a wicked idea formed in my mind. "How about this: if I win, I get to use my leather cuffs on you." I gave her a wolfish grin, enjoying how her breath caught at the suggestion.

"And if I win?"

"If you win, I'll take one of those Pilates classes when it's safe for you to be out and about again."

She smirked. "Sounds like I win either way."

I growled low in my throat, my hands finding her hips. "Careful, my lovely Lioness. Our friends will be here soon, and if you keep talking like that, we might not make it to dinner."

The sound of motorcycles in the distance signaled our guests' approach.

"Let the games begin," she said with a wink.

Chapter Nineteen

Someone would notice the shift between Reaper and me within the first ten minutes. The axis of my world now turned around him, and I noticed small movements that betrayed my feelings. Rhetta would surely notice how I responded to his presence, shifting toward him in the room. Linc would probably see how Reaper brushes my arm when I walk by as if he can't help but touch me.

It's noticeable in our silent communication. The smirk on his face. The small sounds that unintentionally escape from the back of my throat when I think of his body hovering over mine.

He'd set a wager, and now I wanted to win—though I was okay with losing because his prize intrigued me, too. The thought of those leather cuffs sent a shiver of desire down my spine. We didn't need to hide what we were becoming, but my competitive streak ran strong.

Hawk's excited barks announced the arrival of our first guests. The pup raced to the Harley, tail wagging at Rhetta and Thane. My best friend held a plastic bag filled with my favorite snacks.

"Oh. My. God." I began pulling sweet and savory treats from the bag. "You brought me Sour Patch Kids, chips, and peanut butter–filled pretzels? Thank you! Finally, some real food for this house. I was starting to worry I'd have to carve a shiv out of a celery stalk to intimidate Reaper into bringing me some real snacks."

Reaper shook his head as he glanced between Thane and Rhetta. "That woman is a trash panda. She lives off of sugar, carbs, and iced coffee."

I shrugged, carrying my bounty toward the cabin. "Guilty. Not all of us can survive solely on vegetables, rice, and grilled chicken breast. Glad you don't want any of this, because I am not sharing, Mr. Sad Kale Smoothie."

Rhetta followed me into the kitchen with Hawk in her arms and leaned in, speaking in a low, conspiratorial tone. "So, what's it like living with the notorious Reaper?"

I tried to stop my smile. "It's been fine. He's nice."

Rhetta gave me a suspicious glance as I stopped myself from elaborating. I wanted to give Linc a fair chance so I could win our bet.

"I like the quiet. But I'm definitely getting bored."

Another Harley roared up the driveway. "That must be Linc."

Hawk's ears perked up at the sound, and he raced to the door again, ready to greet our new arrival.

The resemblance remained undeniable, but where Reaper's face presented a study in hard angles, Linc's held a boyish, almost innocent quality. He was shorter than his brother. Leaner, too, with a wiry build that suggested restless curiosity rather than raw strength. Linc had the same dark eyes as his older brother, but they seemed brighter, with a youthful light untouched by the shadows Reaper carried. He appeared less guarded, reflecting the unwavering protection he'd always known as the youngest.

Linc grinned, slipping on a baseball cap, as Rhetta and I approached. "The infamous Eva," he said, reaching his palm out for a handshake. "I've heard so much about you."

"From what I understand, a lot of what you know wasn't easily found. I'm impressed. It sounds like there might even be a few things I could learn about myself. Maybe you can show me my file, and we can swap notes."

Linc let out a surprised laugh. "Oh, so Reaper told you? It's all part of working for the Mavericks. We had to make sure you wouldn't run to the police the first time you learned about our nefarious enterprises."

I smirked. "The only nefarious thing I've seen is your brother measuring ingredients on a scale like a culinary psychopath."

"Says the woman who thinks a 'balanced meal' means a slice of cold, leftover pizza in each hand," Reaper snarked.

I found myself caught up in a whirlwind of laughter and banter as the evening unfolded. Reaper stood at the grill, wielding his tongs with the same relentless focus he brought to everything—eyes narrowed, jaw set, and flipping steaks with precision. Who knew watching a man obsess over perfect grill lines could be so damn sexy?

A slow warmth spread through my chest as I watched the group. Thane and Rhetta moved around each other with the kind of practiced ease that only came from years of shared secrets. Linc never let a moment go by without stirring the pot as he recounted stories from their childhood. And Reaper served as an axis, the center of the friendship and chaos. A steady anchor.

This gathering differed from any I'd attended before in my old life. No one here cared about small talk or keeping up appearances. No forced pleasantries or pointless chit-chat. No awkward silences. Only an easy rhythm of people who knew each other's scars and still chose to show up. I didn't have to measure my words or keep my guard up. I could just be me. For the first time in a long while, I wasn't bracing for judgment or waiting for the other shoe to drop. Instead, I found comfort sitting at the rough log picnic table surrounded by tall pines.

"Roman, can you pass me the ketchup?" I asked. His given name slipped out before I could stop it.

The conversation at the table screeched to a halt. Everyone's eyes moved to me. Rhetta's jaw dropped, and Linc's eyes widened with surprise.

A low chuckle rumbled in Reaper's chest as he slid the ketchup across the table. He looked way too pleased with himself, like a fox who'd just found the henhouse wide open.

Oops. I'd grown so comfortable I'd forgotten the weight his real name carried.

"Roman?" Linc asked, glancing between his brother and me, his eyebrows disappearing under his hat. "Only Mom calls you that."

Heat crept up my neck, but before I could stammer out an explanation, Rhetta's face split into a delighted grin.

"You guys are hooking up, aren't you? I thought I was imagining the chemistry, because I was sure you would have told me by now."

Reaper's hand found my thigh under the table. He squeezed it as he smirked at me. "I win."

I rolled my eyes. The thought of his "prize" sent my heart racing. A warm flush of anticipation moved through my body.

"You won what?" Thane asked, leveling a knowing look at Reaper.

"A bet," I clarified. "We bet on who would notice first. Linc, I'm disappointed in you. I thought you'd be the first to call it."

Linc pressed the palms of his hands on the table and leaned back. "I called it days ago."

"So I won?" I asked, glancing between Reaper and Linc.

"Technically, no," Reaper said, giving me a dirty grin. "Linc made his comment before anything happened. So, I still win. I collect my prize tonight. Hope you're ready."

I bit my lip, my belly tightening. The table stayed silent for a beat before Rhetta spoke up.

"I'm going to assume this prize isn't something we should discuss at the dinner table?"

I nodded, glaring at Reaper in silent communication to keep his damn mouth shut.

"That's fine, sugar. You can text me about it later," Rhetta said with a laugh.

After we'd had our fill of steak and potato salad, we moved to the benches around a bonfire as dusk melted into the night. Reaper settled beside me with his thigh pressing warmly against mine. Without a word, he snaked his arm around my waist, pulling me tight to his side. The heat of his body seeped into mine.

The flames crackled and danced, casting wild shadows over the faces of our friends as they told stories. The air turned crisp, nipping at my cheeks and raising goose bumps along my arms. Reaper noticed instantly. He stood, striding into his cabin and returning with a heavy wool blanket. He draped it over my shoulders with a tenderness that made my heart stutter and tucked it snugly around me.

He leaned in, his lips grazing my temple. The simple, gentle gesture sent a jolt through my entire core. I couldn't help the slight, involuntary hum of happiness that escaped me—a soft sound I hoped only he could hear.

The conversation paused again, and I felt every pair of eyes around the fire zero in on us. I glanced up to see Thane and Linc staring, mouths slightly open and beers forgotten. Rhetta's smug grin stretched across her face as if she watched her master plan finally come together. Reaper just smirked, his fingers drumming on my hip. I fought the urge to squirm from the thrill of being claimed so openly.

As the night wore on, the fire burned lower, and the conversation faded into comfortable silence. Linc was the first to leave, promising to return for lunch sometime next week to regale me with more stories of their youth. After a final round of drinks, Rhetta and Thane also stood to head home.

"Have fun," Rhetta jeered as she hugged me goodbye.

Thane made no comment but raised a brow at Reaper in a way that promised they'd be talking about the revelation of our new relationship soon.

As they pulled away on their Harley, Reaper's hand found mine. A different kind of anticipation fluttered in my stomach as his fingers intertwined with my own.

Chapter Twenty

Before Thane's taillights faded into the night, I dragged Eva into the cabin. Hawk snored in his crate, exhausted from playing an endless game of fetch with my brother.

I pressed Eva against the wall. "Are you ready?" I murmured, kissing her neck and pulling back to glance into her eyes. At this point, I didn't expect fear or hesitation, but I wanted to make sure there wasn't even a shred of uncertainty before we started.

She lifted her chin to meet my gaze. "I'm excited I lost for once in my life. That's a first."

I grinned and guided her toward the bedroom, tugging her shirt over her head as we moved. The nightstand drawer slid open, and I lifted out a pair of smooth black leather cuffs. I hovered over her, watching her chest heave in anticipation.

"You sure you know what you're doing with those, or do you just like to play tough?" she taunted.

My lips quirked up in a dangerous smile. "Careful, Lioness. Keep mouthing off and you'll find out just how tough I can be."

Eva's breath hitched and she bit her bottom lip. Her pulse fluttered under my fingers as I tightened the soft leather strap around one wrist, then threaded it through the headboard's slot. Her other hand followed, wrists now pinned above her, body stretched out and waiting.

I paused, letting my gaze linger across her curves. Tension coiled between us before I moved to peck kisses along her jawline. "If at any point you're uncomfortable or want me to stop, just tell me. I don't want to do this if you don't like it."

She nodded, the sparkle in her eye telling me she was enjoying it already.

I kissed her chest and ran my fingers down her sides. She panted with each touch. Her nipples pebbled, and I sucked on each one as she arched her back to move closer to me.

"Fuck," she whispered as she writhed, the restraints pulling taut above her head.

I pecked another kiss between her breasts as I began to move down to her belly, which had started to tense in anticipation. I unzipped her blue jeans, pulling them off and tossing them to the floor.

I continued downward, pausing at her hips to scrape my teeth against her. She let out a slight sound. I smirked, recognizing it as the same one that had escaped from the back of her throat when she sat beside me at the fire.

"I bet you were thinking about this moment all night. How often did you imagine yourself in my bed while we sat with our friends this evening?"

Another slight sound escaped her before she responded. "All fucking night."

I pressed her legs open and began to kiss at an excruciatingly slow pace up the insides of her thighs, moving from left to right before stopping to hover right above her center. I stared up at her face, my hot breath blowing over her sensitive skin.

She squirmed beneath me, the anticipation killing her. This had become my favorite part: watching her unravel as she waited for what would happen next. It was beautiful and brutal to experience this woman, the one who always sought control, offer it up to me, piece by piece.

"Roman, please," she begged.

To watch her surrender to the moment, to unravel, felt intoxicating. In an agonizingly slow move, I pressed my mouth to her clit, flicking my tongue as she arched her hips upward and moaned my name again. I hooked my arms beneath her thighs, lifting her as I circled her flesh in slow, deliberate strokes.

Eva moaned as I slipped one finger inside her and then another. She gasped as I curled them, the pleasure and tension rising. I continued my relentless assault, and the bed creaked as she pulled at the restraints and dug her heels into the mattress.

I paused as she edged toward her release. She whimpered, lifting her head to offer me a heated gaze. "Why are you stopping?"

I gave her a devilish grin. "Because it's my prize, and I get to say when you come. I'm the one in control here."

Eva smirked, a rebellious glint in her eyes. "You mistake anticipation for control. I'm the one who decides whether you get to watch me come."

I laughed, loving the defiant response I'd come to expect from her. I kissed up her body, starting at her hips before moving to her ribs. I traced her tattoo with my fingers and then nipped at her breasts before standing up to slide off my jeans.

I paused as I stood before her, my eyes admiring every curve. A fucking goddess.

"Are you going to stand there and eyeball-fuck me all night?" she asked in a challenging tone.

I stroked my cock as she watched me with a hungry gaze. "If that's what I want, yes," I replied huskily before I lowered myself over her again, our lips meeting.

Who was I kidding? She held more control than I did now, because she had edged into my heart. Hovering above her, I kissed Eva and slid the tip of my cock against her. She arched into me, but I held myself just out of reach.

She growled. "Would you just fuck me already?"

I smirked. "You're quite demanding."

Her lips quirked into a smile. "I prefer to describe myself as assertive."

"Hmm, I do like that about you."

She arched into me again, using her legs to try to pull me into her.

"Say please," I commanded.

"Fucking please," she moaned.

"Good girl. I told you that you'd beg for me," I said as I sank into her to the hilt in one smooth move.

Eva met me thrust for thrust, wrapping her legs around my hips as she arched her back to take me deeper. She pulled against the restraints, wanting to touch me. As she tumbled closer to her orgasm, the number of times she swore increased by the second.

"Fuck. Fuck. Fuck," she chanted. "Don't stop."

Her entire body shook as she came. My strokes became faster, my release closely following. I spilled into her, groaning her name before I gradually came to a stop. I brushed a hair away from her eyes as she smiled up at me.

"Maybe I should lose more often," she said with a chuckle.

* * *

We spent all of Sunday in bed. Not just fucking, though there was plenty of that. In between tangling in the sheets and showering, we lay talking about everything—books and movies, favorite foods, childhood memories. She traced the tattoos and scars on my chest with her fingers as I answered questions I'd never let anyone else ask. We'd drift to sleep, only for one of us to wake the other for another round. By the time the sun started to set, the room smelled like sweat and sex. If anyone had told me I'd spend a whole damn day wrapped up in a woman, talking about favorite songs, I'd have laughed in their face. But with this woman, it felt right.

Eva slept deeply when I rose for work on Monday, her hair

splayed across the pillow. She looked so damn peaceful it made something tight and unfamiliar twist in my chest. I stood over her for a minute, just watching her breathe. If the guys ever caught me getting sentimental over a sleeping woman, I'd never hear the end of it.

I forced myself to leave and padded quietly into the kitchen. I released Hawk from his crate, his boundless energy refilled overnight. I fed him after taking him outside, and gave him a small lecture about keeping quiet for another hour so Eva could sleep in.

I reached for a pen and a battered notepad, hesitating for a second. I wasn't the type to leave notes. Hell, I barely texted. But I found myself scribbling anyway.

Fed Hawk breakfast. Don't let him hustle you for seconds. Wish I was still in bed with you. — R

I read it over, lips quirking. Jesus fucking Christ, I sounded whipped. Still, I left the note propped against her coffee mug.

As I pulled on my cut and headed for the door, I glanced back at the bedroom. The urge to crawl back in beside her was strong—almost enough to make me call in sick.

After a meeting with the building inspector, I headed to the clubhouse to have lunch with Thane. The familiar sight of bikes lined up outside greeted me as I pulled into the lot. Inside, the clubhouse stood in quiet contrast to the tension that brewed beneath the surface as we prepared for our upcoming meeting with the Rangers. Thane occupied his usual spot at the bar as he nursed a beer.

"How's 'playing house' going?" Thane grinned as I approached. "Did you have a good night with whatever fucked-up idea you had to claim as a prize from your wager with Eva?"

I scoffed, grabbing a seat next to him. "Of course. Had I known she would enjoy it as much as she did, I would have asked you to leave earlier."

"You should bring her to the club dinner tonight."

"You think that's a good idea? The contract is still out on her."

Thane shrugged. "I can't think of anywhere safer than a building filled with armed men who won't hesitate to pull a trigger if anyone threatens her. I can tell this is more than a hookup for you. It would be good for her to get to know everyone better."

He had a point. Eva itched to be somewhere besides the four walls of my cabin.

"I'll see if she wants to come. She's a bit of an introvert, but I'm sure she'd like to talk to someone besides me."

Thane let out a rumble of laughter. "Why do I get the sense the two of you aren't doing much talking anyway?"

I flipped him off. "Enough about Eva. Is everyone ready to head to Austin?"

The humor vanished from Thane's expression. "Yeah, but this could go south fast. That's why I want you to lead the operation."

I nodded, the familiar adrenaline rush coursing through me at the prospect of action. "Send a message to Hickok that we'll meet in one week. That buys us time for planning. We'll need intel, manpower, and a solid exit strategy."

As I headed out to check on the drywallers at one of the houses down the street, I shot Eva a quick message.

> **Me:** Want to go to the clubhouse for dinner tonight?

She responded immediately.

> **Eva:** YES!! Can we bring Hawk?

> **Me:** Sure. We'll just have to take my truck.

> **Eva:** Or you could get a sidecar. I could buy Hawk some of those cute little goggles.

> **Me:** I am not putting a sidecar on my Harley. Be ready at 5:30, Lioness.

A smile tugged at my lips as I pocketed my phone. This evening would give Eva the chance to integrate with my world.

Chapter Twenty-One

I buzzed with excitement to get out of the cabin for a night. I'd texted Rhetta, convincing her to stop at my house to bring me a few things I'd need to be ready.

"All right, spill," Rhetta demanded as soon as she walked through the door. "I want all the juicy details about you and Reaper."

Hawk bounded over, tail wagging as he greeted her.

She followed me through the cabin and dropped the bag on the bed.

I glanced at her as I finished applying mascara, careful not to smudge the smoky eye makeup or the dark, sultry lipstick. "What's there to tell? You already figured out that we're hooking up."

Rhetta rolled her eyes. "Oh, please. I want more than that. How's the sex? What was this elusive prize he won Saturday night?"

I couldn't help the grin that spread across my face as I dug through the bag. I pulled out the outfit I had in mind for tonight.

"The sex ... mind blowing. Like, earth-shatteringly good. He cuffed me to the bed and ... I don't even know how to describe the experience."

"I knew you had a kinky side hidden under that business suit!

But, come on, it's more than just sex, isn't it? I noticed how you two were looking at each other. I've never seen either of you like this before."

"Yeah, this thing with Roman feels different."

"I still can't believe you call him that. Most of the guys in the club don't even know his real name."

A small smile played on my lips. "I know we're moving really fast. But I've never experienced anything like this before."

"I felt the same when I first met Thane. It was like everything just clicked. We moved fast, too, but when you know, you know."

"And you've never regretted it?"

"Not for a second. Sure, the club life can be tough, but Thane and I are a team. We face everything together. You know, Reaper doesn't let many people in. His childhood was rough. He took care of his mom and Linc. They even spent some time in a shelter before his dad went to prison."

A pang struck my chest, pieces of Reaper's life he hadn't told me falling into an unfinished puzzle. "He hasn't talked about that yet."

Rhetta nodded. "He wouldn't. I only know what Linc has shared with me. But I'm so excited. You fit into this world so well."

I stepped into the bathroom to change. The tight black top I chose featured embroidered flames licking up my sides. I paired it with a leather miniskirt to show off my long legs and favorite black cowboy boots.

Rhetta blew a low whistle when I opened the door. "Damn, girl. Reaper's not going to know what hit him."

My confidence surged. "That's the plan."

"I'm so happy you moved here. It's like you were made for the Mavericks life."

"We'll see."

"You know what this means, right?" Rhetta said with a laugh. "You're going to be an old lady."

I wrinkled my nose. "That sounds so antiquated and ageist."

Rhetta chuckled. "I know it sounds weird, but it's a term of endearment in the motorcycle club world. It's not about age. It's about status and respect."

I eyed Rhetta, thinking of the property patch she wore across her back.

"I'm not anyone's property. I've worked too hard to be my own person."

"I get it. I really do. But it's not about ownership in the way you're thinking. It's about protection and commitment."

I raised my brows skeptically.

"We both know you'd never stand for being controlled. And Reaper wouldn't try. He would always respect your independence. The 'property' thing is more about keeping you safe. It's a sign that you're off limits."

Some of my reservations eased. "Roman hasn't mentioned it, but I'll try to keep an open mind if he does."

"*When* he does," Rhetta clarified. "He's probably just nervous about how you'll react. He has never given a woman his property patch. I'm not even sure he's ever had a serious relationship."

"Really?"

Rhetta nodded. "It's a big deal. Just try to be open to the idea, all right?"

"Fine," I grumbled. The idea of being Reaper's "old lady" thrilled and intimidated me. It represented a level of commitment I hadn't considered before.

She scanned my body from head to toe before grinning. "He's going to eyeball-fuck you so hard you'll get pregnant."

I laughed. "Let's not get ahead of ourselves. It's way too soon to talk about having babies."

Rhetta gave me a sad smile. "One of us needs to, and we both know I can't."

A pang of guilt twisted in my chest. I'd forgotten about the health challenges she'd endured—the endless rounds of doctors, the pain, the hysterectomy that had shattered her dreams of motherhood. I stepped forward and wrapped my arms around her. "I'm sorry. I didn't mean to—"

She waved me off, but I could feel the tension in her shoulders. "Don't. You know I'm happy for you. Really."

I squeezed her tighter, smelling leather and the faint scent of Thane's cigarettes that clung to her. "You're the best, you know that? And if I do have little Reaper babies, you'll be the best aunt they could ever ask for."

Rhetta pulled back and smirked. "Damn right. I'll teach them how to flip you off before they're out of diapers."

I laughed. "I have no doubt that you'll actually do that."

"I need to head out," Rhetta said as she gathered her things. "I left Maisie in charge of the kitchen, and she's entirely too nice to the prospects. They've probably eaten everything in the fridge, and I'll have to buy more groceries to feed everyone tonight."

As the door closed behind her, I took a deep breath, excitement coursing through my veins. Tonight, I would take on the world—or at least, the Mavericks' world. I'd worry about my potential old lady status and the idea of a family for another day.

As I waited, a message from Matt came through.

> Matt: I just landed at IAH. Story got blown all to shit because someone assassinated the oil executive, so my schedule has opened up. Ruth Wass lives outside of Houston now. She agreed to meet us for coffee at 3 p.m. tomorrow at Maisie's Bakery, which I think is near you.

I sighed, conflict churning in my gut. On one hand, this could be the break we needed to expose Hale. On the other, Reaper would be furious at the idea of me meeting someone in public while a price remained on my head. I'd have to make a serious case for him to understand why this mattered so much. I sent Matt a quick response.

Me: Let me check with my personal bodyguard.

Matt responded within seconds.

Matt: I can't tell if you're joking or not. You need to be there. We have to get this story published before Hale hurts anyone else.

Reaper's truck rumbled up the driveway. I shoved my phone into my purse, pushing the dilemma to the back of my mind. I couldn't wait to watch his jaw hit the ground.

Chapter Twenty-Two

I leaned against the hood of my truck, texting a subcontractor, when the door to my cabin opened. I knelt to greet the fur missile barreling toward me and nearly fell backward when I noticed a pair of soft black cowboy boots and bare legs before me.

My gaze continued upward to the soft black leather miniskirt that accentuated Eva's ass. Her slim waist was wrapped in flames that licked up to her breasts in a deep V. Her hair framed her face in soft curls, and she'd colored her lips a sinful, deep maroon.

She embodied a dark goddess who I would kneel before until the day I died. For a moment, I forgot how to breathe. My heart hammered, and possessiveness and pride surged through my chest. This fierce, beautiful creature belonged to me.

"Fuck," I managed to say, my voice hoarse. "You look ..."

Words failed me. How could I describe the reaction in my heart, mind, and gut? Like I simultaneously burned in a fire and drowned in a lake. Like I wanted to show her off to the world but also hide her away.

Eva smirked, enjoying my reaction. She sauntered to me with lethal grace.

I straightened. "You're going to cause a riot," I said, only half joking. The thought of other men gazing at her sent a spike of jealousy through me.

"Good thing you'll be there to protect me then, huh?"

"Always," I promised, meaning it more than I'd ever meant anything in my life.

I leaned in close as I opened the truck door and inhaled her intoxicating citrusy scent. "We could always skip the dinner. Stay here instead."

Eva's laugh carried through the air. "Nice try. But I've been cooped up too long. Let's have dinner with your friends, and then we'll come back so you can find out what I've got underneath this little get-up. Or, maybe what's not underneath."

I groaned and shifted uncomfortably. Now I'd wonder about that all night. Did she wear lace under that skirt, or nothing at all?

I couldn't stop glancing at Eva as we drove to the clubhouse. The way the warm sun caught her hair, the curve of her neck as she stared out the window, the slight smile on her lips. I'd fallen for her. Hard and fast.

"So, I need to ask you for a favor," Eva started, her tone careful.

"Right now, I would burn the world down for you, babe."

"I need to be at a meeting tomorrow at three at Maisie's Bakery. Matt is meeting one of Hale's victims there, and she's willing to talk on the record. I need you to take me. You can bring the whole damn club to protect me if you want, but I need to do this. I need the closure, and this girl probably does, too."

My grip on the steering wheel tightened. "No. It's too dangerous. I can't allow it."

Eva's head whipped toward me, and her eyes flashed in fury. "Excuse me? You don't 'allow' me to do anything. You do not control me."

"I'm not trying to control you. There's a contract out on your life. You can't just—"

She cut me off. "I've been taking care of myself long before you came along. I don't need a keeper."

"This is about keeping you alive. In case you've forgotten, the Abells want you dead. The story is not worth your life."

"And what about the girl? What about getting justice for what Hale did? I have to expose him."

"We'll find another way. One that doesn't place you in the crosshairs. Let Matt do the interview."

"Matt is coordinating it, but I have to be there, or else she doesn't talk."

"Then she doesn't talk." I regretted the words as the hurt flashed across Eva's face.

"Wow," she said, the anger in her voice replaced by disappointment. "I thought you, of all people, would understand why this is important."

Her words hit me like a punch to the gut. I took a deep breath as I tried to formulate a calm and measured response. "I do understand. But you have to see it from my perspective. If anything happened to you—"

"I get that you want to protect me. But you can't lock me away forever. If you care at all for me, you'll respect that."

Every instinct screamed at me to keep her safe. I needed to shield her from any potential harm. But if I tried to control Eva, I'd lose her.

I let out a heavy sigh. "Fine. But I'm coming with you. And we're bringing backup. Non-fucking-negotiable."

A small smile of victory tugged at her lips. "I can live with that."

We pulled into the clubhouse parking lot, and I turned to her, cupping her face. "You're going to be the death of me, my Lioness."

"But what a way to go, right?"

I couldn't help but laugh. I pulled her in for a kiss before we walked into the clubhouse with Hawk biting at his leash.

As we said our hellos, I couldn't tell what excited the guys more— meeting the woman who dominated my thoughts or playing with her energetic puppy. Hawk's tail wagged as he soaked up the attention.

We navigated the room, Eva's confidence radiating as she shook hands and exchanged greetings. I introduced her to Bones, our resident mechanic, and Archer, a sniper I'd served beside in Iraq. Her quick wit matched their rough humor.

"So, you're the one who's got our VP all tied up." Bones grinned, his grease-stained hands crossed over his chest.

Eva smirked. "Well, usually I'm the one who's tied up, but that's between us."

They roared with laughter. Pride and affection welled in my chest as I watched her interact with my men. I also couldn't help but notice the glances some threw her way. I caught more than one gazing appreciatively down her body as we moved through the clubhouse. A surge of possessiveness rose in me, and I tightened my grip on her waist.

Eva leaned in close. "Easy there. Don't get jealous. They can look as long as they don't touch."

"Doesn't mean I like it. If anyone even thinks about touching you, I'll kill them."

She rolled her eyes and patted my shoulder as if she thought my response was an overreaction. I mean, it was, but I was also completely serious.

Eventually, Rhetta swooped in and pulled Eva toward the bar. "All right, boys. I'm stealing Eva for some girl talk."

As they walked away, Eva threw a wink over her shoulder that had my blood heating.

Thane sidled up to me with a knowing grin on his face. "She's something else. You thinking of giving her your patch?"

"Yeah. Just hope she's ready for what that means."

Thane lit another smoke. "It's about damn time you settled down. You're too old to get away with being a manwhore like Hatchet."

I chuckled. "You were more of a manwhore than Hatchet before you met Rhetta."

He slapped me on the back. "Yeah, and then I got old. I needed a drama-free zone and someone to keep me in line. Make sure I take my vitamins and shit so I don't die. I think you've found that now, too. You're nearly forty. You won't live past fifty if you don't settle down."

Thane stepped away, and I joined Merrick, Hatchet, Archer, and Bones in a corner.

"We need to talk. Eva's got a meeting tomorrow at Maisie's Bakery. One of Hale's victims is willing to talk to her for their investigation."

Merrick's eyebrows shot up. "And you're letting her go?" His tone was laced with a protective edge that indicated he considered Eva under his watch because she was with me. It was a hell of a shift, considering he'd been just as dead-set against Thane hiring her as I was.

I snorted. "She can be very convincing. I need you guys there to help protect her."

Hatchet nodded. "We'll set up a perimeter. Merrick and I can be inside, blending in with the customers." He flashed a charming smile at one of the women nearby. She giggled and playfully rolled her eyes.

"Focus, Hatchet," Merrick growled.

"I'll have eyes on the street," Bones added. "Full surveillance setup."

Merrick ground his teeth. I recognized the skepticism in his eyes.

"What? Speak the fuck up, Merrick. I can tell you're not saying what you really think."

"It's a bad idea. You're exposing her—and us—to unnecessary risk. Can't we arrange for the victim to meet somewhere more secure? Maybe here?"

I shook my head. "The location is already set. Her journalist buddy arranged it."

Merrick's eyes narrowed. "What if it's a trap? We've made a lot of enemies lately."

"You think I haven't considered that? I don't like this any more than you do. But Eva won't back down. We either help her, or she'll go rogue."

Merrick held my gaze for a moment longer before nodding reluctantly. "If you're sure about this, I want to get the keys to the store from Don tonight. I'll have Linc set up some extra cameras, and we'll rearrange the seating to keep her away from windows."

He paused, his eyes meeting mine. "Man, if I were you, I'd even put a vest on her."

I turned to watch Eva and Rhetta at the bar. The sight of her so carefree and beautiful tightened my chest. I hated agreeing to this, but stopping Eva wasn't an option.

"Do it. Archer, I want you and Jay watching everyone through a fucking scope. Green light to shoot anyone who is remotely a threat to her."

Hatchet nodded, already pulling out his phone. "I'll go get the keys from Don now, and we'll meet you there in an hour. That should be enough time for Linc to grab whatever cameras and shit he needs."

"One more thing. If anything goes sideways, Eva's safety is the priority. Get her out, no matter what. Understood?"

A chorus of affirmatives met my ears. Some of the tension left my shoulders. No questions asked, my brothers had my back—and now, they had Eva's, too.

"Fuck," Bones breathed. He nodded his head toward the commotion near the bar. "VP, you're going to want to get over there right now. Someone is about to get their ass kicked, and by the looks of things, your girl might win."

Chapter Twenty-Three

Rhetta had stepped away to take a call when a hand groped my ass. But when I turned, it wasn't Reaper.

Adrenaline and anger flooded into me as I shoved my palms into the chest of the biker. I didn't recognize him from the introduction round earlier. He'd probably just walked in and had no idea I'd arrived with his VP.

"Sweetbutt, you can't come in dressed like that and then play hard to get," the man said, stepping back toward me.

I reached into the back waistband of my skirt where I'd tucked the weapon I always carried. In one fluid motion, I flicked open the switchblade and pressed it against the man's chest, just enough to draw blood. The sharp tip pierced through his shirt, and his eyes widened in surprise.

"You fucking touch me or any other woman in this clubhouse again without consent, and I will slice you from your nuts to your throat," I hissed, my voice low and dangerous.

I added more pressure to the blade, pressing it upward to cut him a centimeter deeper. A small crimson stain began to spread on the white T-shirt he wore below his prospect cut.

The man moved to shift back, but instead of walking away, he reached for the gun tucked in the back of his dirty blue jeans.

Fuck. Of course, I would bring a knife to a gunfight.

"You think you're tough, bitch?" he sneered, his hand on his weapon. "Let's see how tough you are when—"

Before he could finish his threat, a familiar voice boomed through the clubhouse.

"Danny, get your goddamn dick fingers off your weapon and back the fuck away from my girl," Reaper roared, grabbing the prospect by his neck and lifting his feet off the ground.

The clubhouse quieted as all eyes shifted to where we stood, my blade now pointed to the ground, dripping with Danny's blood.

Merrick and Hatchet moved with purpose behind Reaper. Hatchet's face was set in a hard line, and Merrick's eyes blazed with a fierce glint. Seeing how quickly the men shifted from party to protect surprised me.

"We'll take care of this, VP," Merrick said as he tapped Reaper's outstretched arm. "You get back to enjoying the party with Eva. Wouldn't want to get blood on that pretty little outfit of hers."

"Honestly, it looks like Eva could have handled this on her own." Hatchet chuckled. "I'd like to know how she planned to use that blade next. Or maybe where."

Merrick shot Hatchet a warning glance, his expression unyielding. "It's not her job to hold dick weasels like this accountable. It's ours. We've got this."

Reaper released the prospect, and he crumbled to the ground. He delivered an aggressive kick to Danny's ribs before turning to draw me into his arms.

My glare at Danny remained cold before I shifted my gaze to his eyes.

"What happened?" Reaper demanded.

I shrugged, aiming for nonchalance. "Oh, you know, just teaching Danny here about consent and personal space."

Reaper's jaw clenched.

I sighed and gave him the rundown. "He grabbed my ass, and when I pushed him back, he told me I couldn't dress like *this* and then play hard to get. He came back toward me, so I pulled out my knife. In hindsight, I should have brought a gun, but I'm not sure where I'd carry one in this outfit."

Reaper's eyes darkened further, not amused by my attempt at humor. "Get him out of here," he commanded as Merrick and Hatchet picked Danny up. "Strip him of his cut. Make sure he spends the next month thinking about his mistake with every breath he takes."

Hawk nipped at Danny's heels as Merrick and Hatchet dragged him away. Reaper tightened his arms around me. I could sense the tension in his body.

"Hey, I'm okay. Really. This isn't my first rodeo with handsy assholes."

"That doesn't make me feel better."

"No, but I can handle myself."

"You were nearly shot," he countered.

"That's a bit of an exaggeration. I had it under control. Besides, isn't that why I have you? To watch my six when I'm busy being a badass?"

That finally got a small smile out of him. "You're impossible."

I wrapped my arms around his neck and pulled him closer for a kiss. "Yeah, but you like it."

The entire clubhouse watched. "All right, boys, the show's over," I said as I glanced around the room. "Unless someone else wants to take me on?"

I twirled the switchblade in my fingers, and the tension broke. Laughter rippled through the room, and conversations resumed. The party atmosphere returned nearly as quickly as it had stopped.

Reaper reached for my switchblade and stepped toward the bar.

"You need to give her your property patch, man," Bones muttered to him as we moved past. "If she'd been wearing your colors, Danny wouldn't have even thought about touching her."

Reaper stiffened beside me and tightened his grip on my waist. I glanced up and caught a flicker of uncertainty in his eyes before he masked it. I turned to face him to broach the subject, but before I could speak, Thane clapped Reaper on the shoulder.

"Damn, brother. Your girl's got some fire in her." He grinned at me. "I didn't like that prospect anyway. You did us a favor, weeding him out."

Linc approached the bar as Reaper splashed bleach onto my blade. "You know those are illegal in most states?"

I scoffed. "They've been legal in Texas since 2013."

Linc grinned as he glanced back at his brother. "I think you've truly found your match."

Reaper handed the blade back to me. "Having a knife is smart. But maybe we should get you something with a bit more range."

I raised an eyebrow. "Are you offering to take me gun shopping?"

"Maybe. We'll see how you handle yourself at the range, first."

"Prepare to be impressed."

He grinned. "If you're so confident, let's set another wager."

"Absolutely. I'll win this time."

After years of training with my dad and his crew, I had exceptional aim. The shooting range had become my sanctuary as a teenager. It served as a haven where I could channel my focus and unleash my inner badass. While I may have presented myself as a polished PR professional, I had more than a few tricks up my sleeve—skills that would serve a purpose now that I found myself entrenched in the Mavericks' world.

Reaper raised a brow at my expression. I smirked as his eyes darkened, a slow smile spreading across his face. Without warning, he grabbed my hand, his grip firm but gentle.

"Come with me."

My heart raced as he led me through the hallway, past familiar rooms, until we reached a door I'd never noticed. He pulled out a key, unlocked the door, and pressed me in.

My eyes crossed the clean room. Weapons hung on the wall, and a desk with two large filing cabinets sat tucked in the corner. A sofa rested on the other side of the room beside a small safe.

The door's lock clicked behind me before Reaper pulled me close, his hands sliding down to grip my hips.

"Lioness," he murmured, his lips brushing against my ear. "I need you."

I shivered at his words, heat pooling in my core as I felt his hard cock press against me.

"Did watching me cut up a prospect turn you on?" I asked with a breathy laugh.

"Watching my woman take control turns me on."

I raised a brow. "Then I'm taking control tonight. Sit."

He smirked at my commanding tone but made no move to sit.

I pushed him back roughly until his calves hit the sofa and stared into his eyes as I unzipped his jeans. I slid them to the floor, along with his boxers, before pushing him back.

I knelt before him, taking my tongue and running it up the underside of his cock. He hissed, and I lifted my gaze, giving him a feral grin. I had never felt such power and desire.

I gathered my long hair and piled it at the top of my head. "Hold here so this stays out of my face," I ordered.

Reaper's palm gripped my hair, and he shivered as I continued to stroke him with my hand, not breaking eye contact as my tongue swept across the tip of his cock. I slid him between my lips and let a small moan release from the back of my throat, sending a vibration that caused his breath to hitch again. I continued to stroke, using my hands and my mouth, upping the tempo until I could feel his orgasm building, the head of his cock growing in my mouth. His grip tightened in my hair as he leaned his head back, letting out a shuddering groan as I sent him over the edge.

"Fuck me," he swore as his saltiness filled my mouth.

I swallowed and grinned up at him. "Maybe I should take control more often."

He pulled me up, shifting my skirt above my hips so I could

straddle him. His hand brushed against me, and he gave me a wicked grin. "No panties?"

"I didn't think we'd make it through the night without fucking. Figured this would make it easier."

He kissed me, gripping my ass. "Just when I think I couldn't want you more." When he slipped his fingers against me, I could feel my wetness.

"Oh, Lioness. So ready every time I touch you," he said, strumming his thumb against my clit. I began kissing his neck, moaning with every stroke of his fingers. He hardened beneath me again.

I ground my hips into him, his hard cock at my slick entrance. I pushed down and paused, gazing into his eyes.

"I'm falling so hard for you," he said. "I would give you anything you asked for. Anything."

I smirked as my movement took away his ability to form a coherent thought. "All I want is you."

I continued to drive my hips against him and buried my face in his neck as our pace quickened. A wave of pure sensation crashed through me, triggering his own release as my muscles clenched around him.

"Lioness," he groaned into my ear. "You are mine."

Chapter Twenty-Four

My stomach was tangled in a knot of nerves from the moment I opened my eyes. Eva tried to lighten the mood with a joke here and there but fell into an introspective silence as I fitted her with a Kevlar vest I'd grabbed from the clubhouse.

"Stop fidgeting," I murmured, adjusting the straps to ensure a snug fit. I ran my hands along the edges, checking for gaps or loose areas. "You'll have thirty minutes. Get the story, and then I'll escort you out the back. From there, we'll drive for a bit until I'm sure no one is tailing us."

Eva glanced up as she buttoned her shirt over the vest. "I'll be fine. I'm not the President of the United States. I appreciate what you're doing here, I really do, but this is overkill."

I kissed her forehead as I ran my hands down her arms. "I hope you're right. But, if you're wrong, we're ready."

Linc had spent the evening before setting up a handful of cameras—both inside and outside of the building. I wanted to be ready for every possible scenario. And, if my actions seemed too paranoid, we could all laugh about it over beers later that night when she returned safely to my cabin.

Merrick texted me the all-clear for our arrival. Jay and Archer lay prone on nearby roofs, giving them a birds-eye view through the scopes of their rifles. Bones sat outside in an SUV with dark-tinted windows.

Hatchet and Merrick planned to sit in the corner booth with coffees and donuts, watching every customer who entered the door. Linc would keep an eye on the cameras. And I planned to sit behind Eva to watch her back.

I'd suggested I sit beside her, but she had valid concerns I might intimidate her source.

"If at any point I get up and ask you to leave, you need to listen to me," I reminded her as we headed to the bakery in my truck. "The guys are keeping watch, and they'll flag me if anything suspicious happens. The story is not worth your life."

Eva nodded, her expression determined. "I understand. But this is how I stop Hale from hurting any other women. He needs to be held accountable. It's the only way."

I glanced at her, my jaw clenching. I could think of much safer ways we could hold that motherfucker accountable once Dixon found him. I had several ideas on how I wanted to stop Hale fucking Abell from abusing other women and how I wanted to make him pay for how he hurt her.

I gripped the steering wheel tighter. I felt torn between admiration for her bravery and fear for her safety.

"Everything will be fine. And, if anything goes wrong, I've got my own personal army of Mavericks to back me up."

I smiled at her declaration. My men would protect her. "Damn straight."

Everything appeared clear as we approached the bakery, but my instincts remained on high alert. I helped Eva out of the truck, my hand lingering on her lower back as we walked toward the entrance.

"You have thirty minutes. Not a second more."

Eva nodded in agreement. The warm aroma of cinnamon and sugar enveloped us as we stepped inside. Matt sat at a table, a notepad and pen before him. Eva squeezed my hand once before walking over to join him.

I took my position at a nearby table behind her, my senses hyper-aware of every movement and sound in the bakery. My phone buzzed with updates from the team.

> Linc: All clear on cameras. No suspicious activity.
>
> Jay: Eyes on all entry points.
>
> Bones: No movement outside. We're good.
>
> Archer: Clear from my angle.

The weight of my concealed weapon pressed against my side, providing a cold comfort. I scanned the room, my military training kicking in as I noted exits and potential threats.

Chapter Twenty-Five

"Everything will be fine," I assured Reaper from inside the bakery.

Reaper grunted in response and kissed the top of my head.

Matt sat alone at a table in the corner. His eyes widened as he took in the sight of us together. His gaze flicked from my face to Reaper's cut, to our interlaced hands, and then back to me. A mix of shock and confusion crossed his expression.

"I didn't realize you were bringing company."

Reaper bristled at the tight concern evident in Matt's tone.

"This is Reaper." I squeezed his hand before letting go and sitting.

Reaper nodded at Matt in a wordless greeting before moving to a nearby table. His watchful eyes scanned the room.

As I sat across from Matt, he leaned in, his voice low. "What's going on? Are you okay? That guy's a member of the Mavericks."

"He's not just a member. He's the vice president. He's been protecting me."

"Protecting you? You can't be serious. These guys are dangerous. They're criminals."

"You don't know them. You can't judge someone based on stereo-types and headlines alone. There's more to the Mavericks than meets the eye."

"This is insane. You can't actually think staying with an outlaw biker gang is a good idea? You need to leave with me right now. I can help you."

"Absolutely not. And it's not up for discussion. I'm here for Ruth's story, nothing else."

Matt's jaw clenched. "Are you … with him?"

"I am. But that's really none of your business."

"But you—"

I cut him off. "I know you have questions. But right now, we need to focus on Ruth and her story. That's what's important. She should be arriving soon. My relationship with Reaper is none of your concern."

Matt flexed his jaw as he took in my response. His hand moved to his phone, and he sent a quick text before clunking the device on the table.

I stood and walked to the counter, ordering an iced coffee from Maisie before returning to my seat.

The bakery door opened, and a petite young woman with long, blonde hair entered. Ruth Wass was twenty-two, but her wide green eyes and nervous demeanor gave her an even more youthful appearance.

"Ruth?" I stood and offered the woman a reassuring smile. "I'm Eva, and this is Matt."

"Thank you for meeting with us," Matt added.

Ruth's eyes darted around the bakery as she sat. "Thank you for listening to me."

As she settled in, I could feel Matt's gaze burning with unan-swered questions.

Ruth began to share her story. Her soft voice shook as she recounted her time as Hale's intern during her senior year of college.

"It was just little things at first. He'd comment about my appearance. Sometimes, he would stand too close or find excuses to touch me. I tried to brush it off. I told myself I was being oversensitive."

She took a shaky breath before continuing. "Then, one night, I worked late. He came into the office drunk. He ... he tried to force himself on me. I managed to fight him off. I ran away and filed a police report that night."

Ruth's eyes hardened as she recalled what happened next. "The very next day, Benjamin Abell called me. He said I had two options—he could pay off my student loans if I dropped the charges, or he'd make sure I never worked in this industry again if I didn't."

My blood boiled as Ruth finished her story. "I had over $250,000 in student loans. I ... I dropped the charges."

As I began to ask a follow-up question, a barista in her mid-forties approached our table with our drinks. Her salt-and-pepper hair was weaved back in a tight French braid, and deep lines were etched across her forehead. Her hands shook as she set our drinks on the table. Suddenly, her hand hit my iced coffee. The contents spilled across my lap.

"Oh, I'm so sorry!"

"It's okay." I cursed internally as the cold liquid seeped through my jeans.

"There are paper towels in the restroom. It's just down that hallway."

I excused myself, promising Ruth I'd be right back. Maisie approached the table with a towel as I headed to the hall. I overheard her apologies for the mess as I slipped into the two-stall women's bathroom. I did my best to soak the coffee with paper towels, but my jeans remained damp.

After two minutes, I determined drying my pants would be impossible. As I grasped the door handle, a sharp prick pierced my neck. Before I could react, the world began to spin, and darkness crept in at the edges of my vision. The cold tile floor rushed to meet me.

Chapter Twenty-Six

I drummed my fingers on the table, waiting for Eva to return. Something about the situation unsettled me. I grew uneasy as each second passed. I glanced at Matt. He fidgeted in his seat under my stare. His eyes darted between the hallway to the bathroom and his phone.

I turned to Maisie as she walked past with a handful of coffee-soaked towels. "Is the new girl nervous about working here or something?"

"New girl? Oh, you mean Lenora? She's worked here for two years."

My instincts kicked into overdrive. I strode toward the bathroom. My gut churned as my hand instinctively moved to the Glock holstered at my hip.

I flung open the door to the women's restroom. "Eva?"

The empty bathroom seemed clear, except for a few damp paper towels in the trashcan. Steps sounded behind me, and I whirled as I drew my Glock on Maisie, holding a crying Lenora.

"She says the man who was reading his paper and drinking coffee when you arrived took Eva," Maisie explained. "He threatened

Lenora and told her all she needed to do was spill something on your girl and get her to the bathroom."

The woman sobbed her apologies, but I didn't have time to listen. Panic clawed at my chest at the nightmare unfolding before me.

"Merrick, Hatchet," I shouted. "Someone took Eva. Get the rest of the guys in here. We have five minutes to coordinate."

Archer, Jay, and Bones arrived in the building within a minute, standing in a circle at the center of the bakery with Hatchet, Merrick, and I, with Linc on speaker.

"The cameras flickered out at 3:12 p.m. and came back on as I checked the settings. They had someone jam the signal," Linc explained.

As I turned back to the main area, Matt began to stand. His eyes darted around the room.

I stood before him in three quick strides and shoved my Glock hard into his ribs.

"Who else knew we'd be here today?" I growled.

Matt's eyes widened in fear. "I ... I don't know what you're talking about."

"Wrong answer," I snarled. I gripped my pistol tighter and brought the butt down against the top of Matt's head. The sharp thud of metal meeting bone echoed through the bakery. Matt's knees buckled and blood blossomed along his hairline.

"Hatchet, detain this piece of shit. We're taking him with us."

I turned to Maisie. "Keep an eye on Ruth. She might've been used as a pawn, but I don't want her leaving yet. Get your husband to come in for a bit. I need the guys with me."

My mind raced as I pulled out my phone. I toggled to the Find My app to check the AirTag I'd slipped into Eva's back pocket this morning. She didn't know about it. She would've accused me of being paranoid if I'd told her, but now I kicked myself for not being even more cautious.

"I can track her location," I said, my voice tight with fury. "They're heading east on the highway."

"Let's move," Merrick said, already heading for the door.

"Merrick, Hatchet, you ride with me. The rest of you can follow with Bones. Bring this fuckhead, too." I shoved my gun into Matt's ribs before spinning to the door.

Cold determination settled over me as we piled into our vehicles. The panic and fury bubbled beneath the surface, but my training began to kick in. Eva needed me to be focused, to be the strategist and fighter I'd trained to be.

"Linc, get me everything you can on Matt's recent communications. I want to know who he's been talking to," I said into the phone as we peeled out of the parking lot. "He texted someone right after I walked in with Eva. I want to know who and what he said."

As we sped down the highway, my knuckles white on the steering wheel, I offered a silent promise to Eva.

I would find her.

And God help anyone who stood in my way.

Chapter Twenty-Seven

Darkness enveloped me as I came to with my hands bound behind my back. The rough rope cut into my wrists as I struggled. My cell phone remained in my purse at the table, leaving me no way to reach Reaper. I tried to steady my breathing, fighting against the rising panic. My body slammed into the cold metal of the car as it jolted to a stop. Light flooded in as the trunk opened. I squinted as my eyes adjusted.

The man who pulled me out looked familiar. He'd sat at the table closest to the door when we walked into the bakery, hiding behind a newspaper. He'd smiled at me then. My skin crawled at the memory of the innocent gesture.

"Rise and shine, bitch," he sneered. He yanked me from the trunk, and I cried out as he gripped my arms too tight.

My legs wobbled from the drugs and confinement, but I forced myself to stand tall. He dragged me into what appeared to be an abandoned warehouse. My heart pounded, but I kept my face blank, refusing to show fear. I strained to remember every piece of self-defense advice my dad had drilled into me. Fight to survive. Don't make it easy. Make them regret touching you.

I bucked my entire body against the man, attempting to knock the back of my head into his chin. The man picked me up, my legs dangling before he threw me hard against the floor and kicked my side for good measure. I curled in pain before glancing up.

In the center of the room stood two figures I recognized all too well—Hale and Benjamin Abell. The devil himself and his evil spawn. My stomach churned at the sight of them, rage coursing through me.

The man kicked me again before picking me up and shoving me into a chair, securing my already bound hands to the back and tying my ankles to the legs. I struggled against the restraints cutting into my wrists, but they held firm. The cold metal of the chair seeped through my clothes, sending a shiver down my spine.

Hale approached first, his face twisted in a mask of red-hot anger. Without warning, his fist connected with my cheek, the force of it snapping my head to the side. Pain radiated through my jaw. Copper exploded in my mouth, and my vision swam.

"You stupid bitch," he snarled. "Did you really think you could dig up dirt on me and get away with it?"

I spat blood onto the floor and glared up at him. "Fuck you."

Hale's face contorted with rage as he punched me again in the stomach. The air rushed out of my lungs, and I gasped for breath. I clenched my teeth and refused to cry. This man got off on the pain of women, and I wouldn't give him the satisfaction.

He shook his hand. The Kevlar vest had taken some of the blow, and I hoped his knuckles had broken on impact.

Benjamin stepped forward. His calm demeanor contrasted with Hale's fury. He brushed his hands over his jacket as if he were about to negotiate an acquisition, not torture a victim of kidnapping.

"Ms. Harland. I'm afraid your investigation will never see the light of day. You should have taken the settlement. Why couldn't you just let it go?"

I laughed, my tone bitter despite the pain spreading through my body. "Let it go? Do you think I could just forget about all the women you've hurt? All the careers you've tried to destroy?"

Hale grabbed a fistful of my hair and yanked my head back. His fist connected with my face again. My lip split, and blood trickled down my chin as I met his gaze with unwavering defiance.

"That all you got?" I taunted through gritted teeth, my voice raspy. "No wonder you have to force yourself on women. You hit like a girl."

Hale roared and raised his fist again, but Benjamin stepped forward and grabbed his arm.

"Enough," Benjamin snapped. "We need her coherent for now. She can't talk if you knock her out. Please use your head for once."

"If you'd let me handle her my way, we'd have answers by now," Hale muttered.

Benjamin narrowed his eyes. "Your way got us here. My way keeps you out of prison and our companies out of the headlines."

I sagged in the chair as Hale reluctantly stepped back and began pacing like a caged animal. My body ached from the assault and my vision blurred as my left eye began to swell shut.

"She needs to pay," Hale snarled.

Benjamin's tone chilled the room. "Son, if you'd learn to control your temper and keep your dick in your pants, we wouldn't be here. Again."

Hale clenched his jaw. "If you'd offered her a bigger payout, it wouldn't have gotten this far."

Benjamin shook his head and tossed me a bored glance. "He doesn't get it. No, you're the kind of woman who only cares about your version of justice. I bet I could've offered you double, and we'd still be here."

"You're right," I said. "It's not about the payoff. It's about stopping your piece-of-shit son from hurting more women."

"Think you're some kind of heroine?" Benjamin crouched in front of me, his expression almost pitying as he spoke in a smooth, controlled voice. "You're going to tell us everything we need to know

—who else you've talked to, what they've said, and what information has been shared about these sources with any media outlets."

I straightened as much as I could in the chair despite the pain radiating through me. "I'm not telling you shit."

Benjamin sighed as if disappointed by my response. "Matt says you had more women you've been coordinating with on this little story. But you refused to give him their names." He tilted his head, examining my response.

I froze at his words. Matt? He was behind this? For a moment, the world seemed to tilt. My mouth went dry and I tried to swallow, but it was like choking on sand.

Benjamin's lips curled into a smug grin as realization dawned on my face. "Your friend Matt was easily persuaded to help us find you." He chuckled before continuing in a mocking tone, "It's amazing how easily you can blackmail someone who has a severe gambling addiction and a mountain of debt."

The betrayal hit me like a physical blow. Matt had been one of my best friends since college. The friend who'd held my hair back after too many shots of tequila. The one who sent me DoorDash when he knew I'd worked a twelve-hour day during a crisis. The weight of his treachery settled in my chest, making it hard to breathe. And now, because of him, I was about to die for something I thought we both believed in.

Hot tears pressed behind my eyes, but I refused to let them fall. Not when Benjamin and Hale sought to find a weakness in my armor. I'd die before I gave them the names of the women who'd spoken to me. I'd always known trusting others was dangerous. I just never thought it would be Matt holding the knife embedded in my back.

A flicker of movement near one of the broken windows caught my attention. At first, I thought it was a shadow. Relief flooded through me as Reaper appeared on the other side of the grungy glass, his face a mask of focused intensity. A sob escaped involuntarily from deep within my chest before I could stop myself. The triumph on Hale's face told me he mistook the sound as me breaking down.

My eyes locked with Reaper's for a split second, rage and determination etched into every line of his face. I raised three fingers, hoping to signal how many men he'd face inside. Not that it mattered. These three men in suits would be no match for a handful of hardened bikers and veterans. Reaper nodded at me in understanding.

Then chaos erupted.

Glass shattered into the open space as Reaper burst through the window. Merrick, Hatchet, Jay, Archer, and Bones poured in from different entry points. The men moved in a coordinated, lethal manner that left me knowing this wasn't the first time they'd worked together like this.

The man from the bakery barely had time to reach for his gun before Bones tackled him to the ground. Fists flew as they rolled across the concrete floor.

Hatchet went straight for Benjamin. The businessman was no match for the biker. He tried to run but found himself cornered and knocked to the ground. Hatchet crushed his face into the concrete with a satisfying thud.

Merrick's fist connected with Hale's jaw with a sickening crunch. He dropped like a rock and scrambled backward on all fours before pulling a hidden knife from his boot. He lunged at Merrick, who easily dodged. The blade whistled past his ear. Merrick grinned at Hale as if he liked the promise of a fight. They circled each other, Hale lunging and slashing while Merrick weaved and blocked.

Through it all, Reaper homed in on me. His knife flashed as he cut through my restraints, and I fell into his arms. My limbs shook with relief.

"I've got you, my Lioness," he murmured into my hair. His arms tightened around me. "You're safe now."

I clung to him and buried my face in his chest as tears streamed down my face. The adrenaline keeping me defiant faded, leaving me weak and shaky.

Nearly as quickly as it'd begun, the fight was over. My heart hammered against my ribs as I took in the groaning bodies sprawled across the dirty concrete floor, guns held against the back of their skulls. Their bravado was gone, replaced by well-deserved fear and pain. They'd been no match against the Mavericks. A savage satisfaction twisted inside me. The men who'd terrorized me now sat at the feet of my rescuers, and they wouldn't be merciful.

"Zip-tie these fuckers and take them to the junkyard," Reaper ordered. His voice sounded colder than it had been moments before. "I'll meet you there."

He pulled back, his hands cupping my face as he assessed my injuries. I tasted the blood on my split lip, and my sight was clouded with tears as my eyes swelled.

I swallowed hard. "Matt betrayed me. He's the reason they found me."

A muscle twitched in Reaper's jaw. "I suspected as much. He's in the back of the SUV."

His words were both a comfort and a fresh wound. I fought back tears.

"I'm taking you back to the cabin. I need to take care of this situation."

He wanted to handle this the outlaw way.

"I'm coming with you," I demanded in a hoarse, shaky voice.

"You don't need to be here for this," Reaper said, his tone quiet and gentle. "You don't need to see what we'll do. Let me handle it."

I shook my head. "I need to see this through. Please. I want to talk to them. All of them. I need to confront Matt."

Tension still radiated off Reaper, and his eyes raked over the bruises forming on my face before he reluctantly agreed. "All right."

My body sagged as relief washed over me. Reaper wrapped an arm around my waist and guided me out of the warehouse to his truck. Merrick followed to join us while Jay, Bones, Archer, and Hatchet stuffed the three men, bound with zip ties, in the back of the SUV.

Reaper's truck peeled out of the gravel parking lot with the other guys closely following. The adrenaline coursing through my veins began to slow, and I could feel the tender swelling on my face. I flipped down the visor and gasped at my reflection in the mirror.

"There's Advil in the glovebox. It should help with the swelling. I'll get you some ice from the breakroom when we get to the junkyard."

I shuffled through his glove box to find the bottle, swallowing three before leaning back against the headrest. "So, what's the junkyard? Is that code for something?"

"It's an actual junkyard owned by Bones. It has a warehouse we use for these … situations. And, conveniently, there is an incinerator nearby."

"I'm going to recommend we don't do PR for the junkyard then," I said with a tight laugh.

Reaper glared at me, his expression furious. "I can't believe you're making jokes right now."

I could tell I walked on thin ice. I patted his arm. "I'm fine, Roman. The last time I faced Hale, I spent a week in the hospital. This time, I get to walk away. This time, I won. And it's because of you. Because of the Mavericks."

He started to respond, but his phone interrupted him. "Linc, what do you have?"

"I finally managed to hack into one of Abell's servers. There's enough evidence here to put them both away. I'm emailing it all to Eva right now."

"Thanks," I chimed in. "What about Matt?"

Reaper's grip on the steering wheel tightened as his brother shared what he'd discovered.

"Benjamin started to work with the journalist to track you down after the night you disappeared with Reaper."

I swore. The mention of Matt's betrayal sent a fresh wave of pain through my chest. My throat tightened as I processed the information. I'd trusted him.

"I can't believe it," I whispered to myself. "We've been friends for years. How could he do this? How could he sell me out like that? How could he put my life at risk?"

"Matt texted someone from the coffee shop right after you walked in to inform them that you were there with a Maverick. I have a few more things to track down, so I'll call back with an update as soon as I can."

I wiped the tears running down my face.

Reaper took my hand and squeezed it. "Sometimes people surprise us in the worst ways."

"I know. It's just ... I trusted him. I never thought he'd be capable of something like this."

"Money and fear can make people do terrible things," Merrick chimed from the back seat. He caught my eye in the rearview mirror. "Doesn't excuse it, but it explains it."

As we drove in silence, I reflected on the moments Matt and I had shared over the years. Late nights working on stories. Celebrations after breaking big news. Supporting each other through personal crises. This deception tainted the memories.

Merrick's gaze lingered on me in the mirror. "Don't waste time replaying every conversation and interaction from years past. Some people are loyal until they aren't. You might not ever know when Matt decided to betray you or why. No matter what, the Mavericks will always be loyal to you. Reaper, me, the club ... we've got your back."

Hurt and anger swirled inside me as a new resolve formed. Matt's betrayal only reinforced why this story held such importance. It showed just how far Hale and Benjamin would go to bury their secrets.

Gravel crunched beneath the truck's tires as Reaper pulled into the junkyard parking lot. The other SUV rumbled ahead to the large warehouse. I watched Bones key in a code to open a tall garage door before the vehicle disappeared inside.

Reaper's knuckles turned white on the steering wheel as he guided us toward a squat, weathered administrative building.

"Stay here. I'll be back in a minute. Merrick, you can head to the warehouse to get set up."

Merrick stepped out of the truck and turned to face me. "Matt will answer to me personally for this."

I swallowed hard. "Merrick, you don't have to—"

He cut me off with a slight shake of his head. "I do. You're with our VP. You might not be his old lady yet, but we all see the direction the two of you are heading. That means you're family. No one threatens our family and survives."

I watched the dust settle as Merrick strode away. His promise offered a vow of protection and retribution. A small sense of reassurance settled into me.

I pulled my phone from my pocket and toggled to Linc's email with shaky fingers. The evidence became more damning as I read on. More than twenty women had been paid to keep quiet. My eyes skimmed over emails, financial reports, and records, each more incriminating than the last.

Reaper's return jolted me from my digital dive. He handed me a bag of ice, and the cold seeped through a rag.

"For your face," he murmured. He brushed a strand of hair from my forehead with a gentle touch.

He drove a short distance to the warehouse as I held the cold pack to my eye. We entered through a rusted side door, the air heavy with tension and anger.

Hale, Benjamin, Matt, and my kidnapper sat zip-tied to chairs like macabre puppets. Merrick stood over a nearby table of sharp tools. His fingers traced their edges with anticipation.

Benjamin and Hale glared at me with undisguised hatred and malice. Matt's eyes stared at the floor, downcast in shame and regret. My kidnapper had passed out.

"Eva, I am so sorry," Matt began, his voice quivering. "Please, give me a chance to explain—"

I cut him off. "Hatchet, please shut him up for me."

Hatchet grinned at Reaper with undisguised glee as he ripped off a piece of black duct tape from a large roll and slapped it over Matt's mouth with a satisfying smack.

Merrick's eyes gleamed with a cold intensity different from the warmth and reassurance he'd shown me in the truck. It was a terrifying juxtaposition to the man who offered me comfort only minutes ago. He picked up a set of bolt cutters and tossed me a sinister grin that promised justice.

"Well, well," Benjamin sneered. "If it isn't the little bitch who couldn't leave well enough alone."

"You keep calling me a 'bitch' like it's a bad thing. It's not. Bitch means I'm not your victim anymore. I'm still standing. I survived. And you're about to find out just how much of a bitch I can be."

Benjamin narrowed his eyes. Blood, dirt, and grease stained his beige Brioni suit, and bruises and scrapes colored the right side of his face from where Hatchet had pressed it into the concrete floor.

"You think this changes anything, you stupid cunt?" Hale snarled, his words dripping with venom.

Reaper tensed beside me. He stood ready to unleash hell, but I wanted to go first. I wrapped my hand around his arm. The corded muscles beneath his cut tightened. I glanced up to give him a silent request to stand down. It was my turn.

I reached for a beautiful Damascus hunting knife sitting at the center of their tableau of torture. I wrapped my palm around the rosewood and bone handle, ignoring the look of surprise on Reaper's face.

I paced in front of Hale and Benjamin. The click of my bootheels echoed in the cavernous space.

"We know everything. We have enough evidence to bury you both." I twirled the knife in my hand as I considered how I might use it. I pulled out my phone and began to read from the files Linc had sent to my email. Benjamin's skeptical sneer faltered, and the color drained from his face with each damning detail.

"And over twenty women have been paid off to stay quiet for

what you've done to them. Verbal abuse. Assault. Blackmail. And not a shred of empathy for what you've put us through."

Hale spat at me. A glob of saliva landed at my feet.

A strange sense of calm washed over me. It settled into my chest, and the corners of my lips quirked up as what I needed to do next became crystal fucking clear. Hale's reign of terror ended today. I returned the knife to the table.

"Reaper, your gun." I stretched my arm toward him with my palm open while maintaining eye contact with Hale.

I glanced back at Reaper after a beat. He stared at me with an expression of curiosity and concern.

"Please?"

He pulled his Glock from its holster. The metal gleamed under the harsh fluorescent lights. He placed it in my outstretched hand, and his fingers lingered as if reluctant to let go. I gripped the cold metal in my hand and smiled in thanks before returning my gaze to Hale. My voice echoed through the warehouse, steady and even.

"I could turn you in and let you be completely humiliated by the media circus. I'd call every reporter I've ever met. Let the nation watch the Abell Enterprises scandal unfold. And then I'd send you letters every month while you rotted in prison, just to make sure you never forgot me."

I paused as I collected my thoughts, dragging the muzzle of the weapon down Hale's chest. Even though he sat tied up, part of my mind still screamed that I faced danger this close to him. The gun provided a comforting weight in my hand.

"In fact, I will leak every piece of evidence I have against the two of you. But first, I'll ask a hacker to charter an empty plane with your names on the manifest to a country with no extradition."

I pressed the Glock harder into Hale, a twisted satisfaction filling my chest as he flinched.

"When I anonymously send a package of files to every journalist I know, everyone will assume you fled the country. No one will even consider looking for your bodies. And, hopefully, every victim will get some sense of peace knowing you're no longer a threat—even if they don't know you're dead."

Their eyes widened as they understood they would never leave this warehouse alive. I lowered the weapon and tilted my head as I reveled in the heady feeling of power.

"You see, that's the only option. I don't trust the police. They can be bribed. I don't trust the judges that will set bail far too low. I don't trust the lawyers. They'll certainly fuck this up. And I don't trust that you wouldn't do it all again. I don't trust anyone will hold you accountable."

I leaned in close and dropped my voice to a whisper. "Do you know what that means?"

I didn't wait for Hale to respond. I didn't need to. I raised the gun and shot him point-blank in the head.

The sound rang through the enclosed space, and the reek of gunpowder filled the air. Hale's body slumped forward as the blood poured from his skull.

"You bitch," the senior Abell growled, his eyes wide with fear.

"Oh, shut the fuck up," I said, my voice cold as I aimed at his head. "You're just as guilty as your son."

I pulled the trigger again. Silence followed, broken only by the ringing in my ears and the ragged sound of my breathing.

Justice, in its darkest form, had finally been served.

I'd played judge, jury, and executioner.

And I didn't feel sorry.

Not even a little.

Chapter Twenty-Eight

My sweet Lioness.

Ruthless. Cold. Beautiful.

A stunning and terrifying goddess of vengeance.

I didn't expect her to take justice into her own hands, but I was damn proud she did.

And by the looks my men gave me, they were just as surprised and impressed.

"That was ... unexpected," I said evenly as she lowered the gun.

Her hands didn't shake, and the darkness glowing in her eyes held a steely resolve that sent a shiver down my spine.

"I'd be charged as an accessory anyway." She smirked. "Might as well get the glory."

Her past had forged her into a fierce survivor with a dark streak, but her response still shocked me. It shouldn't have. She had good reason for her distrust in law enforcement and lawyers. Throughout her entire life, she'd been failed by the system time and time again. Killing Hale and Benjamin here before they had the chance to weasel away was the most logical conclusion to the day's events.

Matt struggled against the restraints, his eyes white with terror.

Eva stared at him uncertainly, her need for retribution warring with their long friendship. It hit me then. She thought she needed to be fiercely independent, always shouldering her burdens alone. But she didn't have to anymore. I'd be damned if I let her carry this weight by herself.

I touched her shoulder. "Let us handle this one, Lioness. This is not a weight you need to bear alone."

Merrick stepped forward. "We can take everything from here, VP. Go home. We'll handle the rest."

Eva bit her lip in thought, then nodded. "Thank you."

She glanced at the Mavericks surrounding her—a pack I had no doubt would follow her every order now that they'd watched her reveal her ruthless side.

"I owe you guys. For finding me. For saving me."

Merrick shook his head, a rare smile softening his hardened, scarred features. "You don't owe us. You're a part of our family now. We protect our own."

"And we could never let anything happen to you," Archer added with a snicker. "Reaper's a lot more pleasant now that you're around. We wouldn't want to lose that."

"And, with him off the market, it means more ladies for me," Hatchet added.

I chuckled, wrapping my arm around Eva and guiding her to my truck. Her body seemed fragile under my arm, like she might shatter if I let go. But she held more strength than anyone I'd ever met. Still, her bruised and battered face stirred something primal in my chest. A dark rage simmered just beneath the surface, one I'd need to let out through my own method of revenge.

I shot Merrick a text, asking him to kill the Abell lackey who had kidnapped Eva but to keep Matt alive overnight. Barely alive would be fine.

Next, I dialed up the club doctor. "Meet us at the clubhouse in twenty," I said, my tone clipped.

Eva protested. "I'm fine. Really."

I glanced down at her, noting the faint tremble in her hands despite her brave words. My chest tightened at the sight.

"Humor me," I said, my voice softer this time but firm enough to leave no room for debate.

As we reached the truck, I opened the door for her and helped her climb in. Despite my careful movements, she let out a low moan of pain as she settled.

As I slid into the driver's seat and started the engine, my mind churned with thoughts I couldn't shake. That bastard. I should've figured it out sooner. How he'd responded to Eva when we'd walked into the bakery had been more than jealousy and surprise.

The image of her tied to the chair in the warehouse flashed through my mind, and a fresh wave of fury rolled over me. I'd failed to keep her safe and hated myself for it.

Eva shifted beside me, pulling me back to the present. She stared out the window, her ghostly pallor reflecting in the glass.

"How'd you find me so quickly?"

I smirked. "I put an AirTag in your back pocket this morning when you were getting ready."

Her head snapped toward me, her eyes widening in surprise. "You what?"

I shrugged. "I needed to have every angle covered. I was planning to tell you tonight so you could laugh at how overprotective I am. But, it turns out my paranoia was warranted. Again."

She let out a dark, low laugh before stopping to hold her side with a grimace. "Can't argue with that."

Thane and Rhetta stood waiting by the door when we pulled into the clubhouse parking lot. Rhetta rushed forward when Eva stepped out of the truck, wrapping her in a protective hug. She pulled back as Eva winced in pain.

"She needs to be checked out," I told Rhetta as I nodded toward Doc waiting inside.

Rhetta didn't hesitate, guiding Eva with a reassuring arm around her shoulders while I hung back with Thane.

Thane watched me with a grim expression as he lit a smoke. "What happened?"

I recounted everything—from Matt's betrayal to Eva's retribution. Thane's expression darkened with each word, and his jaw clenched so tight I thought he might snap his teeth.

"Damn. Eva took them out herself?"

"She didn't hesitate."

Thane let out a low whistle. "That's one hell of a woman, brother. She's got more fight in her than half our prospects."

"Yeah. She's a renegade. I've never met a woman so fearless. And she has a ruthless sense of justice like I never imagined."

"You sure she can handle the aftermath? The toll that pulling the trigger can take on a person?"

My jaw tightened. "Based on the look on her face afterward, I think it'll only bring peace."

"She's got more in common with us than I thought," Thane muttered.

Doc emerged a few minutes later. "She's okay. Bruised ribs, some swelling, but nothing was broken. The adrenaline's wearing off, but she'll be fine with rest. I offered her something stronger for the pain, but she refused."

Relief flooded through me with a touch of annoyance. Of course she would refuse the pain meds.

Eva stayed lost in thought on the quiet drive back to the cabin. Hawk greeted us with excited yips as we entered, his tail wagging. She winced as she knelt to scratch him behind the ears, and I clenched my jaw so hard it ached.

"Let's get you cleaned up," I said, guiding her toward the bathroom. Something twisted in me at the sight of blood smeared on her skin.

I eased her out of her clothes, wincing at every bruise revealed beneath them. Deep purple marks mottled her ribs and arms. I wanted to shoot another bullet in Hale just for good measure. I kept my movements calm and slow, despite the boiling rage within me.

Each cut, scrape, and bruise was a debt Matt would pay back in his blood.

I stripped down, sensing how drained the day had left her. The shower hissed to life as I led her under the spray. Warm water poured over our bodies, turning the white tile pink as blood and grime washed down the drain. Grabbing a washcloth, I wiped away the blood from her face, careful not to press too hard on her split lip.

The silence filled the small bathroom thicker than the steam curling around us, and I fought the urge to ask if she was okay. I wanted to rinse away every mark and memory of what she'd survived. I pressed a hand to her back and guided her to let the water soak her hair. Her eyes fluttered closed as I worked shampoo into her scalp, my fingers moving in slow, soft circles. She leaned into my touch, and, for a moment, the rage inside me quieted.

After rinsing her hair, I turned off the shower and wrapped her in an oversized towel. She still hadn't spoken a word.

"You're the strongest woman I know, my Lioness," I murmured, pressing a kiss to her forehead. "I'm never letting you out of my sight again."

She managed a tired smile and leaned into my chest as I wrapped my arms around her. We stayed like that for a minute before I helped her into one of my hoodies and guided her to the living room.

We sat in comfortable silence, Eva curled up on the couch with Hawk at her feet and a stiff drink in hand, until my phone buzzed.

"Linc," I answered gruffly.

"It's done. I worked through Benjamin Abell's contacts and canceled the contract. She's safe now. I also moved some of his money into an offshore account. You know, a small settlement for Eva for everything she's been through."

I relayed the news to Eva, and relief flooded her features. The tension coiled tight in my chest for days began to unwind.

Eventually, exhaustion caught up with us. I led Eva to the bedroom. Hawk padded along behind us and, for once, we let him sleep at our feet rather than in his crate. As we settled into bed, I pulled her close and breathed in her scent to reassure myself she was safe.

She fell asleep within minutes, but I lay awake. My mind raced as I rehearsed every way I could make Matt pay. Eventually, exhaustion dragged me under where my dreams twisted as my past and present collided, turning memories into monsters. Images of my childhood blended with the horrors from the day before. Details long forgotten rose to the surface and intermixed with the fear and fury that coursed through me when I saw Eva's bruised body tied to a chair.

A jolt ripped me from sleep. My heart hammered against my ribs, and sweat beaded on my forehead as I sat up with a jerk. I couldn't tell where—or when—I was for a moment as the remnants of the nightmare clung to me.

"Roman?" Eva's sleepy voice cut through the darkness. "What's wrong?"

I tried to steady my breathing. "Just a nightmare. Go back to sleep."

She propped herself up beside me. I could see the concern in her eyes at my strained tone, even in the dim light.

"Tell me about it. Please?"

I hesitated. Eva's hand found mine in the darkness, our fingers intertwining.

"It was about my old man. He was a drunk and an addict. He was always losing his shit on us and our mom. One time, when I was twelve, he really lost it."

She squeezed my hand in silent encouragement.

"He beat her senseless, then tied her to a chair. He locked me and Linc outside. Linc was only seven. Kid was scared out of his mind."

The memory flashed through my mind vividly, as if it had happened yesterday instead of years ago. I dragged in a shaky lungful of air that tasted faintly of her grapefruit shampoo.

"There was this biker going down the street. A Maverick. I flagged him down. Begged him for help. It was Don. He broke in, saved our mom, and beat the living shit out of my old man."

I fell silent for a moment, lost in the recollection. "He called Maisie to get my mom to a women's shelter. Seeing you tied up like that brought it back to the surface of my mind. Even some details I'd buried so deep that I'd forgotten."

Unshed tears shimmered in her eyes. "I'm so sorry."

My throat tightened. I wasn't used to being comforted. I glanced at the clock on the nightstand. It was early morning. Sleep would need to come later.

"You should get some more sleep. I've got some things I need to take care of."

Eva wanted to argue, but I kissed her before she could protest. "I'm all right, I promise. Just need to clear my head and take care of some things. I'll be back in time to make you breakfast."

"Pancakes."

"Anything you want."

"I want real pancakes. Made with flour and sugar. Not monkfruit and whatever weird health flours you have hidden away."

I chuckled as she settled back onto the pillows. "Pancakes covered in maple syrup and blueberries, and dusted with powdered sugar. I'll make the sweetest, most calorie dense damn pancakes you've ever had."

The floorboards creaked under my feet as I moved through the quiet cabin. I grabbed my jacket from the back of a chair and shrugged it over my flannel shirt. My fingers brushed over the worn leather, tracing the familiar patches. The weight settled on my shoulders, heavy with what I knew I needed to do next.

I pulled out my phone.

Me: On my way.

Merrick: We're ready for you

The ride to the junkyard blurred in the pre-dawn darkness. The thunderous roar of my bike always served as a balm to the unhealed wounds in my heart after my nightmares.

My resolve hardened as the cool air cleared the last cobwebs of sleep from my mind. I couldn't protect my mother back then, but I sure as hell could protect Eva now.

Merrick and Hatchet stoically stood guard at the junkyard. I sensed their anticipation despite the dark circles under their eyes.

They'd left Matt untouched, which I knew had taken a lot of control for Merrick. He felt personally responsible for the safety of every member of our family. The dark desire I had to kill Matt was reflected in his eyes, too.

"How's Eva?" Merrick asked.

"She's holding up. But she's got a lot to process. So do I."

I knew my men could see the haunted look in my eyes as I considered what could have happened.

Hatchet nodded toward Matt. "I know what will make you feel better." He gestured toward the table of torture.

"Go stand guard. Make sure we're not interrupted."

Hatchet raised an eyebrow, a hint of a smile on his lips. "I'm always missing out on the fun stuff. I care about what happened to Eva, too. I should at least get to cut one finger off."

Merrick chuckled. "Don't worry. We'll make sure you get your turn. I wouldn't want you to get rusty."

Hatchet snorted. "Rusty? My skills are sharper than ever."

I shook my head. Hatchet enjoyed inventing new ways to hold traitors accountable. His methods were as creative as they were cruel. Last year, when we caught a prospect stealing bike parts from our warehouse, Hatchet had turned torture into a performance. He'd taken his time, savoring every whimper and plea as he pressed the edge of a dull set of scissors to bone and muscle, chewing through flesh instead of slicing.

"Let's get started. I need to be back in time to make breakfast for my woman."

I stalked toward Matt, my boots crunching on the gritty floor. He sat slumped over in the chair. Fear filled his eyes as he stirred and recognized me. Good. He should be afraid.

A cold, calculated rage settled over me. "Eva might have hesitated. But we won't."

He tried to speak, but the duct tape muffled his words. I ripped it off, and he cried out in pain.

"Please. I'm sorry. I didn't want her to get hurt. I just—"

My fist connected with his jaw. The satisfying crunch of bone reverberated through the warehouse. His blood sprayed from his mouth, splattering across my knuckles and the floor.

"You handed her over to them," I snarled, punctuating each word with a blow. "Right now, she can't breathe without feeling the pain from her bruised ribs. She can't glance in the mirror without thinking about how you—someone she saw as a friend and ally—betrayed her. You handed her over to a predator who would have killed her. And now, I am going to make you wish you were dead."

Matt's face had become a messy web of blood and bruises, but I was far from done. I nodded to Merrick, who handed me a pair of bolt cutters. The cold metal fit in my hand, a tool to carve out my vengeance.

"How should we start? How about a finger for every text you sent to Hale about Eva? How about your tongue for betraying her? Maybe even your eyes because of how you judged the woman I love for being with me?"

His screams echoed off the metal walls as I worked, methodical and relentless. By the time I finished, Matt struggled to remain conscious. His broken, bloody mess of a body slumped in the chair. I stepped back, wiping my hands on a rag with a sense of cold satisfaction.

"End him."

Merrick nodded and pulled a pistol with a suppressor from his hip. The silenced shot barely echoed. It seemed anticlimactic after all the screaming and begging.

Hatchet stepped back inside with a rusty meat hook swinging from his hand. "Damn it, Reaper. I had some fun ideas for this."

"Sorry, brother. I guess you'll need to add it to your collection."

Hatchet's teeth gleamed in the dim light as he showed his most menacing smile. "Next time, Merrick is keeping watch."

"When it comes to Eva, there'd better not be a next time."

We worked in silence as we cleaned up. I hauled Matt's broken body to the incinerator. The metallic tang of blood and death clung to my skin and clothes.

Merrick methodically scrubbed the tools with bleach. The sharp chemical stench burned my nostrils.

I grabbed a fresh change of clothes from my bike and slipped into the admin building's shower to scrub away the blood and sweat until my skin burned. I tossed my flannel and jeans, splattered with evidence, into the fire. The flames licked them clean of any trace of my connection to Matt's death. As we finished, the sun rose over the horizon.

I offered a smile to my brothers. Words weren't needed, because the same grim satisfaction reflected in their eyes.

A sense of peace washed over me as I swung my leg over my bike. Now, I could focus on the future. Our future.

I revved the engine and sped down the road toward the cabin. An overwhelming need to protect Eva, to keep her safe from any threat, big or small, surged through me. I'd die before I let anything happen to her. She belonged to me to protect, to cherish; I'd kill again if necessary to keep her safe.

And I knew what that meant. It was time to offer her my patch. It was the highest commitment I could give her. It would mean fully bringing her into my world, with all its dangers and complexities.

But it would also mean protection, respect, and a spot by my side no one could question. It would mark her as mine in the eyes of the club and our rivals. And as Thane prepared me to move into the role of president someday, I needed to be sure she was ready for what that meant.

Yet I still hesitated. I felt torn between my desire to claim her and my respect for her autonomy. Eva was fiercely independent. How would she react to the idea of wearing a cut labeling her as my "property?" I winced at the imagined conversation as I heard her voice in my mind.

"Property? I'm not a piece of real estate," she would likely say.

The patch would keep her safe and make her untouchable to our enemies. But at what cost to her sense of self? Would she view it as protection or a prison?

Maybe I was overthinking. She'd faced down threats with a steel spine. Perhaps she'd embrace the patch for what it truly meant—not a mark of ownership, but a symbol of partnership, of her place with me and the Mavericks.

Or maybe she'd laugh in my face and tell me where to shove our outdated ideas of possession.

Chapter Twenty-Nine

Reaper hovered for a week, treating me like I couldn't do anything myself. Even though there was no longer a threat to my life, he barely left my side. He spent most of the day poring over blueprints on the counter and barking orders over the phone to his employees and subcontractors. The handful of times he needed to leave for a few hours, Rhetta mysteriously showed up with a new movie to watch or a bottle of wine.

"You need to chill the fuck out," I said after the thousandth time he insisted he do something for me I could manage myself. "I'm not made of glass. You know better than anyone that I am tough as hell."

He also had utterly refused to have sex with me, worried about how to maneuver around my bruised ribs and battered face. At this point, my injuries appeared more painful than they felt.

"I'm going crazy. Let's go somewhere," I begged. "Any-fucking-where."

Reaper finished sending a text before wrapping his arms around me and kissing my head. "Fine. I've been wanting to show you something anyway. Grab your jacket. We'll take the bike."

The air whipped through my hair as I wrapped my arms around

his waist, the memories of our first ride flashing through my mind. I reached down, stroking his thigh like I had that first night, and giggled as he tensed.

For a while, we rode nowhere in particular—just enjoying the freedom of the road and the roar of his bike.

He slowed as we pulled onto a dead-end gravel road, turning down a long, winding driveway. At the end sat a beautiful mid-century home with a work trailer beside it, the Grimm Construction logo emblazoned across the side.

"Whoever owns this house is lucky," I commented, admiring the wraparound cedar porch and blooming crocuses.

He grinned at me. "I own it. I buy a house or two every year to flip. I've been working on this one for the past few months, and it's almost done. Just needs a fresh coat of paint, a refinish on the wood floors, and some new carpeting."

He ushered me inside, and I twirled in a slow circle as I took it all in. A spiral staircase stood to the right. In the middle of the open-concept living room sat a double-sided stone fireplace. The kitchen, bright with gleaming stainless-steel appliances, featured an island slab longer than the entire kitchen in the house I owned.

Reaper swept me over with a nervous gaze. "Even though you're safe now, I don't want you to move out. I want you to move in with me, but the cabin is small. We could make this our home. Or we could sell it, and I could build you the home of your dreams. Whatever you want."

I smiled, wrapping my arms around him. "My home is anywhere with you. I would love to build our life together here."

Reaper pressed a kiss to my lips. "Good. This is the perfect place for a family. Five bedrooms, three full baths, and a home theater."

I tilted my head. "Five bedrooms is a bit presumptuous."

He grinned, unrepentant. "Not if you want a guest room, a home office, and a couple of rooms for the little ones."

I swatted his arm. "You're getting ahead of yourself. I'm not decorating a nursery just yet."

"In that case, let me show you the dining room, where I have a surprise."

He guided me, his hand low on my back, to a sunny room surrounded on three sides by floor-to-ceiling windows. A bottle of champagne cooled on ice in the center of an oak table. Beside it floated three balloons with two red velvet cupcakes and a wrapped gift on the gleaming surface.

I glanced at him in surprise and laughed. "What if I'd said no?"

He shrugged as he reached for the champagne. "Then I wouldn't have shown you the dining room." He popped the cork, pouring the bubbly liquid into the glasses. "And I'd have had to call Rhetta to ask her to pick this stuff up so I'd never have to come back to this house again."

Reaper picked up the gift, pausing to collect his thoughts. His eyes met mine, filled with an intensity that caught my breath in my throat.

"I can't imagine my life without you. These past few weeks, I've fallen for you. Hard. You're it for me, my Lioness. I hope this gift shows you how serious I am about our future together."

The vulnerability on his face struck me, and I leaned up to kiss him and took the gift from his hands. It felt light, and the box thunked as I shook it. I tore the paper and opened it to reveal a folded leather cut.

On the back, the Mavericks Motorcycle Club logo appeared cradled by a bottom rocker with "Property of Reaper" embroidered in white thread.

He held his breath, uncertain and hopeful, as I smiled at him. I slipped it over my shoulders and then wrapped my arms around him.

"So, I'm officially an old lady?" I asked, running my hands over the smooth black leather. "I love it. I love you."

He pulled me close, and his lips brushed my ear. "I love you, too. More than I ever thought possible."

Reaper stepped away and pulled a swatch pad from the counter-top. He flipped through the samples before handing them to me.

"Now, how about you pick out the paint colors and carpeting for our new house? We should be able to move in within a few weeks."

I grinned, already imagining our life together in this beautiful home. But, at that moment, I didn't care about the details. I set the swatches aside and kissed him.

"First, I think it's time you stop treating me like I'm made of crystal. I've got a new cut to christen, after all."

I watched his gaze as I slipped the cut off my shoulders and pulled my shirt over my head. I unclasped my bra and threw it behind me before putting the cut back on. The cool leather was a delicious contrast to the heat building within me.

Reaper stood watching me in quiet fascination. I could see the hunger and lust in his eyes.

"Are you going to undress, or are you just going to stare at me?" I taunted.

I kicked off my boots and shimmied out of my pants, standing before him in just my cut and black lace boy shorts.

Reaper stepped forward, his calloused hands gripping my hips. In one fluid motion, he lifted me onto the table, nearly spilling the bottle of champagne.

His lips traced my jawline, each kiss sending shivers down my spine. "You are mine." He tugged on the leather. "And now everyone will know it. And that makes me so fucking happy."

He crushed his lips to mine in a searing kiss as his hands moved up my thighs. His fingers swept across the lace of my panties, and I moaned into his mouth.

I wrapped my legs around his waist and pulled him closer. His hardened cock pressed against me. The rough denim of his jeans brushing against my bare skin only heightened my arousal.

I pushed my body against the hard planes of his chest. My fingers fumbled with the buttons, desperate to feel his skin against mine. "Too many fucking clothes," I murmured against his lips. "Take them off."

Reaper smirked at my order. "Patience, Lioness."

"We both know I'm not a patient person."

He let out a low chuckle as his hands roamed my body. "You're so beautiful," he murmured against my skin. His large, calloused hands cupped my breasts. "So perfect."

"Please, stop teasing me."

With a groan, he positioned himself between my thighs. And then, in one swift motion, he drove into me. We both gasped at the sensation.

As we moved, the world and every bit of the terrifying past month faded away. With every thrust, every touch, every whispered word, we fell deeper into each other.

After we reached our peak together, we stayed there in comfortable silence. The future would bring new challenges and new dangers. But for now, at this moment, wrapped in Reaper's arms, I was safe, cherished, and at home.

Chapter Thirty

It would be a long day, but I wanted to settle one last piece before hitting the road with Thane and Merrick. For our confrontation with the Rangers to go according to plan, I needed to leave by 4 p.m.

We'd finished lunch when Eva's phone buzzed in her back pocket. Her smile faltered as she glanced at the screen. I watched her face crumple as she answered. She listened, agreeing with the person on the other line, and then thanked them before hanging up. Her eyes filled with tears as she glanced at me, then at Hawk, sprawled across her feet.

"Hawk's been adopted," she choked out. "We have to take him to meet his new family today."

My heart clenched at the pain in her voice. I'd planned this surprise for days, working with the shelter to make it official. But seeing her like this, I almost regretted not telling her sooner.

The drive to the shelter was quiet. Eva stared out the window, one hand stroking Hawk's fur as if she could memorize the feel of him. Every so often, she'd sniff and swipe at her eyes, trying to hide it.

"This is always the hardest part of fostering. You love a dog like your own and then you say goodbye so they can be with the humans they're meant to be with forever."

I reached over and squeezed her knee, offering silent reassurance. I didn't trust myself not to spill the secret if I spoke.

At the shelter, Eva climbed out and clipped Hawk's leash with shaking hands. I watched as she led him to a grassy area, her shoulders hunched as she tried to hold back tears. Hawk, oblivious to the emotional turmoil, pranced beside her.

She led him to a patch of grass, crouching to rub his ears, whispering something into his fur I couldn't quite hear. I stood back, giving her a moment, until a shelter worker approached me, a bright yellow folder in hand.

"Here you go," the shelter worker said, pressing the folder into my palm. "Everything's in order."

I nodded my thanks and made my way over to Eva and Hawk.

"Sir?" the worker called, holding a cheerfully bright yellow bandanna. "I forgot we need to put this on him. Our adoption coordinator will be right out to take a family photo of the three of you."

Eva turned, confusion etched across her face as the worker tied the "I'm Adopted" bandanna around Hawk's neck. Her gaze darted between me and the shelter worker, brow furrowed.

"What's going on?"

I smiled, holding up the folder. "Hawk's officially ours. I adopted him—so he could stay with the humans he's meant to be with forever."

Eva's eyes widened, fresh tears of joy spilling over. A brilliant smile lit her face. Then, she punched me hard in the chest, knocking me off balance.

"You sneaky bastard," she laughed through her tears. "I can't believe you did this."

I wrapped my arms around her before she could punch me again, holding her tight as she pressed her tear-streaked face into my shoulder. Hawk wriggled between us and thumped his tail wildly against our legs, determined to join the hug. When he didn't immediately get the attention he sought, he nipped at my ankle.

* * *

Eva watched me as I loaded ammo into my extra magazines, her eyes following my practiced movements with growing concern. Once I'd holstered my Glock, slipping the spare ammunition into my pockets, I added a small Ruger pistol to my boot. When I pulled out the Kevlar vest, her brow furrowed.

"Where are you going that you need to wear that?" she asked, her voice tinged with anxiety.

I clenched my jaw, caught off guard by the question. How did other Mavericks handle this? The unfamiliar territory of having someone to answer to caused me to hesitate.

"Just some club business."

Eva's eyes narrowed. "Club business requires bulletproof body armor?"

I slipped on the vest. "It's standard procedure when we're heading out of our territory. It's a meeting with the Rangers. Things have been ... tense lately. The vest is just a precaution, nothing more."

"Tense enough that you're expecting gunfire?" she pressed.

I turned and cupped her face in my hands. "I promise, it's nothing I can't handle. I've been doing this for years."

She leaned into my touch, but her expression told me she was unconvinced. "I understand there are things you can't tell me, but ... is this dangerous? Really dangerous?"

I hesitated. I felt torn between my instinct to protect her from worry and my growing desire to be honest. "There's always an element of risk. But we're prepared. I personally planned this operation."

"Just ... come back to me, okay? In one piece. No new holes, please."

I kissed her, trying to convey everything I couldn't say in words. "I always do, my Lioness. I'll be home late. Don't wait up."

As I headed for the door, I could sense Eva's eyes on me. The weight of her concern crept into an unfamiliar, almost uncomfortable territory. I'd never considered how my actions might affect someone else before.

I paused at the threshold and glanced back at her. "I love you."

"I love you, too. Be safe."

As I closed the door behind me, I couldn't shake I'd left too much unsaid. But the mission demanded my full focus. I couldn't afford to be distracted.

* * *

We arrived at the Rangers' clubhouse outside of Austin an hour earlier than they expected.

Our intel proved accurate, and we breached the perimeter with ease. Each man moved with practiced stealth, and our boots barely sounded on the gravel as we approached.

A sense of déjà vu washed over me as we moved toward the clubhouse. It reminded me of leading high-stakes military operations in Fallujah—except there was more freedom and fewer rules of engagement. The familiar adrenaline rush coursed through my veins and sharpened my senses.

I nodded to Hatchet when we reached the main building. He ignited the charges where we'd planned, his hands steady and sure. The controlled explosion sent vibrations through the ground, creating the distraction we needed as we breached the door.

It splintered under our assault. Wood fragments flew through the air as we burst inside. Hickok and Poe stood frozen in shock at the unexpected assault.

"This ends now," I growled with my gun trained on Hickok's president patch. "Your dealers stay out of Houston, and the attacks on the Mavericks stop. We'll forgive your club for attempting to hijack a load of weapons, but only because your men already paid in blood for that mistake. Tonight, I'm giving you three options: keep your drugs out of Houston, patch over, or die."

The fluorescent lights buzzed overhead. Hickock's eyes narrowed, and a sneer twisted his features.

"You think you can come in here and dictate terms? Fuck you, and fuck Houston. We'll ride and deal wherever we damn well please."

His hand blurred as he reached for his weapon. Time slowed, and I reacted on instinct as I squeezed the trigger. Two shots in rapid succession.

But Hickock moved faster than I anticipated. Another sharp crack split the air, and a searing pain exploded in my thigh. The bastard had gotten a shot off, too.

Hickock stumbled backward with his eyes wide open in shock as he realized I'd hit him square in the chest. He gasped in one last breath before his lifeless body slid down the wall, leaving a crimson smear in his wake.

Poe stood with his arms crossed. He raised a brow at Merrick, Thane, and Hatchet, who all had their weapons trained on his chest.

"Jesus Christ," Poe said, glancing between his fallen president and me. "Looks like I just got a promotion."

"Congratu-fucking-lations," I growled.

"Listen, I never wanted any of this. Hickok had it in his head that we needed to expand our territory. I never agreed. A patchover would be more fight than it's worth, so you have my word. The Rangers will stay out of Houston. I'd like to call a truce."

I ground my teeth as I breathed through the searing pain and kept my Glock steadily aimed at his chest. "See that you do. There won't be options next time. Just consequences."

Poe nodded once, keeping steady as we backed out of the room. He may have just agreed to peace, but I wouldn't give him the opportunity to shoot me in the back.

As we stepped out of the clubhouse, the cool evening air did little to ease the burning in my thigh.

Merrick's gaze flicked to my leg. "You good?"

I grunted and leaned against my bike for support. "It's not bad. Through and through."

Hatchet approached with a smirk as he took in the sight of the blood seeping through my jeans. "We should patch you up before we ride. I don't need you splattering blood all over my bike. I have a date when we get back."

"I'd hate to inconvenience you."

Hatchet smirked at my sarcastic tone. I reached for the first aid kit I'd added to my saddlebag after my last gunshot wound on the road.

"I don't think it's considered a date if you don't even know her name," Merrick said.

I could see the flicker of amusement in Hatchet's eyes.

"I have a text with her address and an open invitation to show up when we get back to town."

I rolled my eyes. Hatchet's voice was laced with a confident swagger only he could pull off.

"And I don't need her name. She answers just fine to 'sweetheart.'"

Hatchet's attempt to distract me from the pain was welcome. A small part of me appreciated his effort to shift the focus away from my wounded leg and onto his latest conquest.

I pulled out my knife and used the sharp blade to slice through the denim of my jeans. Blood oozed from the entry and exit points. I grabbed a pressure bandage, pressing it against the injury. I hissed through clenched teeth as I began wrapping gauze around the stinging wound on my thigh. The pain burned intensely, but I'd had worse.

Thane watched with a grim expression. "You're getting too much practice at this, brother."

"Occupational hazard."

"How's Eva going to react?"

"Not real fucking happily, I'm sure." I grimaced as I swung my leg over my bike. "She had a lot of questions before I left. How much do you tell Rhetta?"

"It's a delicate balance, man. I give her enough information so she's not blindsided, but not so much that she's constantly worried. Rhetta knows the risks, but I spare her the gory details."

"And when shit like this happens?"

"I'm honest, but I downplay it. She doesn't need to know every close call. It's about protecting her, you know? Both from the danger and the constant fear."

I grunted as I mulled over Thane's approach. Walking this precarious line would prove challenging, especially with someone as sharp and inquisitive as Eva.

Thane clapped me on the shoulder. "You'll find the right balance. It's okay to keep some things to yourself. It's not lying. It's shielding her from the worst parts of our world."

I let out a bitter laugh. "Fuck. She is not going to agree with that philosophy."

"We both know she's tougher than she looks. She'll be able to handle whatever you tell her."

I sent a quick text to Doc and dry-swallowed a few Tylenol. He'd stitch me up when we got back to the clubhouse. I started the engine, wincing as the vibrations set off a ripple of pain. I dreaded the conversation to come, especially since I'd promised Eva that the Kevlar vest was only a precaution.

As we rode away from the Rangers' clubhouse, the rumble of our bikes cutting through the night, a mixture of satisfaction and concern swirled within me. While we had neutralized the immediate threat, I considered how short-lived the peace between our clubs could be. But for now, we had secured our territory.

Houston belonged to the Mavericks, bought and paid for in blood —theirs and mine.

Chapter Thirty-One

I jolted awake at the sound of the front door opening, my heart racing as I glanced at the clock. 3:47 a.m.

Reaper had been gone for over twelve hours, and the gnawing worry in my gut gave way to a fitful sleep sometime after 1 a.m.

I threw off the covers and opened the bedroom door just as Reaper had reached for the handle. My relief morphed into anger, concern, and frustration.

His jeans were torn and caked with dried blood, and a white bandage was visible through the rip. His face looked drawn, dark circles under his eyes speaking of exhaustion and pain.

"What the actual fuck?" I demanded. "What happened?"

"Long night. Shit went a bit sideways."

My temper exploded. "That's all you're going to fucking give me?"

He moved past me into the bedroom, and I noticed his limp.

"It's nothing. You should go back to sleep."

"Like hell I will. You're hurt. You've been shot again, haven't you?"

Reaper sighed as he sank onto the edge of the bed. "Yes, I was shot. It went all the way through. Didn't hit anything vital. Doc patched me up before I came home."

"What kind of club business involves you getting shot in the middle of the night?"

I stood in front of him, my arms crossed on my chest. His eyes flashed with irritation.

"This is my responsibility as VP. Sometimes it gets messy."

"Who the fuck shot you?"

"The Rangers' president."

Rage coursed through me. "That motherfucker. I'll kill him myself!"

"You're too late. I already did."

"Damn it. This is exactly why I wanted you to tell me what you were planning this morning. You could have died tonight, and I wouldn't have known a damn thing about it!"

He ran a hand over his exhausted face. "I didn't even think to tell you. I've never had to do this before. Sometimes, I don't even think about the danger myself."

"Well, you'd better start thinking about it," I snapped, but some of the fight had left me. "I deserve to know when you're in the line of fire."

Reaper nodded as he reached to take my hand. I let him, despite my lingering anger.

"You're right. I need to do better. But there are some things I can't share. Not won't—can't. For your safety and for the club's."

"I can't be kept completely in the dark. I need to know when you're in real danger. Not every detail, but enough to know what I'm dealing with. Enough to not be blindsided when this happens."

"Fair. You have to understand that this life … it's not always black and white. Sometimes, the less you know, the better."

I jabbed a finger into his chest. "I'm not some delicate fucking flower that needs to be shielded from the realities of what you do as a Maverick. I can handle more than you think."

Reaper's arm wrapped around me. He pulled me close despite my half-hearted resistance.

"I know you're strong. This isn't about that. It's about keeping you safe. About not causing unnecessary fear and anxiety."

"What about keeping my heart safe? I've already lost my mother and Jace. The fear of the unknown is worse."

The memories of losing my mother and big brother sent a sharp stab of grief through me. Reaper stiffened as he considered my request, and his eyes softened as he gazed at me with love and empathy.

"I promise to tell you what I can. But you have to promise me you won't push for details I can't give you."

"I can live with that. As long as you're honest with me about the big stuff. Like, oh, I don't know ... getting fucking shot?"

He grinned. "Deal."

"Let's get you cleaned up." I guided him toward the bathroom. "Pants off."

He raised a brow at me suggestively, and I laughed. "You're not getting in bed covered in blood. I'm going to help you clean up. Nothing more. You're injured."

Reaper ran his hands down the thin tank top I wore. My nipples pebbled at his touch, and I smacked his hand away.

"I'm still mad at you. Now, fucking take your pants off so you can come to bed."

Reaper complied, sliding his ripped and bloody jeans to the floor before sitting on the toilet seat. With a hot washcloth, I wiped the dried blood from his leg.

"Exactly how often are you dodging bullets? Or failing to dodge bullets?" I glanced up at him, trying to sound firm, but a slight shake in my tone gave away my fear.

"Every so often. Less than when I was a Marine, if that helps."

My eyes narrowed at his evasion. "It doesn't. I know that being a Maverick is dangerous sometimes. I need to know what I'm signing up for. Am I playing nurse weekly? Monthly? A few times a year? You've been shot twice since we met barely a month ago."

"Hmm, I quite like the idea of you playing nurse. Can you wear the little outfit?"

His attempt to defuse the discussion ignited anger in me. His focus on some juvenile fantasy rather than addressing my very real concerns felt not only disappointing but outright infuriating.

"I'm being fucking serious here." I squeezed my hand over his bandaged wound with just enough pressure to remind him of the pain. He winced. "My bedside manner will get worse if you don't take this conversation seriously. You promised you would be honest with me."

As I knelt before him, tears pricked in my eyes in frustration. I stood to turn away to hide the welling emotion, but he pulled me back to face him. "I've taken five gunshots since joining the Mavericks. One to my vest when I was an enforcer. A graze on my side, and another to the vest when I was sergeant at arms. And two this month."

I bit my lip as I considered how each close call could have taken him from me.

"The Rangers agreed to a truce. They know we're bigger and badder, and their new president will keep them out of Houston. The war is over."

I stood, allowing him to use me as leverage to do the same, and helped him limp to the bed. As we settled in, I turned to face him, my expression serious.

"I need you to understand something. I love you, and I need to know when you're walking into danger. I can't be left wondering if you're coming home every time you leave. Can you promise me that?"

He stayed quiet for a moment. "I can't promise you there won't be danger. I can't promise you I'll always walk away without a mark. But I swear to you, I'll never keep you in the dark again." Reaper pulled me closer, and his lips brushed my forehead. "I love you, my

Lioness. You deserve the truth—even when it scares the hell out of me."

* * *

I stood in a kaleidoscope of terror and pain.

My mom's shrieks echoed through our old house. The grunt of her husband pounding the chef's knife through her chest and belly sounded through the kitchen.

I wanted to get to her, but the hallway stretched before me. I tried to run, but my feet were cemented to the ground.

Suddenly, Hale's face loomed above me on the cold concrete of a parking garage. His fists were everywhere, his hand around my throat as he suffocated me. I tried to scream, but no sound came out. I tried to fight back, but I stayed frozen in place.

The scene shifted, and I sat bound in a dark room, every predator I've ever known surrounding me. Then, Reaper stood before me. I called out to him in a warning and screamed. Bullets blasted through his chest.

"Eva, wake up. You're okay."

I jolted awake and gasped for air. Sweat soaked through my tank top and pillowcase. My ears rang with memories of my mom's screams. My body ached, both in memory of Hale's attack and from the hits he'd delivered the day before.

Reaper's strong hands gripped my shoulders. His voice cut through the fog of my dreams. I sat up as he clicked on the bedside lamp. I blinked as reality seeped back in. He pulled me against his chest, and the terror began to wash away, but the anguish remained.

"It was just a nightmare. You're safe."

I clung to him and trembled as he stroked my hair. I focused on the steady thrum of his heartbeat under my ear.

"Do you want to talk about it?"

I pulled back and shook my head.

Reaper pursed his lips as he watched me. "Your brain's still processing. It's been a hell of a month."

Tears streamed down my face. "I thought I was stronger than this."

He gently wiped a tear from my cheek and then kissed it.

"Hey, you're the strongest woman I know. But you've gone through a hell that would break most people."

I nodded. I wanted to believe him. My life had been a shit show of death and destruction for two decades.

"Maybe you need to talk to someone," he suggested carefully. "Not a therapist, obviously, given ... recent events. But me, Rhetta, or even Linc. Did you know he has a degree in psychology?"

I raised an eyebrow. "Seriously?"

"Yeah, along with his computer science degree. He got the brains in my family." His expression turned serious. "Taking a life affects everyone differently. Even when it's justified."

I swallowed hard. "What's your body count?"

His gaze sharpened as his eyes narrowed. "You mean how many people I've killed?"

My voice came out as a whisper. "Yeah. I've ... I've killed three people now. That's a lot for the average person. Is that a lot for a Maverick?"

Reaper remained quiet for a moment. His jaw flexed. "My first kill was as a Marine. Being in a war zone makes it different, somehow. Easier to compartmentalize." He paused, his eyes distant. "My first as a Maverick ... that was a shock to the system."

I waited, sensing his hesitation. He met my gaze.

"As a Maverick, I've taken twelve lives. All for different reasons. But all because they threatened something important to me."

"Including Matt?"

I bit my lip. Did I want an honest answer to that question? Despite his betrayal, Matt had been one of my best friends for the better part of a decade.

Reaper searched my eyes and let out a long sigh. "Technically, yes. Matt was shot by my order to Merrick."

The admission hung in the air between us. I didn't recoil or judge. Instead, a strange sense of understanding settled over me.

Reaper and I were marked by violence. We carried the weight of lives taken out of necessity.

"How do you live with it?"

Reaper's arms tightened around me. "You remind yourself why you did it. You hold onto the people you love. And you don't let it define you."

His words sank in, and the adrenaline from the nightmare faded. Reaper sensed my exhaustion creeping back and shifted me back to the bed.

"Sleep, Lioness. I've got you."

As I drifted off, a sense of safety enveloped me, one I hadn't known in weeks. The nightmares might come again, but I no longer faced them alone.

Chapter Thirty-Two

The dust motes danced in the living room as the afternoon sun filtered through the window. We finally settled in our home after a month of picking paint colors, wrangling movers, and navigating Eva's particular packing preferences.

Settled. The idea was foreign.

For most of my life, "home" became wherever the Corps shipped me or whatever corner of the clubhouse I could carve out. Now, home was this—a messy stack of blueprints for my next job threatening to spill onto the coffee table, sour candy on the countertop, and the thump-thump-thump of Hawk's tail against the hardwood floors.

I'd always thought settling down meant giving something up— freedom, control, my independence. But with Eva, I'd gained more than I ever thought possible. She didn't just fit into my world. She enhanced it. And for the first time in my life, I wasn't just living day to day. I thought about the future.

I found her in the kitchen, arguing with the dishwasher. The woman could wrangle millionaire CEOs and New York Times editors, but a goddamn appliance reduced her to sputtering frustration.

I leaned against the doorframe, enjoying the sight of her with flour dusted across her black tank top. She'd attempted—and failed—to bake a cake this morning.

"Need backup, Lioness?" I asked, a smirk tugging at my lips.

She shot me a withering glance. "This is why I don't cook or clean. This fucking thing. I need a doctorate to turn it on. It's started flashing lights at me. I think it's mocking me!"

I stepped into the room and opened the dishwasher. I rearranged a few dishes, closed the door, and pressed a button. The machine whirred as it started.

"You like control over everything. Even the appliances. But honestly, you load the dishwasher like a raccoon on cocaine. That's probably why it won't work for you."

She ignored the dig. Probably because I was right.

"What's the point of having smart appliances if they don't work?"

I chuckled and pulled her into my arms, kissing a floury cheek.

"We need to go buy a cake, by the way." She gestured to the chocolate-covered catastrophe on the granite countertop.

I smirked at her. "I'm sure the one you baked doesn't taste bad. It just looks ..." I paused, unsure of how to describe her baking disaster. "Like I should probably be in charge of desserts from now on."

Eva halfheartedly punched me. "It's fine. Kenna and I will just go out for dessert this weekend. She won't be surprised that her celebratory cake was a massive failure."

Eva's best friend from college, Kenna, had left the East Coast to help manage Eva's growing roster of clients in Houston and San Antonio. Her consulting business—now renamed Lioness Communications—had grown faster than she'd ever expected.

I watched with pride and awe as she juggled client calls, strategy sessions, and proposals while settling into our new life together. I'd even let her take the lead on the business side of Grimm Construction, and I'd hired two new project managers just to keep up with the contracts. I admired this side of her I hadn't appreciated before—the sharp, ambitious businesswoman who could command a room even from miles away.

We'd planned to help Kenna move into Eva's old house. When we pulled up to the small home on my bike, now vacant and waiting for its new occupant, the memories of the night I'd saved Eva's life blasted through me. It was more than just a memory. It served as a goddamn before-and-after snapshot of my life.

If I'd let her take a fucking Uber home that evening, she'd be dead. And ... fuck, the thought alone made my gut clench.

Fifteen minutes after we arrived, Kenna pulled in behind the wheel of a rental truck smaller than I expected. Turns out you can't amass a lot of stuff in a D.C. studio apartment.

Kenna stood barely five feet tall, petite, with curious green eyes, a sprinkle of freckles across her cheeks, and shoulder-length auburn hair. She looked more like a librarian than a savvy consultant, wearing a blue polka-dot sundress. But I'd learned long ago that appearances could be deceiving.

I observed with amusement as she and her best friend-turned-business partner argued about the best way to organize a closet in between debating brand taglines for a new client. It was refreshing to witness Eva in her element. After watching her adapt to my world, I was intrigued to glimpse a part of hers. She appeared more animated, and the dark, warped sense of humor she shared with Kenna some-times startled me.

I'd recruited Merrick and Hatchet to help with the heavier pieces of furniture. They'd agreed, probably because they liked being around Eva. She had a way of speaking her mind, a frankness that amused them—primarily since she remained the only person who could get away with the pointed comments she lobbed at me.

Merrick tripped over himself to carry a vintage table for Kenna. She seemed more intrigued than intimidated by his massive size, scars, and stoic stare.

"Careful with that," I warned. "It's probably worth more than your bike."

Linc's background check on Kenna had uncovered a few interesting facts—including that her family was beyond rich. She likely had expensive taste. With an enormous trust fund in her name, Kenna only worked because she wanted to.

Kenna laughed. "It's just an old piece I brought from home. Are you sure you don't need any help? It's the least I can do."

Her eyes lingered on the tattooed biceps straining against Merrick's shirt sleeves. She made no secret of admiring my men as they helped move her furniture.

Merrick grunted. A rare hint of shyness colored his cheeks. He didn't clam up around women. Hell, for the past few years, he'd rarely acknowledged them, preferring his solitude over relationships. It was a subtle shift, but I noticed it.

Hatchet stepped in, hoisting a bulky armchair over his blond head like it weighed nothing. "I got this, ma'am. Where does it go?"

I shot him a sharp glare. Hatchet caught it and hesitated. For a split second, the cocky tilt of his mouth faltered. He could chase any piece of ass in Texas, but I didn't want him crossing the line with Eva's best friend.

Kenna's gaze followed him. "Wow, impressive. Let me show you." She flashed Hatchet a grateful smile.

Eva nudged me with her elbow as she helped me move the endless boxes of books to the living room. "Hatchet likes her. I think they'd be adorable together."

I let out an exasperated sigh. "You and Rhetta and your goddamn matchmaking."

Eva grinned, undeterred. "She's my best friend, and I want her to find someone worthy here. I think a Maverick is just what she needs to move on."

I let out a long sigh. Eva stood ready to meddle, just like Rhetta had been with us.

* * *

After Eva and I returned to our house after a long afternoon, I found myself in the kitchen, making her favorite pasta with salmon and a lemon-cream sauce—even though Eva had insisted ordering pizza would be fine. Despite feeling tired and sore, I wanted to prepare something nice to celebrate. Kenna planned to join us after a quick shower following a sweaty day.

Eva wanted to help, but cooking wasn't exactly her forte—a fact evident when I asked her to add the noodles to the water. I'd assumed she understood the simple assignment until she snapped them in half before dropping them in the pot.

I stared at the mangled mess. "The fuck are you doing?"

Eva blinked. "Is it that big of a deal?"

I clenched my jaw in irritation. "Yes, it's a big deal. You don't break linguine noodles in half. Why don't you go drink some wine and wait for your friend on the front porch?"

Eva giggled. Despite my annoyance, I found the sound endearing. As she turned to leave, she reached over the cutting board and swiped a handful of freshly shredded parmesan. She popped it into her mouth with a mischievous grin.

"You goddamn food shark!" I yelled and swatted her ass with the wooden spoon sitting on the countertop. "Get out of here."

She laughed and sashayed out of the kitchen. Hawk trotted at her heels with hope for cheese crumbs. I groaned and got back to cooking. I loved her, but I was considering banning her from the kitchen.

Kenna proved just as fiery as I'd expected when she joined us for dinner. After a few glasses of wine, she became even more lively. Her eyes sparkled as she and Eva shared stories and memories.

"How did you and Eva meet?" I asked, curious about the friendship between these two strong-willed women.

Kenna grinned. A hint of nostalgia colored her expression. "We were rivals. Both majoring in PR. Neck and neck every time a professor had a friendly competition. Both vying for the best internships. Honestly, I hated her."

Eva chuckled. "The only person I know who is more competitive than me is Kenna."

Kenna continued her story, leaning forward. "A professor paired us for a class project, and we became allies. We were strong on our own. But together? We became a fucking force to be reckoned with."

I could imagine it. Eva and Kenna in their twenties, planning their careers, plotting to take on the world with their combined ambition and talent.

"So, Reaper, when will you ask Eva to marry you?"

I choked on the sip of beer I'd just drunk. The liquid burned as it went down the wrong pipe. Coughing and sputtering, I tried to regain my composure while Eva patted my back.

"Jesus, Kenna," Eva chided. "You can't just drop bombs like that."

Kenna shrugged. "What? It's an honest question. Now that I see you two together, it's crystal clear to me. Eva, I've never known you to be so in love."

"Fuck me," I rasped. I attempted to clear my throat, but my eyes were still watering.

Eva's hand remained on my back as it tensed. We hadn't discussed marriage yet, and now her best friend had caught me off guard.

"We, uh ... we haven't really talked about that," I admitted, glancing at Eva.

Her cheeks flushed, but whether from embarrassment or the wine, I couldn't tell.

"Oh, come on," Kenna pressed, leaning forward. "You're telling me that you gave her your property patch—which is patriarchal as fuck, by the way—and let her customize this Barbie dream house, and you adopted a dog together, and you've not thought about putting a ring on it?"

I found myself in the hot seat, caught between Kenna's relentless questioning and Eva's uncertain gaze. I had thought about it. More than I cared to admit. But my world didn't exactly lend itself to white picket fences and happily-ever-afters.

Eva groaned. "Seriously. Let's change the subject."

I caught Eva's eye and brushed my hand over her thigh under the table. We had a lot to talk about, but not now. Not in front of her best friend. I wanted to claim every piece of Eva, and I'd even had Linc stalk her online shopping browsing to see what style of jewelry caught her eye. Last week, she'd clicked on a few vintage pieces with colored gemstones. I'd already decided I wouldn't give her a traditional diamond, but my plans were murky beyond that.

"Okay, fine. So, tell me about the Lone Star Mavericks," Kenna demanded. "Eva tells me you're one of its leaders."

I paused as I considered how much to reveal. "It's part brotherhood, part business. We're a tight-knit group that shares a passion for motorcycles and the freedom of the open road. As for the business side, we have our hands in various ventures—some of which Eva has supported. But at our core, we're about loyalty, respect, and taking care of our own."

Kenna poured herself another glass of wine and took a long sip. Her gaze didn't waver. "It was nice of Merrick and Hatchet to help today. What exactly do they do for the club?"

I shared a glance with Eva. They typically handled the ... less palatable aspects of club business.

"Merrick is our sergeant at arms. Hatchet supports him as our enforcer. Essentially, they maintain order and provide protection when needed. Enforce the rules. Generally, they just get shit done."

Kenna leaned back and swirled the wine in her glass. The intelligent spark in her eyes told me everything I needed to know about her. She wouldn't press me, but she'd certainly do her own research tonight.

"We're planning to go to the club tonight for drinks, if you'd like to join us," Eva said. "It would be good for you to meet some clients."

A few hours later, Thane and I sat at the bar as we watched Eva take her friend through a round of introductions.

I smiled at the familiar scene. We'd come far in such a short time.

Kenna held her own amongst the leather-clad men and the noise.

Her extroverted, bubbly energy balanced the gritty men she met. Unlike Eva, who was drained by these sorts of interactions, Kenna seemed to grow more excited by the minute.

She befriended each biker she met, but her subtle interactions with Merrick and Hatchet caught my eye. They engaged in a strange dance of attraction and polite conversation, a delicate balance of flirtation and restraint. Kenna's body language subtly shifted when she addressed either of them—a slight tilt of her head or a touch that lingered a moment too long. A twinge of concern hit me at the smoldering attraction in their own expressions and gestures.

Often quiet and reserved, Merrick softened around the edges when Kenna spoke to him. His usual scowl gave way to the ghost of a smile. His eyes followed her movements with intensity. His posture relaxed as they talked, his shoulders easing from their usual tense position.

Hatchet, on the other hand, exuded charm and easy grins. But tension appeared in his jaw when Kenna's attention shifted to Merrick. A competitive edge tinged his banter, a barely concealed desire to outshine his brother. Hatchet's eyes sparkled as he regaled Kenna with stories, but there was an undercurrent of seriousness I didn't often see in him. A desire to win her over.

Eva noticed it, too. I found her eyes flicking between the two enamored men, then up to meet my knowing stare. The tension grew thick enough to cut with a knife. The air crackled with unspoken attraction and rivalry.

As Kenna continued her animated conversation, Eva excused herself and walked to the bar to get them drinks. She leaned in to kiss me.

"They're smitten." Amusement laced her tone.

"Yeah," I muttered. "And that's exactly what worries me."

Eva chuckled. "Maybe we should make sure she doesn't wander down any dark hallways. I hear those can be dangerous."

I grinned, thinking about the first night we met—the irresistible pull that had drawn me to the consultant I didn't think we should have hired.

The tension didn't leave my shoulders. Love and lust had a way of complicating even the strongest bonds, and I didn't need Merrick and Hatchet at war with one another over a woman.

As Eva gathered the drinks and returned to her friend, I couldn't help but wonder how this would all unfold. One thing remained certain—with Kenna in the mix, life at the Lone Star Mavericks Motorcycle Club was about to get much more interesting.

Epilogue

Eva paced the living room, a ball of nervous energy. I'd tried involving her in the cooking process but kicked her out of the kitchen within fifteen minutes. She remained a terrible sous chef, snacking on all the carefully measured ingredients I had on the counter.

The scent of roasting turkey and herbs filled the air, and a pumpkin pie sat cooling on the counter.

"Would you calm the fuck down?" I yelled over the sizzle of onions in the pan. "You're making me nervous, and I don't do nervous."

Had I known she would be this neurotic, I wouldn't have agreed to host Thanksgiving at our new house. We'd moved in only a few months ago, the sharp scent of fresh paint still lingering in some rooms, and her father had been itching for a visit. That had escalated into a whole family ordeal, with additional settings for Linc, Mom, Rhetta, and Thane.

"I can't help it," Eva shot back, running her hands through her hair for the hundredth time, messing up her styled curls. "What if your mom hates me?"

I stopped and turned to face her, incredulous. "Are you fucking kidding me? My mom already loves you. She asks to speak to you every time she calls."

Eva bit her lip, unconvinced. "Yeah, but that's over the phone. What if she meets me in person and decides I'm not good enough for her son?"

I wiped my hands on a dish towel and strode over to her, placing my hands on her shoulders. The soft fabric of her maroon sweater warmed my palms. "If anything, she'll wonder what the hell you're doing with me."

Just then, the doorbell rang, its chime echoing through the house. Hawk bounded down the stairs, his nails clicking on the hardwood, tail wagging. Hot on his heels ran Poppy, our Dutch shepherd foster pup, all gangly legs and floppy ears. Eva's eyes went wide with panic. I gave her shoulders a gentle squeeze.

"Breathe, my Lioness. It's just family. I've watched you stab a prospect before. I think you can handle this."

She nodded, taking a deep breath. "Right. It's just our family."

I couldn't help but smile. *Our family.* I marveled at how much had changed since the start of the year. Here we were, hosting a Thanksgiving dinner like some normal, suburban couple.

As I opened the door to greet our guests, I caught sight of the small bump just beginning to show under Eva's sweater. Our little secret, for now. Though Mom would probably figure it out before dessert.

"Hawk, Poppy, sit!" Eva commanded, her voice stern. Both dogs skidded to a halt, planting their butts on the floor, though Poppy's tail wiggled against the hardwood.

I opened the door, and Mom pushed past me, making a beeline for Eva. Before she could even get out a nervous "hello," Mom had enveloped her in a tight hug.

"Oh, honey, you're even prettier in person."

Eva's face flushed red, but the tension left her shoulders.

Mom turned to me, her eyes twinkling. "Roman, dear. It smells amazing in here." She pulled me into an embrace. "She's lovely," she whispered. "Don't mess this up."

Linc followed with a bottle of wine in each hand. He handed them to Eva with a wink. "You can't spell 'family' without alcohol."

Eva laughed, the sound genuine and relaxed despite her earlier anxiety. "That makes absolutely no sense at all."

Linc scooped up Poppy, the brindle-colored pup wriggling in his arms. "So, when are you two making this little girl officially part of the family?"

"She's just a foster," Eva insisted.

Linc gave me a knowing grin. "Sure, sure."

The doorbell rang again, setting off another round of excited barking. I opened it to find Joel, Eva's dad, standing on the porch. His eyes crinkled as he smiled, taking in the chaos behind me.

"Joel, come in," I said, ushering him inside. "I'd like you to meet my mother, Susan."

As they exchanged introductions, the door swung open again. Thane and Rhetta walked in without knocking. I caught the expression on Joel's face—a mix of surprise and uncertainty. Eva clearly hadn't filled him in on all the details of our life yet.

Thane and Rhetta hung up their cuts and greeted everyone, hugging Susan like old friends.

"Joel," I said, sensing an opportunity. "Mind giving me a hand in the kitchen?"

Rhetta, already in on my plans for the night, chimed in. "Great idea. Eva, let's open that wine Linc brought. I picked it out for him, so I know it will be good."

I smirked as Eva grabbed her wine glass, already filled with grape juice, ever so prepared to keep our secret for now.

After removing the turkey from the oven, I turned to Joel, pulling out a small velvet box. Joel's eyes widened as I opened it, revealing a vintage-style emerald ring.

"I want to ask Eva to marry me tonight," I said, my voice low. "I hope I have your blessing."

Joel's face broke into a wide smile. "My daughter has never been so happy. You absolutely have my blessing."

Silenced filled the kitchen for a moment, and then Joel cleared his throat. "So, your best friend is the president of a motorcycle club. Eva hadn't mentioned that."

I couldn't help but chuckle. "I noticed you caught that and figured she hadn't told you anything yet. I think she wasn't quite sure how. To keep it simple, Thane's the president of the Mavericks. And I'm his VP." I paused, choosing my words carefully. "I do everything in my power to keep Eva safe from that part of my life. But honestly, she doesn't need protection. That daughter of yours is a force of her own."

Joel nodded, a mix of pride and concern in his eyes.

"She doesn't need a knight in shining armor because she's too busy forging her own goddamn sword," I said, admiration coloring my tone. "She's tougher than most men I know. I'm not the only one who watches out for her, though. Every single Maverick stands ready to protect her."

Joel's expression softened. "She is a strong woman. I raised her that way. But life has hardened her more than it should have."

I nodded as I added a bit of salt to the bowl of mashed potatoes. "I know. She's been through more hell than she deserves. I'll do every-thing I can to make sure she never has to worry again, though."

I handed him the bowl of potatoes and picked up the platter holding the turkey, carrying it to the dining room and placing it at the center of the table. The spread of food displayed before us could belong on the cover of Southern Living magazine.

As we gathered around the table, the warm glow of candles flickered. I took in the sight before me. While I considered all my men family, Thane was as important to me as Linc. Seeing our parents at the table and Eva's glowing expression fulfilled me in a way I'd yet to fully comprehend.

I stood and raised my glass. "I just want to say how thankful I am for all of you—especially Eva." I turned to face her. My heart thundered as nerves I didn't know I had surged to the surface. "You're my Lioness. Fierce, protective, and loyal. You face every challenge head-on with a courage that never ceases to amaze me. Your strength isn't just in your ability to stand up to danger, but in the way you love."

The ring box weighed heavily in my pocket. "Before we carve the turkey, I just have one question ..." I dropped to one knee in front of the only person in this world I would kneel before. The room fell silent as I pulled out the vintage ring, its teardrop emerald surrounded by marquis diamonds catching in the candlelight. "Will you marry me?"

The room fell silent, all eyes on Eva as tears welled up in her eyes. "Yes, Roman," she whispered, then louder, "Yes!"

As cheers erupted around us, I slipped the ring onto her finger.

The long weekend with our family had filled our home and hearts.

Our family. It still struck me as strange, but it was something I could grow accustomed to.

Susan and Dad left this morning, promising to return for Christmas. I'd started shopping online for the perfect special gift to reveal the big news to them.

The weight of the ring on my finger still felt new, catching the light as I twisted it. I couldn't stop smiling from the joy radiating from within. I watched Roman move around the kitchen, cleaning up the last dishes from our Sunday brunch.

"I still can't believe this is real." My hand instinctively moved to rest on the swell of my stomach.

Roman turned, his eyes softening as they met mine. "Better start believing it, my sweet Lioness. You're stuck with me now."

I laughed, the sound bubbling up from somewhere deep inside. "Stuck with you? I think you've got that backward. You're stuck with me. You're about to marry a woman who can't cook, hates to clean, and is a better shot than half your club."

He crossed the room in a few long strides, pulling me into his arms. The familiar scent of leather and his cologne enveloped me, grounding me in the moment. "That's why you're perfect for me. I can do the cooking. We have more than enough money to pay for a maid if you want. And I love that I can trust you to shoot straight."

A wave of nausea washed over me, a reminder of the morning sickness that had been plaguing me. I took a long, shaky breath, Roman rubbing my back in understanding. "You know, when I first came to Conroe, I never imagined this was where I'd end up," I murmured against his chest.

Roman pulled back, raising a brow. "You mean an old lady hosting Thanksgiving dinner for our mismatched and broken family while carrying an outlaw's babies?"

I nodded. "Exactly. But I wouldn't change it for the world."

Roman's chest rumbled with a low chuckle. "And I never imagined I'd be lucky enough to meet a woman like you, let alone start a family with her. Life's funny that way."

I pulled back, seeking his eyes. "Do you ever wonder what would have happened if you hadn't been there that night?" The night he'd saved my life. Twice.

He shook his head, his expression serious. "I don't waste time on 'what ifs.' All I know is that meeting you changed everything. You became my world. And now, you're giving me even more."

Tears pricked at the corners of my eyes, hormones amplifying my emotions. "After losing Mom and Jace, I thought I'd never have a family again. But you, the club, even Hawk and Poppy ... you've all become my home. And now we're creating our own little family."

Roman's thumb brushed away a tear that had escaped. "Home isn't a place, Lioness. It's wherever we are together. You, me, and our little cubs."

A sense of peace settled over me as I leaned in to kiss him. This life wasn't the one I'd planned, but it turned out better than anything I could have imagined.

Our story didn't resemble a fairy tale. It felt messy, complicated, and at times dangerous. But it belonged to us, and I wouldn't change a single chapter.

Damascus & The Wildfire
Lone Star Mavericks MC Series, Book 2

Love blooms in the wreckage.

When Kenna Walsh trades her polished D.C. life for the wide Texas skies, she isn't looking for love—just a fresh start. Three years after losing her fiancé, her heart still feels hollow. But when she's hired to plan the Lone Star Mavericks' fiftieth anniversary party, she's pulled into a world built on loyalty, violence, and a code she doesn't yet understand.

Merrick, the club's quiet, battle-scarred sergeant-at-arms, carries his own ghosts and keeps the world at arm's length. Hatchet, their reckless enforcer, meets the darkness with a grin and refuses to let Kenna disappear into the shadows. And for the first time in years, her heart isn't just waking up—it's at war with itself.

When a violent street gang threatens everything the Mavericks stand for, Kenna is drawn deeper into a brotherhood where loyalty is everything and trust is hard won, forced to navigate not just the threats outside the clubhouse, but the fractures within it.

And as danger closes in, she finds strength in places she never expected—and faces a choice that could change the course of her future forever.

Read **Damascus & The Wildfire** on Amazon Kindle or purchase signed copies directly from the author at rachelesterlineauthor.com.

* * *

Dear Reader:

Buying direct from rachelesterlineauthor.com is the best way to support my work as an independent author. It ensures the most support goes toward my next release, and allows me to give back to you! Every order placed here is hand-packed by me and includes bookmarks and stickers as a thank you for your support.

Sincerely,
Rachel Esterline

Subscribe for Updates and Bonus Content

Visit rachelesterlineauthor.com/subscribe to receive updates about release dates, event announcements, and bonus content, and more.

* * *

ABOUT THE AUTHOR

Rachel Esterline is an independent author based in the Lansing area in Michigan with her partner-in-crime of more than twenty years, Jeremy, and their two rescue dogs—Kimber and Ranger—whose wild spirits and stubborn loyalty wind their way into every canine character she writes. She has two degrees from Central Michigan University—a bachelor's in integrative public relations and a master's in higher education administration—and her Accreditation in Public Relations from the Public Relations Society of America.

instagram.com/RachelEsterlineAuthor

facebook.com/RachelEsterlineAuthor

tiktok.com/@RachelEsterlineAuthor

Book Club Experiences

Kick your book club into high gear with an author-led experience.

I love connecting with readers and bringing the gritty world of my motorcycle club romances right to your group. Depending on the group, I can offer:

Interactive Activities: Fire up your creative side with MC-inspired extras—like a road name generator, story-based mad libs, coloring pages, games, and more.

Custom Stickers and Goodies: Every club deserves its colors. Deck out your meeting with themed stickers and bonus swag that make your gathering unforgettable.

Live Q&A Sessions: Let's ride together for a live conversation about the book. I'm available to join your meeting in person (within driving distance of Lansing, Michigan) or virtually for an interactive, behind-the-scenes chat.

Visit **rachelesterlineauthor.com/book-clubs** for info.

About the Malinois & Dutch Shepherd Rescue

Malinois and Dutch Shepherd Rescue, Inc. (MAD Rescue) is a 501(c)(3) nonprofit organization dedicated to saving Belgian Malinois and Dutch Shepherds who have been surrendered, abandoned, abused, neglected, or impounded. Operated entirely by compassionate, like-minded volunteers across the United States, MAD Rescue relies on a network of dedicated fosters and donors to provide care and second chances. Visit **madrescueinc.org** to learn about volunteering, fostering, or adopting.

From left to right: Kimber, Jeremy, Rachel, and Ranger in October 2023, following Ranger's official adoption from the Malinois & Dutch Shepherd Rescue.

Acknowledgments

Throughout my career, I've always been a storyteller—but always the stories of others as a news writer, magazine editor, social media manager, and PR professional. I've written speeches for CEOs, planned press conferences for legislators, launched startup brands, and created content for universities and nonprofits.

In late 2024, I started to write every morning for myself. Before work, I'd huddle beside a fire in my basement with my dogs still asleep to craft the stories in my head.

At first, I told no one—not even my husband. I figured my interest would fizzle out, and the draft would sit in my Google Drive like all the other fragmented stories I'd tried to tell before. But this time the worlds and characters I created drew me deeper. I started saving notes in my phone as I heard dialogue and watched scenes unfold in my head.

Thank you to **Morgan**, my friend and hype woman who endlessly encouraged me and was the first to read *Reaper & The Lioness*. Thank you to my other beta readers, **Haley** and **Lindsey**, who gave me invaluable feedback that helped me continue to refine my characters. And thank you to **Sarah** of Sarah Davis Photography, who captured photos that made me feel as badass as Eva.

I also appreciate the mighty team of people who helped me bring this book to you. Thank you to **Mel** for creating my logo, my social media vibes, and the cover of this book, and **Evelyn** at Pinpoint Editing, who helped me polish my manuscript.